SNPGRDXZ
AND THE TIME MONSTERS

BOOK 1 OF THE SNPGRDXZ SERIES

_____

PAUL R. LLOYD

Paul R. Lloyd

Snpgrdxz and the Time Monsters
Book 1 of the Snpgrdxz Series

Published by
Paul R. Lloyd Books
P.O. Box 638
Warrenville, IL 60555

ISBN: 978-0-9892934-1-9

THANK YOU

Thanks for choosing the Snpgrdxz series.

Purchase more of my books at www.Amazon.com

CHAPTER 1

CRAZY IS AS CRAZY DOES

From where she stood at the foot of my bed, fifteen-year-old Jennifer Hawkins couldn't miss, but would this sweet girl shoot me?

Yes, I meant that Jennifer Hawkins, the prettiest sophomore at Lincoln High in Wheaton, Illinois, with her skinny-but-tall body, the daughter of Principal Hawkins and old Mrs. Hawkins, the choir director at our church.

"Bryan, I'm sorry you won't understand what I'm about to tell you, but that's all I'm sorry for, you little –" Here Jennifer referred to the male anatomy in a derogatory way. I'm certain she didn't mean my personal anatomy. How would she know? Mine's not like that. Honest.

" – I'm about to blow your head off so you won't survive to shoot me again later. Now you know why I will kill you. I guess that explains everything, doesn't it? There's nothing sweeter than avenging your own murder."

I ducked and covered my head while admiring Jennifer's tight blue jeans and white blouse.

Okay, maybe I wasn't her type. Or she'd prefer a date with Lionel Nipgrinder, the senior quarterback who was unaware of her existence. But these were not reasons for her to shoot me on the Monday night before my junior year. At age sixteen, I was a year older. She should have shown respect for her elders. Instead, she wore an evil grin I hadn't thought she was capable of.

"Why?" I sat up and pointed my hands to the ceiling. Tears welled up in my eyes. I knew nothing about weapons so I had no idea what type of pistol was about to end my brief life but my soon-to-be murderess gave off a perfume that hinted of soaking wet toy poodle or sweet animal perspiration rather than flowers.

The gun Jennifer held had an extra-long fat attachment on the barrel which I assumed meant a silencer. That's what it would be in a James Bond or Jason Bourne movie. Noticing the little add-on made my stomach push up into my heart.

At a moment like this, you're supposed to have a brilliant insight into the meaning of life, but all I noticed was Jennifer's cup size under her white blouse. She must have grown over the summer.

I also couldn't help notice as the sweat poured down the side of my face that James Bond and Jason Bourne had the same initials. Why was that?

What else could I do? Someone, I assumed Jennifer, had switched my bedside lamp on while I slept. But how had she made her way into my house without waking me or my parents or my little sister, Katie? We Ganarskis are light sleepers.

How was she avenging her own murder? Did she mean I had killed her or was about to? Why would I harm the girl I had a crush on? Besides, I couldn't kill a cat or a mouse. I'm just not made that way. I'd slap a mosquito no problem, but Jennifer Hawkins? I don't think so.

I was about to plead my pacifist nature to Jennifer when an Asian girl I didn't know slammed through my bedroom door with my best high school buddy Gilbert Armstrong right behind her. My door banged against the plaster wallboard and flapped back against Gilbert. As he ricocheted off my bureau, my body began to shake.

The force of the rebounding door almost knocked the Army rifle out of Gilbert's hands. I mean the weapon with the bayonet attached. The Asian carried one also with a long banana clip loaded and a bayonet mounted that had a shine on the edge of the blade like she had just sharpened it. Where Jennifer's aroma was sweet but animal like, their aroma was a mixture of the musk of hard sweat and dirt.

"Turpelator will be pissed." Actually, Jennifer dropped the f-bomb before "pissed." In her fifteen years, Jennifer Hawkins had never uttered rough language harder than "crap" in my presence so you can imagine my shock at her little f-ing speech on top of her derogatory comments about my private anatomy which she knew nothing about.

From the dark depths of my parent's bedroom, I heard my dad call out, "Quit making all that noise, Bryan."

Jennifer backed away from the foot of my bed until her back banged into my open bedroom window hard enough for her butt to almost pass through the open window space. She caught herself and bounced off my window before firing without aiming because she was busy focusing her pretty eyes on Gilbert and his Asian cohort. Some people worry about distracted driving. I had to worry about distracted shooting.

Before I could react to any of this, Dad hollered again from his bedroom, "Bryan, cut out the racket already. Your TV is way too loud."

The Asian skewered Jennifer through the chest with a bayonet thrust packing enough force to knock both of them out my open window. The blow shocked my mind off Jennifer's cup size and onto Dad's direct order earlier today to replace the broken window screen in my room or I would have to pay hell or hell would pay me, I forgot which. Either way, you don't ignore one of Dad's mighty commands, but there was the window hole without the screen.

With the aluminum structure of the window destroyed when Jennifer and that Asian terrorist flew through it, I wasn't sure I needed to replace the screen anymore, but I had to keep Dad happy or else.

While I took in the fresh aroma of burnt sulfur and hot lead, Gilbert bellowed through the window hole, "Nice going, Snpgrdxz."

He turned his black, baldy cut head in my direction and smiled a shit eater at me. "This didn't happen, Bryan."

Before I could ask what a Snpgrdxz was, Gilbert left my bedroom the old-fashioned way as he charged out the door.

"For the last time, turn down that TV," Dad hollered.

I had no problem thinking this had been a wild late night TV flick. I wanted it to be a nightmare movie. Wouldn't you?

Maybe I had replaced the window screen, and Jennifer Hawkins' increased cup size was a figment of my imagination. How else do you explain Mr. Turpelator, our high school physics teacher, who flew in through my open window uninvited? I wasn't hyperventilating, but I wasn't playing catch with my breath either.

And why had Jennifer mentioned his name before shooting at me?

Mr. Turpelator hovered above the place where Jennifer had stood with her pistol before the Asian girl gored her. He didn't have a gun, but he opened his mouth about a foot and a half to reveal the longest fangs I had ever seen. He floated closer to me on the bed like he wanted to suck my brains out. His breath made me think of dead rats in the rain. To be precise, the aroma was more like dead rats in the gutter two days after they had drowned in a flood and now the sun beat down on them.

Either my breath was worse than I thought (it was after midnight) or Mr. Turpelator had spotted the big crucifix Grandma Ganarski had hung above my bed the year I received Communion for the first time, no matter that we were Protestants. Either way, he threw his hands up to block his face and flew backwards out the window at a speed that suggested a balloon struck by a pin or a puppet whose strings had been hard yanked.

As I checked the crucifix, I couldn't help but notice that Jennifer had missed Jesus by a quarter inch.

Dad would kill me if I didn't replace the shattered window and clean up the broken glass, but would he be pissed about not replacing the screen? A new window, paid for by my summer job, would include the screen.

I tried to sleep, but what if it hadn't been a dream? Was the girl I was crazy about in high school at this moment bleeding to death right under my second floor bedroom window? If these midnight events were real, then Jennifer's bloodstains would cover the floor and the wall. I'd also find bloodstains around the window, right?

I climbed out of bed and checked my floor. I didn't see any blood, so it must have been a dream except how do you explain the evidence of broken glass, bits of aluminum, and the bullet hole in the crucifix? Besides, the aroma of animal sweat still wafted in the air. But what if Jennifer had been so close to the window when the Asian girl had stabbed her that her lifeblood flowed out the window with her?

CHAPTER 2

ESTABLISH A FEW FACTS

Scuffling noises from the backyard tore my attention away from the broken window. I padded barefoot down the hall to Katie's room. From her window, I glimpsed two shapes next to the storage shed by the back fence. As my eyes adjusted to the dim light, I identified Gilbert and the Asian. They patted down a dirt pile in the shape of a grave where Mom's mums grew in the fall.

"Bryan?" Katie asked.

"Go back to sleep." I rushed downstairs to the garage to grab Dad's flashlight. I tripped over the one-hundred-foot long electric cord Dad used with our plug-in lawnmower. Okay, I mowed the lawn, and yes, I was supposed to wrap up the wire and drape it over the mower handle out of the way when I finished. I knocked over the recycle bin which started the empty cans and bottles clanging around the garage floor. The plastic gallon milk jugs clattered in their muffled plastic wuss noise until they ended up under Mom's Malibu and Dad's Explorer. Dad was going to slaughter me.

From my position with my butt on the garage floor, I heard Mom shriek loud enough to wake the possibly late Jennifer Hawkins. I stood only to discover one of Dad's crushed aluminum beer cans under my left big toe as I danced and hooted out of the garage without the flashlight.

I made my way through the family room into the kitchen. "It's okay, Mom."

I checked my right foot for blood. There wasn't much. The empty was a twelve-ounce can so how much damage could it do? And I didn't think this was the best time to tell Mom that Gilbert and some Asian terrorist murdered sweet little Jennifer Hawkins up in my bedroom.

Besides I was still alive so someone watched out for me. I mean other than Gilbert and his Asian girlfriend. She was attractive despite her warrior ways.

"What's happening down there?" My sister Katie this time. Could Dad be far behind?

On cue, Dad wandered out of the powder room off the kitchen dressed in his t-shirt and boxers trailed by the aroma of long dead pork. "Why are you bothering me with so much racket in the middle of the night?"

"Sorry, Dad. I was checking on a noise in the backyard when I tripped."

"Be quiet and go back to bed so I can sleep undisturbed by the likes of you."

"Yes, sir."

Dad appreciated an occasional expression of respect, which worked wonders when there was more to a story I didn't want to tell. Dad headed for the stairs as I searched the kitchen for a flashlight. I found one in the drawer next to the refrigerator.

I checked the flashlight to see if it lit. You know how it is with flashlights. They sit in a kitchen drawer for years. When you need them, you discover acid leaking out of the batteries. Mom must have been at this flashlight recently because it worked, but the bottom of the drawer had acid stains from the previous set of batteries.

In the yard under my bedroom window, I discovered blood stains and shoe impressions on the lawn. I followed the footprints and blood smears until they vanished at the storage shed by our back fence. Someone had dragged Jennifer's impaled body across the lawn to the dug up spot.

I noticed two shovels and thrust one into the dirt. It hit something below the surface that was too soft for a rock. The sugary animal aroma from my bedroom escaped into the air.

My butt hit the ground. I backed up until I came into contact with the shed. I couldn't breathe. I had liked Jennifer Hawkins since preschool, and had a crush on her since puberty, but never realized how deep my feelings for her went until my chest collapsed around my heart and the tears flowed.

I heard a rustling noise by the back fence. I took a gander in time to spot shadow upon shadow as something dark and mysterious vanished into the night.

***

Where blood had darkened the lawn during the night, black muddy spots appeared like the remains of a well-scrubbed cleanup campaign gone awry. I woke up on the dirt spot next to the storage shed, but was stiff and chilled by an August morning in the Chicago burbs. I searched around the yard again under my window. The lawn had a dish detergent aroma. Bubbles floated over the grass, but there were no blood stains.

I had survived a wicked dream about blood on the lawn, or one of the local coyotes must have caught a bloody rabbit. But who served on the cleanup committee and why didn't they wake me?

I went inside for breakfast. I should have gazed up at my window. So sue me. I'm not a detective. I'm a teenager.

The first day of my junior year of high school was a few days away. And a guy had to eat. This was no time to panic about a nightmare that turned my bedroom lamp on while leaving perfumed soap bubbles on the lawn and a grave by the storage shed.

It didn't take long for the reality of my looming craziness to hit home. The words spoken by my evening visitors were right out of a nightmare where the girl you like tries to kill you so you won't kill her later. What insane logic was that? But upstairs in my bedroom, I had to replace the shattered window and face the reality of a bullet hole in Grandma's crucifix.

***

"You didn't happen to invade my bedroom last night with an Asian beauty queen who rammed a bayonet between Jennifer Hawkins' boobs, did you?" I passed a towel to Gilbert on the bench of our basketball game in the summer league. The season ended with this game, and our school's football players were already gone to their practice so Gilbert and I became the beneficiaries of their basketball game minutes.

"I think I would remember that." Gilbert peeled off his left sneaker and rubbed his foot.

I spun my head to face the other way to avoid the aroma of old gym, but it followed wherever Gilbert's feet went. I turned back to him. "Then my dad drove me crazy."

"Did what?" Gilbert replaced his sneak.

"Drove me nuts. I'm having hallucinations." I yanked a soda out of the ice chest, but before I could pop the tab, Coach Corbin, aka our youth director at church, roared for us to get ready to return to action.

We made our way down to Mr. Romano, the art teacher at Lincoln High, who served as timekeeper for the summer basketball league as well as the regular interscholastic winter league. He stopped the game long enough for us to jump back in.

Later when we returned to the bench for a rest, Gilbert asked, "So this Asian babe? Was she a hottie?"

"Yeah, kinda. I paid more attention to the gun with the silencer Jennifer fired in my direction."

"If she was a hottie, then I went out with her." Off came Gilbert's sneakers again.

It was my turn to scrunch up my face while I sipped the soda I had eyed since the previous break.

Gilbert slapped my back. "Kidding, Bryan, okay?"

"So you're not dating any new girls?"

"I'm not dating an old girl either. Who has money for dates?"

"Then it must have been a wild dream."

Gilbert leaned forward with his elbows on his knees. "Trust me, Bryan, you can relax. Oh, wait. Did your mom dump chemicals into your corn flakes? She's the drug-crazed hippie type, right?"

I pictured my church deacon mom dumping weed into my breakfast bowl. The picture didn't work, but my experience last night didn't fit anywhere near a sane place. "Gilbert, there's a brand new bullet hole in the big crucifix above my bed, and somebody smashed my bedroom window. And I found blood stains on the grass in my yard under my window, but somebody cleaned it up while I slept."

"So how did you get Jennifer Hawkins up in your bedroom past your parents, especially your dad?" Gilbert put his sneakers back on.

"I didn't. I woke up and there she was with a gun aimed my way."

"And what are you doing with a crucifix?" Gilbert tied his sneakers.

I took in the aroma of fresh sweat coming off the basketball court, a sweeter smell than Gilbert's feet. "You've seen it. Grandma got it for my first communion."

"Did you ask Jennifer Hawkins about any of this?"

"Are you crazy? I'm not in her league."

Gilbert gave me a cold stare. "What are you talking about? We're in youth group with her, and we've known her since preschool."

"I can't call her about this."

"Text her."

"What if she's dead? When you wake up insane is no time to text your friends."

CHAPTER 3

MY IRRATIONALITY CONTINUES

In the darkness before dawn on Wednesday, Jennifer Hawkins kissed me awake. She snuggled close on the bed with the aroma of sweet flowers around her. "Darling, I'm so happy we're together again at last."

I turned on the lamp by my bed and sat up certain of my new irrationality. Jennifer wore the same blue jeans and a white blouse she modeled for my Monday night reality dream. "How? Why?"

She kissed with a mouth open, tongue-probing passion that shocked me. Sure, I've known Jennifer Hawkins all her life, and I cried for her when I thought she was stabbed to death by my best friend Gilbert's Asian terrorist girlfriend, although Gilbert didn't have a girlfriend, Asian or otherwise. But where did this sweet Christian teenager learn to kiss like that? No girl had ever pushed her tongue my way before so you can imagine my surprise. She pulled away like she needed air before the next French dive with me.

"Jennifer, I'm so glad you like me, but isn't this a bit fast?"

"Darling, I missed you so much." She brought her open lips almost to mine but stopped. "Did you say 'a bit fast'?"

Not waiting for an answer, she pulled away while the passion on her face morphed into a scrunched up question mark that transformed into an "I screwed up" expression. "Snpgrdxz?"

Jennifer studied my face for something that wasn't there. I have to admit I was happy her lovely, kissable mouth had returned to saying words like "crap" instead of real curses and swears.

It was my turn to speak, but what can a guy say at a tender moment like this? I should have asked who or what was a "Snpgrdxz," but all I could muster was a weak "Huh?" I would have to wait until another time to ask Jennifer to explain Snpgrdxz to me.

Jennifer stomped across the room hands on hips. "I missed. Sorry I frightened you. This didn't happen, okay? And if you see Turpelator, run like hell."

She crept out through my open bedroom door as I considered that it was too late to warn me about Mr. Turpelator.

I went over to the hole where my window used to be and pushed aside the cloth I hung for a covering. The evening breeze wafted in cool, damp, clean suburban air as I gazed at Jennifer running down the driveway.

The Asian girl appeared by the side of the house. She headed towards the shed with two shovels as her short skirt billowed in the night breeze.

Gilbert joined the Asian girl. He spoke barely above a whisper. "Jennifer."

"What?" Jennifer asked in a normal volume.

"We have to get rid of your body before the sun comes up. Can you help us?" Gilbert asked.

"What will you do with it?" Jennifer asked.

Gilbert pointed to the shed. "We can't leave it here. Let's take it out to the woods where we burned those cars that time and cremate her."

"Good idea. But please respect my body," Jennifer said.

"Why don't you come with us to make sure we do it right," said the Asian.

"Okay, but I wish my Bryan were here. He always knows how to do these things right." Jennifer took off around the front of the house. I ran downstairs to open the front door for her before she rang the bell and woke my family.

I had no idea what Jennifer meant about me knowing how to do something right. I'm not the do-it-right sort. I'm more the goof-it-up-the-first-time-and-fix-it-later kind of guy. But if Jennifer Hawkins wanted my help to dig herself up and burn her other body, then I was ready. Insane but ready.

I remembered she snuck into my house earlier with no problem. I ran back upstairs to put my jeans on. For a teenage girl to kiss a guy clad in his skivvies in his bed was one thing. But to answer the front door dressed that way was another. Crazy or not, I had to respect the proprieties.

When I arrived at the front door with my pants zipped and belt buckled, no one was there. I whispered, "Jennifer."

No one answered.

I went outside and checked around, but saw no sign of her.

The squeal of tires caught my attention in time to observe a dark sedan peel out of my driveway and take off up the street. It went too fast to tell the make in the dark.

Jennifer must have changed her mind about inviting me to help burn her extra dead body. I stopped as another hallucination or wild dream invaded my mind. In a dream, would Jennifer Hawkins burn her own dead body? She needed two bodies to pull it off, and she mustn't need the extra one anymore.

I wandered back by the shed to discover an open, empty grave. I shoveled dirt in. As I patted down the last of the muck, my dad arrived.

"What are you up to?" he screamed.

Never was a clever answer so needed and never had one not bothered to show up on time. What could I say? "Nothing."

"Don't you nothing me. You buried drugs or booze. Dig them up and remove them from my property or you move out. Am I making myself clear to you, young man?"

"Yes sir, but this is not about drugs or booze."

My dad turned his back and wandered off in the direction of the house. He mumbled, "Burying dope? Burying booze? It's what they used to do during Prohibition. What's with that kid?"

I returned to bed as the red glow of the morning sun broke over Chicago in the distance. I was more convinced than ever that I needed psych counseling, but who goes to the guidance counselor before the school year begins?

***

When I awoke several hours later, Jennifer's visit seemed like another insane dream or vision, but as I dressed, I realized my bedside lamp was still lit and my jeans bore the telltale signs of mud on the cuffs and knee area. What nightmare invades reality?

You can have hallucinations without dropping off your nut. Two nights of insane visions that disturb the real world don't prove anything, do they?

I spent half the day arguing with myself over whether to speak with Jennifer Hawkins about what happened. I was shy, and she was hot which didn't make for the best combination. On the other hand, I was a junior and she was a sophomore which had to count for something along the lines of a "more mature man" or "big man on campus," right? Although I wasn't sure art club qualified you for BMOC status. Girls dug the BMOC stuff, but in the end I didn't call or text her. Turned out I didn't have to.

The other half of the day, I eavesdropped on the window installer in my bedroom. Mom insisted I clear a path through my dirty laundry and junk for him. I figured as long as I had to pick up clothes, I might as well take the pile down to the washing machine for Mom. The window guy didn't seem to mind the gym locker-room odor I stirred up while picking up my long dead laundry. He appeared old enough to have teenagers of his own so he may have been used to it.

It's a special day when you can make your mom happy while preparing for a midnight visit from the girl you have a crush on at school.

While I had no reason to think Jennifer would stop by my room tonight, I also had no reason to believe I wouldn't see her. After all, I was the one having insane hallucinations that left an imprint on the real world.

Gilbert texted after dinner so we chatted for a while. No surprise here, but he denied digging up dead bodies in my backyard last night. The Asian girl didn't text which made me happy. I would have dropped down dead if she had.

CHAPTER 4

BONKERS

What could make me so bonkers as I climbed into the sack on the night before my first day of junior year? Think what you want. I wasn't crazy, was I?

Without waiting for me to fall asleep on Wednesday evening, Jennifer Hawkins crept through my brand new window, turned on my bedside lamp, and plopped down on the bed next to me. My eyes laser-locked onto the clear, clean skin of her smooth thighs sticking out of her white lacy jammie shorts. Her fat ruby lips curled into a kiss-me smile that brought out her high cheek bones. She didn't wear perfume but should have because she smelled like one of the guys after gym class.

She grabbed my face in her hands to drag my attention up to her sultry green bedroom eyes. "Hi, Bryan. I guess you want to know why I'm in your room the night before school starts, huh?"

"Kinda." I morphed into a puddle of teenaged crazy goo and angst. I didn't know what Jennifer Hawkins had in mind this time, but the crucifix on the wall above my bed still had a bullet hole in it the last time I had checked.

"Yeah, I guess I like you."

"Wow. That's cool, Jennifer, because I sort of like you, too." I ran my hand through her brunette hair and noticed blond highlights that weren't there the last time I had seen her in that other dimension I sometimes visit, the one where she takes pot shots at me and digs herself up for the funeral pyre.

She planted a kiss on my lips that would have blown my socks off if I wasn't already stripped to my undies. We broke apart at the sound of the big crash.

***

If you sneak down to the kitchen for a snack in the middle of the night, why mess up by dropping the plate or the fork? But that's my dad. Or my little sister, Katie. Or Mom. One of them made the big noise in the kitchen. We Ganarski's are a night-snacking family.

"I have to skedaddle." Jennifer placed her index finger over my mouth.

"But Jennifer..." I muffled through her finger. I wanted to ask her about last night and "skedaddle." Where did skedaddle come from? What fifteen-year-old girl says "skedaddle" these days? Isn't it Bronze Age speak? I can hear two Romans guarding Jesus's tomb and when the rock rolls back by itself, one Roman guard says to the other, "Time to skedaddle."

The word is like Latin or the name of some city in Washington State. But it's not uttered by anyone under age fifty. Not today. Not since the nineties, anyway. The eighteen nineties. The word was last used on the *Titanic* by a crew member right before he jumped onto a lifeboat.

But the next thing Jennifer said got my attention because her voice became husky and hoarse. She smiled, her finger still warmed my lips. "Next time you see me in school, Bryan, mosey on up to me and plant a big kiss smack on my lips so everybody will know we are a couple."

"What about your old... I mean father?"

"Especially the old man. He is so antiquarian. Our little PDA will give him a wakeup call."

As Jennifer Hawkins disappeared out my window, I thought about how I've known her forever and how she has always been attractive but on the quiet side despite her good looks.

Kids change over the summer, don't they? Her bra size sure improved. New school year, new Jennifer Hawkins. And a much happier me if I could get past the insanity of these past few nights.

I definitely had to clean my room enough to entertain midnight guests.

The good news is Jennifer Hawkins visited me in my bedroom three nights in a row. We both may still be virgins, but we were moving in the right direction, weren't we?

I spent the rest of the night with a grin that slung off my face and stretched out across the remaining dirty laundry scattered about the floor.

In the morning, I remembered my bedroom was on the second floor and no way did Jennifer Hawkins make that jump out my window.

Paul R. Lloyd

CHAPTER 5

A KISS IS JUST A KISS

Jennifer Hawkins may have been part of an insane dream fantasy, but Maria Gonzalez went missing for real.

When Gilbert and I saw her, Maria puffed on a homemade cigarette, the kind without tobacco. She sat on the curb in the spot where I planned to park Mom's Malibu. Her lacy skirt was a tad wider than a belt making it too short for a kid's dress up doll while revealing way too much black patterned pantyhose with a bunch of runs and holes in the wrong places. She gave off an aroma of sweet herbal smoke mixed with dollar store perfume.

Her hair was the darkest black a girl can buy at the local Walmart. She had the reddest lips Revlon makes. I wasn't sure if the dark circles under her eyes were real or a makeup job. She was long and skinny but not like Jennifer Hawkins. Jennifer made skinny look hot. Maria made skinny look anorexic.

The parking space was the last one available, so I pulled Mom's Malibu in.

Gilbert, who sat next to me, said Maria would move.

She didn't.

Maria's knees touched my bumper. "Nice driving, Ganarski."

"Thanks, I think." I slammed the car door and strode down the sidewalk with Gilbert in tow. I brushed up against a new kid squeezing by on the sidewalk who headed the wrong way.

"Sorry," he said.

I stopped. "Why are you sorry? I was the one who bumped into you. By the way, aren't you headed in the wrong direction? School is this way."

Gilbert was big enough to play on the football team, but he preferred first string in math. He punched my arm, knocking me over about a foot to the left. "He's being polite."

I shrugged. "Oh, yeah. Sorry. I'm Bryan Ganarski and this lamebrain is –"

"– Gilbert Armstrong. And don't pay any attention to Bryan. He thinks everyone is a lamebrain." Gilbert punched my arm again.

"I'm Daniel Brickmaster." The new kid was close to my six-foot height, maybe an inch shorter. He seemed in good physical condition, but not athletic.

Principal Hawkins chose that moment to beam down from whatever planet he goes home to at night. "Do you boys understand the school rules about personal touching?"

"Yes, sir." What I wanted to say was his daughter had violated his no-touch policy when she dropped by my bedroom the past few nights, but I didn't.

Principal Hawkins moved in close enough for me to taste his foul morning breath and sweat as he pointed a long, bony finger over my shoulder. "Then what were you doing with that young lady?"

As usual, I had no idea what Principal Hawkins was talking about. "I didn't touch..." I took a gander over my shoulder to see if Maria was busted, but the curb was empty. When I turned back, Principal Hawkins was gone.

I spun around again to discover Principal Hawkins in hot pursuit of nothing in the direction we last saw Maria Gonzalez.

Gilbert and I strolled through the sophomore hall on our way to the junior area. Daniel, the new kid, clomped along with us.

"Maria may be a Goth wannabe, but she never cuts school. She'll show up for her classes." Gilbert clapped the new kid on the shoulders. "Where are you from?"

"Oh, here and there. You know," Daniel said.

Gilbert and I stared at him like he had arrived from Planet X. I was about to ask for a tighter explanation as Principal Hawkins says when his daughter, Jennifer, flashed her kiss-me smile in my direction.

Unless I hallucinated again last night, Jennifer Hawkins told me to kiss her at school today. What drugs did Mom sneak into my cereal?

Jennifer wore tiny blue shorts and some kind of frilly white blouse as she approached with several of her girlfriends. "Hi, Bryan."

"Hi, Jennifer." My voice went husky. I broke out in the biggest sweat since seventh grade. I couldn't help myself because I had witnessed a strange Asian terrorist girl murder her in my bedroom the other night.

And then Jennifer visited me two nights in a row after that. And she asked me to kiss her the next time I saw her, didn't she?

I have to check out whatever Mom dumps in my food. But I wasn't about to let Mom's diet arrangements stop me.

But should I kiss her? In public? She said she wanted to do a little PDA to show her old man she was ready to date. I hesitated.

I'd be doing her a favor, right?

I gulped.

She had asked me to kiss her, didn't she?

Okay, gumption is something a guy has to work up to.

It boiled down to two choices. Either I kissed Jennifer Hawkins right now or I pooped my pants out of fear and intimidation.

Besides what's the worst that could happen?

I kissed Jennifer Hawkins.

In front of her friends and about half the tenth grade.

I'm not talking a tiny peck here. I pressed in with a lengthy lip smacker as I took in her light aroma of fresh flowers. And I did it in front of my best friend, Gilbert Armstrong. And that new kid, Daniel what's his face.

Who knew Jennifer Hawkins could slug a guy so hard?

From my position flat on my back, I couldn't raise my head high enough to see above a certain light brown birthmark splotch on Jennifer's left thigh. She didn't have it last night. The spot reminded me of a map of Italy with the boot facing the wrong way.

Jennifer dropped down next to me and held my head. "You idiot, why'd you kiss me?"

Okay, so maybe I had hallucinated again last night. Now, what was I supposed to say? "It's something I always wanted to do. I'm sorry. I should have asked you out first and took you on a couple of dates and stuff."

"I can't say I forgive you, Bryan. Then again, I have to, if you say you're sorry."

"Oh, am I ever sorry I kissed you." I rubbed my jaw and enjoyed the warmth of her closeness.

"Don't be too sorry. I liked it. And didn't you say you always wanted to kiss me?"

"Yes, since the day back in first grade when we helped the kindergarten kids learn to use their crayons the right way, and I was assigned to help you."

"You remember that?"

"Yeah."

"Me too. You were cute and oh so mature as a big stud first grader. I am sorry I hit you so hard. It was a kneejerk girl reaction. Try the subtle approach next time, okay?"

"So you'll go out with me?"

"No." Jennifer kissed me quick on the lips, rose up and banged smack into Mr. Turpelator.

Our physics teacher grabbed Jennifer around the waist and hugged her. He ran his hand up and down her back before patting her well below the waist. This inappropriate teacher behavior was more than a bit too cozy for my taste.

Jennifer glared at Mr. Turpelator as she yanked away from him. Mr. Turpelator smiled, patted her head and kissed her hair. "That's an example of what you're not supposed to do in school, chums. Off with you, child."

Jennifer smacked Mr. Turpelator on the face and ran away. Mr. Turpelator sighed, laughed and vanished into the herd of stampeding students.

"What was that about?" Daniel asked.

"I don't know. We witnessed a new Mr. Turpelator," said Gilbert.

I remained on my back smiling up into Gilbert's shocked face. Daniel what's-his-name appeared amazed. I assumed at the time that he had never seen anything this wild before. Of course, I was wrong about him.

***

"You will fail physics. I do not pass dolts. You foolishly signed up for physics when you could have taken a general science course to qualify for graduation. There will be no excuses. You will fail unless you prove to me you are an above average performer. And guess what, chums? By definition less than half of you are above average." Mr. Turpelator finished his lecture about what to expect in physics class on our first day of junior year.

He was tall, gaunt and spoke in the purest monotone, slow and steady. He usually wore black, like today with his black dress shirt and khaki slacks. He came across like a business networker at a funeral home convention. "You may now ask questions," he droned.

Gilbert shot his hand into the air. "Remember last year when I asked you about time travel in chemistry? You said that was physics and we had to wait until we took it."

"Did you have a question, Mr. Armstrong, or did you think question time was for complaints?" Mr. Turpelator glared.

"I wanted to know if we will study time travel. That's physics too, isn't it?" asked Gilbert.

Mr. Turpelator groaned like teachers do when they have discovered their star pupil is slightly less intelligent than your average snail. "Mr. Armstrong, if you set your mind on real physics, you won't have to travel back in time to retake tests. We will have no time travel in my physics class, chums."

"Why not?" Daniel Brickmaster asked.

Mr. Turpelator shifted his shoulders straight, threw his head back and raised his nose to the ceiling. He inhaled long and hard before speaking. "I'm not fond of new students. But because you asked, I'll answer you, old boy. First, time travel doesn't exist. What we have are observable scientific data and the conclusions reasonable people make from data."

"And no UFOs either?" Daniel asked.

"You're not from around here, are you? What's your name?"

"Daniel Brickmaster, sir."

"Please, Mr. Turpelator?" begged Turk Mays. "We want to study time travel so we can go to Woodstock."

"Oh, very well, but only because this is the first day of school, and so many of you live under the delusion that *Star Trek* represents the best that science has to offer. But it's fiction, chums. Forget time travel because four scientific facts make it impossible. These are my four rules of time travel. They won't be on the test, and this is the last time we will discuss time travel in this class, understood?"

A couple of kids replied in the affirmative.

"Very well, here are the rules. I call them the 'You cannots' because you can't do any of these things." Mr. Turpelator wrote the following on the whiteboard:

You cannot:

1. Change the past.
2. Avoid a time loop.
3. Meet yourself or your ancestors
4. Make things better.

Mr. Turpelator replaced the cap on his marker. "Think, people. If you traveled to the past, you would create a new timeline that wouldn't affect your original timeline. As a result you would move forward in time from a new starting point to create history as it happens instead of 'revisiting' it. You can't change anything."

"What's a timeline?" asked Megan Mincheah from the back of the class.

"Timeline?" Mr. Turpelator sniffed the air as he raised his nose to the ceiling and drew a blue horizontal line on the white board. "This line represents your path through normal time from the day you are born to the day you die, one can only hope. Or you can use it to represent existence from the beginning of time to as far into the future as you can imagine."

Mr. Turpelator placed a red X in the middle of the time line. "This is where you are in time. Call it the present. If you want to time travel to the past, you move to a place on the left side of the X. To visit the future, you move to the right of the X.

"The problem comes in when you move out of your normal spot in time and travel to another time." Mr. Turpelator drew a green loop from the X to a point in the past.

"When you enter another period, you create a new track that spins off from your first time." Mr. Turpelator drew a purple line down from the spot where he entered the past and added a new parallel line under the original progression.

"This new line runs parallel to your original or what I called your normal time line. You will move forward in the new timeline. You cannot return to your original timeline because you cannot change it. It already happened, including that you left it.

"Rule two means you would become stuck in an eternal time loop with no exit. The loop begins when you first travel back in time and continues from the time you land in the past until you either die or return to your normal present. Either way, you will always be born again and repeat every life action until you make the decision to travel back in time the first time to complete the loop. Sub-loops occur whenever your time travel activities feedback on themselves."

"Doesn't rule two negate rule one?" Gilbert asked.

"No. In your original time line you will be born and live until you time travel. The fact of your time travel to the past creates a loop repeated in infinity. In effect, you will never die."

"That doesn't make sense," Megan said.

"That's the point, Miss Mincheah. If it made sense, then you could travel in time. But time travel doesn't make sense. Let's see if the other rules will clear it up for you.

"Rule three states you cannot meet yourself or your ancestors. If you contact yourself in the past, you will destroy the universe because the universe cannot sustain a paradox. Something will always happen to prevent it. And if you contact your grandmother in the past, and she dies as a result, you will never be born and so you will disappear forever. No one will have any memory of you. History will reflect your nonexistence. This creates a paradox and a paradox cannot exist. Therefore, you cannot meet your ancestors.

"Finally, rule four tells us time travel always makes things worse. It's not possible to make things better because you will upset the space-time continuum and risk collapsing the entire universe. Nothing is so bad as to risk traveling back in time to make a change. If you do, things will continue to get worse until time ultimately collapses. Time travel causes the end of the world. As we are still here, time travel is impossible."

"Mr. Turpelator, didn't scientists used to say it was impossible for heavier than air objects to fly?" asked Megan Mincheah as the bell rang.

***

By the time we escaped Lincoln High that afternoon, the sun waited for us, the trees stirred, and the ninety-plus temperature blasted our faces. I offered Jennifer Hawkins a ride home.

"I can't, Bryan. You have to stop asking me for a date."

"It wasn't an invitation for a date. It's transportation. Gilbert will ride with us. We're safe."

"I don't think I'm allowed to ride in cars with boys." Gilbert's falsetto pierced my ears as he tossed his backpack on the backseat of my mom's Malibu.

"Gilbert, you ride with me every day." I opened the front passenger door for Jennifer.

"Oh, right. What about Jennifer?" Gilbert jumped in the backseat.

"I don't mind riding in cars with boys, Gilbert. I'm not sure I'm supposed to, and I'm forbidden to date them until I'm older." Jennifer threw her backpack into the Malibu.

"How much older?" I asked.

"Not until I'm forty." Give Jennifer credit. She kept a straight face.

I could feel my jaw bounce once on my chest.

Jennifer noticed I wasn't breathing. "I'm kidding, Bryan. I'm supposed to wait until I'm sixteen."

"Oh. So that's why you said no to me?" I fumbled with my keys and dropped them.

"It's a reason." Jennifer hopped in the front seat while I put my tongue back in my mouth and pushed my jaw closed.

My heart resumed beating. I took in the aroma of sweet flowers that wafted into the Malibu with her.

I located my keys by crawling under the car to coat myself with hot tarmac and gravel. Back in the Chevy, I drove north on Main Street through downtown across the railroad tracks and past the coffee shop and other stores of old Wheaton. Jennifer asked me to turn right at Jefferson. A few blocks later, she said to make another right. She pointed out one of those Victorians from the Middle Ages near the college and asked me to drop her off.

I pulled over to the curb and stopped.

She unlatched the door, but didn't open it. Instead she gazed into my eyes. "Just because I'm not allowed to date doesn't mean I don't like you, Bryan Ganarski."

She leaned across the seat and planted one full on my lips. I forgot about Gilbert in the backseat while Jennifer and I made out for a few minutes. We pulled back from each other. Jennifer flashed the biggest smile ever aimed at me by a girl, giggled once, and stepped out of my mom's Chevy.

"I never did that before." She galloped up to her front porch and disappeared inside her house.

I about peed my pants a minute later when Gilbert said, "Guess you guys are like a couple, now."

I had forgotten about him. But it soon turned crazier. Not as insane as the midnight visits to my bedroom, but almost. As I pulled up to Gilbert's house, Daniel Brickmaster said, "Hey, this isn't where I live."

I slammed on the brakes and checked the rearview mirror. Brickmaster grinned at me. Gilbert had vanished.

***

Two soft, warm, clammy hands covered my eyes. The air filled with the aroma of roses and vanilla trying to cover up the boys locker room. A sultry voice asked, "Guess who?"

31

There was no mistaking the sweet sound of Jennifer's voice, but at that time of the evening, I sat at my computer desk in my bedroom Skyping with Jennifer Hawkins.

"You tell me?" I asked as clouds of insanity gathered about us.

"Come on. You can guess," chimed the false Jennifer of my madness.

I pulled the female hands away and turned around in time to stare at an attractive teenaged belly button. I raised my eyes without leaving my seat in front of my computer. Yep, it was Jennifer Hawkins. Before I could lift my eyes above her shoulders, the Jennifer Hawkins on Skype asked, "Who's that girl in your room?"

I turned back to the screen. Jennifer could see the girl's navel and blouse so I now shared my hallucinations with the real Jennifer. "Let me call you back."

Too late. Real Jennifer had clicked off on me. I was in trouble with her, and we hadn't dated yet. But we sure talked up a storm until this other Jennifer showed up.

"You want to make out?" The girl tilted her head to one side and smiled. She had not noticed the one, true Jennifer Hawkins on my computer screen.

She looked like Jennifer from the top of her brunette hair, the shade of her green eyes and her rosy, high cheekbones. She wore a white blouse like the one Jennifer had on at school earlier, except it was tied at the bottom to reveal a certain quantity of beautiful midsection. She wore short shorts like the ones Jennifer had worn in school. I checked lower, being a leg man. No backwards map of Italy on this Jennifer's left thigh.

"Aha, you're not Jennifer Hawkins," I shouted. Four dark nights of insane midnight visits had pissed me off.

"Sure I am."

I continued to shout while pointing at the intruder, "Second mistake. You should have said you were her twin sister or a lookalike cousin. First mistake is you didn't check to see who I was Skyping with, did you? Who are you?"

The girl bowed her head. She plopped down on my bed and whispered, "Dopey."

Her voice no longer sounded like Jennifer Hawkins. Instead, it had a broken masculine quality like a kid in the midst of puberty.

"That your name?" I asked.

The girl's face melted. I backed up, fell over my desk chair and scrabbled across my laundry piles on the floor like an upside-down cockroach until I banged my head into the wall under my new window.

Okay, I'll confess. I let out a little pee. Not a lot and don't tell everybody either. It was just a bit. Come on, you'd be scared crapless if you gawped at something that looked like the prettiest girl in tenth grade morph into Daniel Brickmaster, the new kid in my junior class.

This afternoon, Gilbert had turned into Daniel Brickmaster. Tonight, imitation Jennifer morphed into Brickmaster. What was going on?

I tried to say, "What the..." but all that came out was "Warrrrllll" and a little more pee. Don't spread it around. You'd have done the same. Don't kid yourself.

I tried to back up but I was already against the wall. Instead, my efforts succeeded in raising my body about two feet up the wall from where I sat on the floor. I banged my head against the window trim, but my feet were planted flat so I pushed myself up to full height.

Daniel Brickmaster was a tad shorter than me, but it didn't matter. I was scared and in dire need of a change of pants before Mom showed up or my sister Katie dropped by unannounced. Or, heaven forbid, the dad of all anger appeared. We were an unannouncing family.

Daniel kept his voice low. "I'm sorry. I've been so careful. I, oh what's the use. I won't hurt you, Bryan. Relax, okay?"

Daniel Brickmaster looked weird in a girl's blouse and shorts. His belly was hairy as were his legs. If this was an hallucination, why would I dress the new kid in girl clothes?

"Ah... I... Ah I..." I'll confess. My language skills were somewhere south of my damp shorts from the new kid's morphing. And this was on top of the midnight visits the previous three evenings.

"I'll explain. Why don't you have a seat?" How come Daniel was so relaxed? Wasn't he the stranger in my strange land?

I picked my chair up and sat down. I tried to push my jaw up to close my mouth but it kept dropping down. "Ca...Can you... ah... you know..."

"You need an explanation, huh?"

"Yeah." I scratched my head.

"First, you have to promise not to tell anyone."

The idea of an unusual secret about a new kid in school delighted me. But then again I may have imagined the whole thing as part of one of Mom's drug experiments, if in fact my midnight visitations were the result of whatever she had dumped into my cereal. I nodded at Daniel. "I promise, but you have to make me a promise in return."

"What?"

"Promise you will never, ever pretend to be Jennifer Hawkins around me again. And never ever stick your masculine tongue down my throat."

"That's two promises, but yeah, it's a deal."

"Okay, please explain yourself."

"I'm a shape shifter."

"Ga-ga-ga?" My mouth stopped working again despite Daniel's transformation.

"You want to know my real name?"

"Ga."

"Snpgrdxz."

"Gesundheit." My mouth worked.

"No, it's my name."

"You're name is Gesundheit?"

"Snpgrdxz."

"Gesundheit."

"No, you don't get it. I didn't sneeze. I spoke my name. Snpgrdxz."

"Sn-what-ix?"

"Say it with me. Snip"

"Snip."

"Grid."

"Grid"

"Ix."

"Nine."

"IX!"

"Yeah, Roman numeral for nine. Studied that in Latin class."

"My name is Snpgrdxz. There are no vowels. We don't use them where I come from."

"Why not?"

"We don't. How would I know? I'm a kid where I come from."

"You're a teenager?"

"Yeah. I'm equal in maturity to an earther teenager."

"But how old are you in actual years?"

"In earth equivalent years, I'm three hundred sixty-seven."

Before I got to ask Daniel how three-hundred-sixty-seven years made him a teenager, I had a new thought. "Your weird name sounds familiar."

"That's not possible. You're the first earther I told my name to."

"Are you a vampire or werewolf? They change shape whenever they want."

"No. I'm not a zombie either. You know me well enough now to not have to worry that I'll eat your brains or suck your blood or tear you limb from limb. In fact, I enjoy our friendship."

"Why me?"

"Long story. Short version is I picked you out because you seemed likable enough. To find a new friend I first pick the town. I'd visited Wheaton before, but never lived here. Then before school begins, I hang out at the local eateries and swimming pools, or wherever the teens hang out. You're not too in and not too out. Your kind makes the best friends. No one asks too many questions, like who's the new kid hanging out with Beau the star quarterback?

"I wanted to have fun with you to see how you would respond, so I pretended to be a girl for you the other night. I overheard you and Gilbert talk about girls the day before in Burger King, and you mentioned how hot Jennifer Hawkins looked. All I had to do was find out who Jennifer was. What you didn't know is Jennifer came into Burger King about five minutes after you and Gilbert left. She was with her girlfriends who were like Jennifer this and Jennifer that and then one of them called her Hawkins so I knew she was the one you liked."

"So you decided to freak me out by becoming Jennifer?"

"I was having fun. Sorry if I caught you unawares."

"I'm okay except my legs are too rubbery to stand on."

CHAPTER 6

YOU AIN'T WILD 'TILL YOU'RE WILD

So was it hallucinations? Dreams? Mom drugs? Invaders from outer space? Insanity? Or a combination?

After school the next day, I discovered Jennifer Hawkins in Mr. Romano's art room conversing with Gilbert Armstrong and Daniel Brickmaster, aka Snpgrdxz, the shape shifter. Or if he wasn't Snpgrdxz, then I was Bryan Ganarski, the hallucinating teenager who imagines things into existence while in his bedroom.

Maybe the insanity wasn't about me. What if my bedroom was haunted or invaded by demon vampires or werewolves or zombies? Laugh if you want, but wait until you turn the lights out in your room tonight. I want to hear you laugh then.

Monday night was a mystery because the terrorist appeared to have skewered Jennifer in my bedroom, but apparently didn't because she showed up alive on Tuesday. I found a blood puddle in the backyard under my window and a grave by the storage shed. And Gilbert had called the Asian girl "Snpgrdxz."

Tuesday night Jennifer treated me like her long lost lover and said "Snpgrdxz" like it meant something, but I didn't know what. And my friend Gilbert and that Asian terrorist yanked Jennifer's body out of the backyard grave for disposal elsewhere. That meant Jennifer had two bodies, the one she lived in and the one she died in. Okay, assume both nights were nightmares, and the mysteries were real-world things like the bullet hole in Grandma's crucifix and the people who mentioned "Snpgrdxz." Maybe I dig graves in my sleep and shoot guns I don't own while doing so.

Wednesday night Jennifer announced she liked me and wanted to be my girlfriend. She asked me to kiss her when I saw her at school. But the next morning when I kissed her, she denied everything. She didn't say "Snpgrdxz" at school.

Last night Daniel the shape shifter alien overage teenager pretended to be Jennifer when he visited me, and he would have fooled me if I wasn't already on the computer with the real Jennifer. He spoke the Snpgrdxz word and told me it was his real name.

I checked with Gilbert who denied dating an Asian girl. Jennifer wasn't murdered, but what was Daniel Brickmaster up to? I checked with him at lunch, and he admitted visiting my room last night, and he was a shape shifter, and his real name was Snpgrdxz. He admitted he took on Jennifer's identity the other night and he was the one who asked me to kiss her in school. Up to that point, I hadn't met Daniel yet. Go figure.

But Daniel denied visiting me on Monday and Tuesday nights. "You're on your own for those bouts of weirdness, pal. Could those nights have anything to do with the men in black? They may want to use you as a go-between or source. I'll be in danger because it means they may be close."

"What are you talking about?" I asked. "I have enough zany stuff screwing up my life without adding the men in black."

"The men in black have chased me since nineteen forty-six," Daniel said. "We'll have to be careful. They could catch me for dissection purposes and you would disappear, another mysterious missing teenager."

"Aren't missing teenagers kidnapped and murdered by perverts who do horrible things to them?" I asked.

"Do you really think there are that many perverts in your world?" Snpgrdxz replied. "I'm serious. It's the men in black."

***

I was no closer to the answers to my insane experiences. To change the subject, I considered why Jennifer Hawkins hung out with a bunch of art club people determined to paint pictures, stay poor and skip school? Okay, so I had a cynical view of artists because, well, I was one. And art club was what kept us after school. The other guys I can understand, but not my Jennifer. We were falling in love, weren't we? Or was yesterday morning's kiss another dream vision? And what about the make out session in Mom's Malibu when I dropped her off yesterday?

Jennifer locked eyes with me and smiled. I took her hand and helped her rise out of her seat. Mr. Romano noticed me with Jennifer. "Remember, Wild Thing, you ain't wild 'till you're wild."

Jennifer nodded her head. "Guess I'm not a wild thing. I'm plain old Jennifer."

Mr. Romano pushed his flowing salt-and-pepper locks back so he could scratch behind his ears. "I can tell a wild thing."

Jennifer stared at Mr. Romano for such a long time he became uncomfortable.

"No, I'm not Wild Thing," Jennifer said.

Mr. Romano laughed.

"Maria Gonzalez is the one you should call Wild Thing," Gilbert said. "She skipped school two days in a row."

Mr. Romano stared at Gilbert with a baffled expression, which is pretty much how he stared at everyone. Except this stare was more confounded than usual. "Maria is as straight as an Aztec arrow. Not a wild bone in her sprocket. She is home sick."

I'm not sure what Mr. Romano tried to tell us with the "sprocket" comment. He could have been reaching for "body" but missed because he couldn't see his words what with the smog wafting around in his brain from his pothead days.

"Ask anyone, Mr. Romano. Maria is as wild as they come." Gilbert waved his hands around.

"When did you become the expert on Maria Gonzalez?" Mr. Romano asked.

"I'm not." Gilbert stood.

"So where is she?" Mr. Romano asked.

"Search me" Gilbert sat down.

"You ready?" I asked Jennifer.

"Yeah."

I kissed her hand.

"Cool." Jennifer headed for the door with me attached.

"Hey, Wild Thing," Mr. Romano called.

Jennifer gave Mr. Romano a cold backward glance.

Mr. Romano said, "Stay wild, baby. We like seeing you here at art club. And remember it ain't a date if you travel in a group. So go for it."

"What?" Jennifer asked.

Mr. Romano said, "Before you love birds head into the bushes or the backseat, how about helping us on this film idea I have for art club this semester?"

"Okay." Jennifer yanked me back into the room while ignoring my protests.

Mr. Romano turned on his video projector. We observed the art room on screen for about a minute with no changes.

"What are we watching?" Daniel Brickmaster asked.

"Good question, new kid," Mr. Romano said. "What does it look like to you?"

Gilbert leaned back in his desk. "The art room? Are we seeing it through the lens of a surveillance camera?

"Exactly, Gilbert. I shot this footage before school yesterday morning. The camera is behind you on the wall by the ceiling."

We spotted a small camera attached to the wall where Mr. Romano had indicated.

"What are we supposed to do with this?" I asked.

"How would you like to make an art film? Your job is to write the voiceover narration for a surveillance video. Nothing happens on screen, so you have to make it exciting with voices, music and sound effects."

"You mean the whole movie is nothing but this static shot? It's like a photograph." Gilbert pointed to the screen.

"Whoa, did you see that?" Daniel shouted.

"What?" Mr. Romano asked.

"A blur crossed the screen like somebody running fast," Daniel said.

"Let's back up and see what we captured so our movie will have action." Mr. Romano stopped the video and restarted it. We stared at the screen this time. Nothing happened for the first couple of minutes, but then we spotted the blur.

"What was it?" Daniel asked.

"What do you think it was?" asked Mr. Romano. "Let's play it again but in slow-mo."

"It looks the same as it does at regular speed," said Gilbert.

Jennifer gasped as the slowed down video showed a creature that could be either a troll or the ugliest dude at Lincoln High. He carried Maria Gonzalez on his exaggerated width shoulders. They moved across the room and into a closet. Maria's eyes were wide and filled with fear. She opened her mouth like she was screaming, but the video didn't have sound.

"Quick call nine-one-one. Maria's been kidnapped by a troll," said Gilbert.

"Dude, who has a phone?" asked Mr. Romano.

I called nine-one-one on my cell.

After giving the dispatcher my name, she asked, "What is the nature of your emergency?" The voice sounded like a computer programed to mimic an interested person. It wasn't a machine sound but not real either.

"My friend's been kidnapped by a troll who dragged her into the tunnels. Come quick." Too much information. I knew it the moment I spoke.

"Did you say a 'troll'?"

See, I told you it was too much info. "Yeah."

"Can you describe this troll?"

"Certainly. Curly black hair, hairy shoulders and back. Oh, and he wore a furry butt cover, like a miniskirt except on a guy. Or a troll."

"How tall was this man?"

"Not a man, a troll. He was about three-feet to three-feet-six-inches tall, something like that. Short. Stocky fellow with extra broad shoulders."

"Did you say three-feet tall?"

"Yeah, thereabouts. Maybe a bit more."

Machine voice sounded a bit more sarcastic than a talking computer. "Where did you say this alleged kidnapping took place?"

"Lincoln High in Wheaton. We're in the art room."

"Right. Listen, kid, it's against the law to call the emergency help line when there's no emergency. No more prank calls, okay?"

"It's not a…"

She hung up on me.

***

I redialed 9-1-1.

This time, I limited my call to the facts the police would accept. I told her the truth. Maria Gonzalez kidnapped.

42

Kidnapper last seen dragging her into the tunnels from the art room of Lincoln High. Kidnapping captured on video.

This time the lady, a different lady, said, "I'll send a patrol car right away."

I hugged Jennifer. "We have to tell your dad."

Jennifer's face took on a concerned appearance. "You believe Maria was kidnapped, don't you? A short kid in need of a haircut dragged her into a closet. I mean calling the police is one thing. Calling them twice is another. All you're doing is breaking the law. But telling my dad is crazy. You can get into a lot of trouble pranking Dad."

I glanced around the room. "Police on the way. Going to Dr. Hawkins office. Be back with the police and Dr. Hawkins so get ready."

***

"Trolls don't exist." Jennifer sidled up close as we strolled to the principal's office.

"I know but he looked like a troll moving fast." I tripped over a joint in a floor tile.

"How do you know it was guy troll and not a girl troll?" Jennifer helped me stand up.

"Too hairy and topless."

"No boobs?" she asked.

"From the back, he was one hairy troll. I don't expect anyone to find boobs on that particular monster's front." I dropped Jennifer's hand and opened the principal's office door for her.

Her dad sat behind his big desk working late as usual.

Jennifer smacked me on the shoulder. "Chicken."

"Can you say 'detention' for me and 'grounded' for you if your dad catches us holding hands?"

"Good points."

Dr. Hawkins gazed up from his laptop. "Hi. What are you two up to?"

"Bryan called the police." Jennifer flopped in a chair in front of her dad's desk.

Sirens screamed by the office window before I could volunteer why I called the police.

"What happened?" Dr. Hawkins pulled the glasses off his nose.

I explained about Maria Gonzalez being kidnapped but left out the part about the troll. Let him figure that out for himself. Not sure he believed me until two uniforms charged in. Having the police show up makes everything real. I told the officers about the video. I was excited as I spoke but I still left out the troll.

Dr. Hawkins led the officers to the art room. The police told us to stay back while they searched. They dragged Mr. Romano into the closet and disappeared down a dark stairway.

"I didn't know that closet led to the tunnels." Jennifer said.

"Lots of tunnel entrances around school," I said.

Dr. Hawkins gazed at me. "Why were you two in the tunnels?"

"We didn't go into the tunnels, Daddy." Jennifer's eyes pleaded for belief.

"We were sitting here in art club when we spotted Maria on Mr. Romano's video, sir," I said.

"What video?" Dr. Hawkins beamed laser detention heat into my brain with his eyes.

"It's a surveillance tape. Mr. Romano wants us to make a film using surveillance footage and add voiceover to tell the story."

"How did you get hold of surveillance video? It's not available to students." Dr. Hawkins' lasers were still on full blast.

"Mr. Romano shot his own fake surveillance video here in the art room. See, there's his camera." I pointed out the camera on the wall near the ceiling.

"Okay. So it's an art project and something just showed up?" Laser eyes beamed at me again.

"Yes, sir. Here, I'll show you." I replayed the scene in slow-mo with the troll and Maria.

"What was it?" Dr. Hawkins asked.

"Looks like a troll to me, Daddy," said Jennifer.

Dr. Hawkins scratched his chin and rubbed his butt. "You kids can head on home." Lasers.

"Police said to 'wait here.'" I wanted to leave to get away from the laser beams shooting brain-draining x-rays into my head.

"Okay. Stay. You called them so they will want to speak to you." Dr. Hawkins swung his laser-cannon eyes around to zap Jennifer. "You can go home."

"Okay." Jennifer smiled at her dad and took off. At the door, she turned and gave me a smile before heading out.

I was alone with Laser Lights for the next four hours. I called home to let my folks know what happened and where I was. Katie answered so I told her. She didn't believe me, but she must have told my dad because he called a few hours later when he got home from work. I explained the situation. He came down to the school to be with me. Dad doesn't trust principals and police. They add up to a ton of trouble when you combine them.

Dr. Hawkins had his long legs stretched out in front of him as he leaned against one of the closet doors. Doors covered the walls in the huge art room at Lincoln High. Most of the closets held art supplies and art junk. The room smelled like acrylic paint and vinegar.

But the closet behind Dr. Hawkins was always locked. The kids figured Mr. Romano kept his beer and pot stashed in there. You never know.

Dad sat in a student desk while I paced in a circle. The sound of footsteps came from the open door I always thought led to a closet. A flashlight beam in the distance showed a tunnel or cave. The little light lit the way for

45

whoever was behind it. A voice, which sounded like one of the cops, I don't know which one, said, "Found something."

About a minute later, the cops and Mr. Romano came out of the dark underground.

One of the officers carried a girl's black shoe in his hand. "We'll need a search party to cover the tunnels."

CHAPTER 7

MR. ROMANO'S SECRET CLOSET

"Dude, you can wander them tunnels for years and not find your way out." Mr. Romano nodded in apparent agreement with his own brain. Which one of us was the "Dude" – Jennifer Hawkins, Gilbert Armstrong, Danny Brickmaster, or me?

We had gathered in Mr. Romano's art room on the second floor of the oldest part of Lincoln High after wandering the tunnels most of Saturday morning. Seemed like the place to stay out of the way of the searchers.

"We have to find Maria." Jennifer folded her arms and harrumphed in her teenage girl way. She was cute, but the look on Gilbert's face said she was nuts. Danny smiled like he was an uninterested observer from another planet, which he was, of course.

Police, fireman, and volunteers wandered through the underground tunnel system. Most of them came back out.

Mr. Romano said, "You kids eat lunch and take a nap. Report back here at three o'clock."

Gilbert laughed. "But Mr. Romano, we're kids. We don't nap."

Mr. Romano shook his head. "Okay, do what you want, but I need a nap. Return at three and we'll take another peek at them tunnels."

Jennifer took my hand and led me out with Daniel and Gilbert in tow. We jumped into Mom's Malibu, which she let me borrow for the day.

"Where do you want to eat?" I asked.

Jennifer had her cell pushed against the side of her head. "My mom says she'll feed us."

"Okay, let's go to your mom's house," said Daniel.

***

"Jennifer Ganarski sounds nice to me," I said.

"Me too." Jennifer tickled my tonsils in front of everyone.

Her mom selected that moment to mosey in from the kitchen. "Jennifer Hawkins, what are you doing?"

The kiss in question began with the invitation to lunch. I drove the gang to Jennifer's house which was one of the oldest in Wheaton. Located on the north side of town, the home featured gables, gingerbread and the other accoutrements of the Victorian era.

Do you like that word "accoutrements?" I learned it in English class last year when it showed up in a book I read. Anyway, fancy wood shingles and bric-a-brac covered Jennifer's house on the second floor and the attic. The first floor was stucco down to the stone foundation. A large porch wrapped around the front and one side of the house. A driveway went to the back of the lot where a two-car garage stood. Several ancient oaks adorned the lot.

Jennifer acted as a tour guide for us. "The house has been in our family since my ancestors built it back in the eighteen forties or fifties. I forgot when. We could never afford a house this big in the Chicago suburbs if we had to buy it today. What's cool is we owned the property before my ancestors built this house. It replaced the original log cabin that stood here from the eighteen thirties. We used to own many acres of land around this side of town also, but my great whatever number of grandparents sold it off as lots way back in the day. Money was tight back then like today."

Jennifer showed us the inside of the house with modern wallpaper and ancient oak trim. The oak floor boards and door trim were wide and thick with fancy turnings or carvings on the trim. The window molding matched as best as I could tell with the curtains in the way. The windows were old with little square stained glass panels around the outside and clear in the center. The stain glass panels were colorful in red, blue, yellow and green.

On the wall by the entrance from the dining room to the kitchen, I spotted a family tree.

Jennifer noticed me studying it. "It goes back to the first member of our family who settled our land. Their names were Joseph and Jennifer Williams. We can't prove it, but our family oral tradition says Jennifer's maiden name was Hawkins, like my last name today. We think Mom may have married a distant cousin."

Jennifer dropped her voice to a whisper, "Another family rumor claims Joseph was a black man, but we've never been able to prove it one way or another. We've never traced our family before old Joe and Jennifer showed up in Illinois in eighteen thirty-eight with their little girl, also named Jennifer."

"Jennifer shows up a lot on your family tree," Gilbert scanned the framed parchment.

"It does. Mom says I'm named for all of them."

Gilbert said, "According to this, we're looking at your Mom's family tree, but your father is the Hawkins. How is that?"

"The name Hawkins shows up several times on the family tree. Dad says it's a kwinky-dink. He's right of course, unless he is a distant cousin as Mom suspects. But how would you plan the maiden name of the woman you choose for your wife? Or in my mom's case, the last name of your husband. I mean no way would my parents or I choose the name

Ganarski for my married name. It would have to happen on its own."

"Put your jaw back where it belongs, Ganarski. She was using you as an example. She didn't propose." Gilbert punched me on the shoulder.

That's when I said the thing about the name Jennifer Ganarski sounding nice and Jennifer went to work on my tonsils with her tongue, and as I said, her mom popped out of nowhere to catch us in the midst of passionate PDA.

Jennifer pulled away from me. "Sorry, Mom."

"You know better than to make a public display of yourself." Mrs. Hawkins crossed her arms to match her cantankerous demeanor.

"But Mom, we're not in public."

Ignoring Jennifer, Mrs. Hawkins said, "Bryan Ganarski, your mother will hear about this."

"Yes, ma'am. Sorry ma'am," I said.

Despite the little PDA episode, Mrs. Hawkins fed us a great lunch of ham and cheese sandwiches.

Back in my mom's Malibu, Jennifer grabbed my neck at the first red light and planted one huge heart-throbber on my lips.

When the light popped green, I asked, "Was that for me or were you pissed at your mom?"

"Both, but mainly because I'm ticked at Mom. At least she didn't ground me."

"Why didn't we hook up before? I've had a crush on you since from forever." I didn't want to admit that my crush kicked in big time during seventh grade when I first noticed she had girl legs hanging down from her butt.

"Bryan, what I said about changing my name to Ganarski was no accident. I've had a crush on you since kindergarten. I waited for you to make the first move and now you did. It's about time, by the way."

"A guy has to work up the guts, Jennifer. It only took me four years."

***

"Trolls?" Jennifer, who started to unfold her arms, froze in mid-unfold. We were back in Mr. Romano's art room where we had awakened him at his desk by strolling into the room in the quiet, normal way of teenagers, also known as loud.

"Wild Thing, I work late some nights. You ever think about what crawls out of them tunnels when there ain't nobody around?" Mr. Romano wandered over to that closet he always kept locked. He fumbled around with his keychain and poked one in the lock to open the door. He rummaged through a stack of old cardboard boxes as a strong musty smell arose in the room.

"You've seen trolls?" Gilbert wanted in on this action. "And you think Maria's kidnapper was a troll?"

"You don't believe your best friend, but the crazy art teacher is somehow believable?" Jennifer pointed an index finger in Gilbert's face.

"Well, I guess…" Gilbert backed up three steps.

"Guess nothing, pal. You owe Bryan an apology." Jennifer's finger hadn't moved.

"You owe Bryan an apology. You're his girlfriend and you didn't believe him." Danny Brickmaster said.

Jennifer harrumphed. "I still don't believe Bryan. I don't believe Mr. Romano either. There's no such thing as trolls. But you believe now, don't you, Gilbert? So you owe Bryan an apology. I can always apologize later if you find a real troll."

Jennifer hadn't denied she was my girlfriend. She was my girlfriend then, right? In public, I mean. It's one thing to say you've had a crush on someone since forever and another to allow the public to hear you say it out loud. My smile tickled my ears.

Mr. Romano poked his head out of the pile of boxes. "Dudes and Wild Thing dudette, we need to get your friend back along with the missing searcher. Don't matter whether we're dealing with a troll or something else. There's no saying no to the call, man."

"No." Gilbert folded his arms.

"I have to be home for dinner so I'll have to decline. Besides, I don't want to be the only girl," Jennifer returned her index finger to the port arms position.

"It's not something we should attempt, Mr. Romano. We're kids." I said.

Mr. Romano stuck his head in another box. "Kids are the only ones who can find her. Think adults believe in trolls?"

"Don't you?" I asked.

Mr. Romano yanked a rifle out of a box and slammed a clip in. "Okay, either we raise an army of burned out stoner creatives or it's just us. I say it's us."

"I'll go," said Danny Brickmaster who obviously didn't understand that quest journeys always begin with a rejection of the call. Didn't he study his literature last year? Or watch *Star Wars*? Right, he wasn't here last year, but you'd think he would have learned something about literature from the movies after the years he spent as a teenager.

Mr. Romano tossed the rifle to me, and I made a lucky catch. I don't know what the trigger hit, but a quick burst of bullets hit the ceiling.

"What's this?" I asked.

"M16." Mr. Romano poked a bit more into one of his boxes and came out with a large wooden mallet. He presented it to Jennifer. "You'll need this, Wild Thing."

Jennifer rose off the floor where she had landed when the bullets flew. She accepted the mallet. "But I'm not going unless you promise to have me home in time for dinner. And you have to promise to find another girl for the trip, one like me so we can be friends."

Mr. Romano reached into another box and withdrew M16s for the rest of the group and one for himself. The M16s matched the rifles my imaginary Gilbert and the Asian girl carried when they burst into my room the other night, except these weapons appeared brand new and clean. Their weapons showed wear and tear like they'd been through a war. But I'm sure those rifles must have been M16s. They were shaped the same. Another difference was Mr. Romano's weapons didn't have bayonets like the ones the other night.

Mr. Romano dug around and came out with a box filled with bayonets. He handed one to each of us. He explored the closet again until he produced a box of ammunition belts loaded with M16 clips. One more box dive led to a sheath with a Bowie knife. He handed it to Wild Thing, I mean Jennifer.

"I'm still not going unless Bryan goes," said Jennifer.

With more box dives, Mr. Romano came up with minor's hats for us and two oil lamps like you see in old western movies. Another box dive produced half a dozen flashlights.

Mr. Romano spun around to reveal this huge grin on his face. "I know the way around them tunnels better'n most trolls. And better'n any zombie I've ever run into down in the tunnels. They're always wandering around lost. So are you ready to lock and load?"

I'm not sure which one of us said it first, but we cried, "Zombies?"

"You carry the crucifix, Dudette Wild Thing." Mr. Romano was half-buried in another one of his boxes with the crucifix stretched in his hand behind his back.

Jennifer grabbed it. "Are you planning to say Mass?"

"Hold on to these, too." Mr. Romano held a fistful of wooden stakes behind his back. Jennifer took those into her arms. She was loaded with stuff now.

"Wild Thing, did you bring a backpack?" Mr. Romano closed a box lid and turned around.

"It's Saturday. I left it home." Jennifer said.

Mr. Romano yanked a box out of his closet. "Grab one."

Each of us took a brand new huge backpack out of the box. They were the kind people used for backpacking into the wilderness rather than what you'll find on a typical high school student's back.

Mr. Romano yanked another box out of the closet. "You'll want these."

We each snagged a sleeping bag and a couple of bungee cords to attach them to our backpacks.

"What'll we need the sleeping bags for?" Jennifer stuffed the wooden stakes into her backpack.

Mr. Romano gawped at her like she was as crazy as her new boyfriend in the days before school began.

Gilbert asked, "Vampires?"

"You never know. I better break out the silver bullets, too." Mr. Romano dove into another box.

"Silver bullets?" Daniel asked.

"Werewolves," said Jennifer. "This is starting to sound like fun. Are you sure we'll be home in time for dinner?"

Mr. Romano reached under his desk and yanked out one of those large plastic picnic coolers. He opened the lid to reveal ice and beer cans. "Everybody grab a beer."

Jennifer pulled out the first one and snapped it open. "I've never had alcohol, Mr. Romano. Are you certain we're allowed?"

"Wild Thing, when you intend to follow where the tunnels take you, don't leave unless you've had a drink first. And trust me, this little beer will not be your last one of the journey. And you have to stop worrying about your supper. I've packed plenty of food in my backpack."

Jennifer snagged my arm while we both sipped our beers. She laughed which made me laugh. "Guess I'm coming with you, Bryan Ganarski."

"Up till now I wasn't going," I said.

Mr. Romano popped a beer. "One last thing before we take off. Leave the electronics behind."

Four groans formed the background music to the stacking of cells, pads and other twenty-first century mobile devices in Mr. Romano's secret closet. We were bound for a road trip without connectivity.

CHAPTER 8

THE TUNNELS

A shadow zipped by behind me. It was darker than the blackness outside of the range of our lamps. I don't know what it was but it smelled evil. We walked single file through the tunnels beneath Lincoln High with me last in line. I made a squeaky noise as I caught my breath.

"What?" Jennifer asked. She padded along in front of me.

"I noticed a shadow?" My voice shook.

"So, are you afraid of shadows?" Jennifer faced me.

"Yeah, it was physical, like a dark creature. Scared the crap out of me."

"Good, then you won't be constipated this trip." Jennifer chuckled and spun around. I'm sure her face reddened because she never says poopy stuff around me, but it was too dark to tell.

A bat nearly flushed my bladder out as it dove out of the darkness in front of us. We ducked and Jennifer covered her hair with her hands as best she could.

When the bat vanished into the black depths behind us, Jennifer asked, "What else is lurking in the dark?"

Mr. Romano said, "You're not the wildest wild thing in these parts, Wild Thing. Be on your guard at all times. Wear your spiritual armor but lock and load."

We hadn't traveled more than fifty paces when Jennifer asked, "How long do you think we'll be gone?"

Mr. Romano said, "Not so much time as anyone will notice. We're looking for Maria Gonzalez, and when we find her, we head home for dinner."

"Then why did Mr. Romano insist on us packing so much gear?" Jennifer asked.

"In case it takes all night?" I tugged on my M16 to make it more comfortable on my shoulder.

"We have enough junk to feed a dozen people for a year. Did you see all the Army chow Tony stuffed into his backpack?" Gilbert asked.

"Are you having second thoughts about this journey?" I asked.

"Only if you are, Bryan," said Jennifer.

"I'm too scared to back out now so count me in. Besides, I know what I want," I said.

Jennifer pushed her open hand against my shoulder. "I know what you want, too. Find Maria and be the big hero. It's a guy thing."

"No, I want to spend as much time with you as I can. My goal is to make you my girlfriend. Finding Maria and becoming a big hero is a side benefit."

"Wow, I'm just in it for the adventure, but you care that much about me?"

"I told you I've had a crush on you forever, Jennifer."

"How long is forever?" Daniel Brickmaster asked.

"Seventh grade."

"I've liked you for a long time, too. But I'm not sure I'm ready to commit to anything more than to start a dating relationship. Let's just see what happens. No big commitments, okay?" Jennifer adjusted her backpack.

"But I can consider this our first date?" I asked.

"If you want, but this is a lousy place to bring a girl on her first date."

About ten minutes later, I heard tiny noises behind me. "Is it safe to walk down here, Mr. Romano? I hear pebbles falling from the ceiling behind us, and it could mean we're about to have a cave in."

"The tunnels have been here for a century or two, maybe longer," said Mr. Romano. "They ain't going anywhere."

Five minutes later, I heard the first footsteps behind me. "We're being followed," I said.

The group stopped to listen.

"I don't hear anything," Gilbert said.

"I heard big feet behind us. I can't help if the thing stopped when we stopped." I smacked a fist into my hand which caused me to drop my flashlight. I bent over to pick it up, but noticed a pair of shoes lit by the flashlight. The shoes were about 10 feet behind us. "Who's there?" I called.

"You see something?" Mr. Romano asked.

"Yeah, right behind us." I flashed my light into the darkness. The others shined their lights as well. The tunnel was empty with no shoes in sight.

"Control your imagination," Mr. Romano said. "There's enough scary stuff where we're going without adding made up nonsense."

I lost track of time, but not before the footsteps started again. They stopped. The sudden silence raised more goose bumps than the mysterious footsteps. After the silence came a slithering sound.

I asked, "Are there snakes down here, Mr. Romano?"

Before Mr. Romano answered, two arms embraced me from behind and yanked me to the ground. In the dim light, I saw a grey old man with red eyes. His breath smelled of dead fish and rats. The thing opened its mouth about a foot to expose two extra-long yellow fangs. The creature rolled its head back as far as it could, so I knew it was about to snap down on my throat. I tried to move, but couldn't. The thing had me in a locked-down grip.

I spotted a female hand come over the vampire's head. It held a crucifix which the hand smashed into the vampire's face. The creature shriveled and flew backwards into the darkness behind us. I followed the female hand up to my Jennifer's smiling face.

"Thanks. You saved my life," I said.

"Then you owe me a kiss, mister." Jennifer knelt and laid a lip lock on me to melt the vampire memory.

A tiny fairy fluttered out of the dark behind us and flittered about like a butterfly until it vanished into the tunnel in front of us. The creature looked like a tiny lady wearing a short dress. Its miniature wings flapped about like a dragonfly's.

"That was Tinkerbelle, right?" Daniel asked.

"Why don't they have black fairies?" Gilbert asked.

"They do," said Mr. Romano.

The fairy hadn't been gone more than a few seconds when we heard a loud buzzing noise.

"Now what?" Gilbert asked.

"Duck," Mr. Romano cried.

I still shook from the bat, the mysterious shadow, the footsteps, the snake and the vampire. I flattened to the ground and in the process, coated the front of my clothes in tunnel mud. The rest of the group screamed as they dropped to the ground. They gasped for air. I caught my breath as hundreds of bats fluttered above us. I couldn't help but wonder if we too should be following their example to escape the tunnels. Where was Mr. Romano taking us? Could we trust this burned out ex-hippie art teacher? And would we be home in time for dinner?

Once the bats vanished, we trudged deeper into the depths of the black underworld beneath Lincoln High. I worried that something else might jump out at us. We were guided by the lamps built into our miner's hats and our flashlights. These light beams bounced off old heavy wood beams. The beams supported the plank ceiling indicating that the material above the wood was dirt. The walls were black Illinois farm soil as was the floor. The ground was damp and we had to watch for the occasional mud puddle.

Mr. Romano led us single file with Gilbert behind him followed by Daniel Brickmaster, aka Snpgrdxz. Jennifer came next followed by yours truly.

The air had a dank and damp aroma.

Ahead of us, I noticed an attractive blonde approaching. She had long, curly hair and wore a red dress like the kind you see the wealthy folks wear on those British soaps about the early twentieth century. Mr. Romano ignored her as she passed him. The others followed Mr. Romano's lead, including Jennifer, which surprised me since she wanted a girl companion on this trek. If you think about it, the blonde was most likely from one of the search parties and somehow became separated. She could be lost.

As she passed Jennifer, I said, "Hi, are you okay?"

Jennifer said, "Yeah, I'm fine."

The blonde stared at me for a moment before a glint of recognition crossed her face. She hugged me. She must have been wandering the tunnels for a long time because she was ice cold.

"Do you need help?" I asked.

"No, thanks, Bryan. You've already done more than enough. I have to run." She vanished into the darkness behind us.

"Thanks for not being jealous when that girl hugged me," I said.

Jennifer turned around. "What girl?"

"The cute blonde in the World War I getup."

"When was this?" Jennifer asked.

"Just now."

"Bryan, you're imagining things. Except for the bats and a vampire, we haven't seen anything in these tunnels yet."

I called down the line, "Mr. Romano, did you see that blonde strut by?"

"What blonde?" Mr. Romano called back.

Gilbert stopped and faced me. "I wish there was a blonde, Ganarski. Jennifer is right. We need another woman for this trip."

As our group moved forward through the tunnels, Snpgrdxz said, "That must have been weird, Bryan, seeing a blonde that no one else spotted. What were you smoking?"

"Seeing her wasn't the weird part. She knew my name." I scratched my head in search of bat eggs and vampire teeth.

Jennifer tripped over a rock but I caught her arm in time to keep her from falling. She thanked me with a kiss which led to a second and third smooch. When we came up for a gulp of our dank and wet air, the others were gone.

"Hey, where are you guys?" I yelled.

"Over here. Don't worry, I'm coming." The voice sounded flat.

"Who was that?" I asked.

"I don't know, but I love his deep, resonant voice," said Jennifer.

Two eyes glowed in front of us. They bounced in our direction. As the eyes floated out of the darkness into the beams of our lamps, we found ourselves gazing at a man with greased down hair wearing a tuxedo.

"We're beginning to see a theme here, Jennifer. Is there a World War I party scheduled for tonight?"

The man approached. "Jennifer Hawkins and Bryan Ganarski, so good to see you two." He smiled without opening his mouth which made me wonder how happy he was to see her. "But you look so young, still. It was Turpelator, wasn't it?"

"How do you know our names?" Jennifer asked.

"You know me, Jennifer. I'm Chauncey Chadsworth from Lincoln High. Don't you remember? Class of eighteen."

"Nineteen eighteen?" I asked.

Jennifer said, "Chauncey Chadsworth from nineteen eighteen? Nope, I can't recall ever meeting you. For that matter, this isn't nineteen eighteen."

"I know, but that's when we met. Now it's time to make you mine, my lovely dearest. I've waited I don't know how many decades for this moment." Chauncey sounded a bit formal but what do you expect with a guy from World War I.

Mr. Romano hollered from down the tunnel, "Wild Thing, the crucifix, quick."

"Why does he want the crucifix now?" Jennifer asked. "It's not even Sunday."

Chauncey chose that moment to open his mouth about two feet so he could show off his huge fangs. Twinkle dust sparkled in our light beams.

Chauncey missed Jennifer as she ducked to snag the crucifix from her backpack. He snagged me by the shoulders and pulled me in close. Have you ever smelled vampire breath? Deep down inside they've been dead for who knows how long. Chauncey's breath gave off the aroma you expect from a grave opened too soon after someone was buried. I tried pushing him away, but was no match for his demon strength.

Jennifer mushed the crucifix into the side of Chauncey's face. With his head in flames, he fell back into the darkness of the cave behind us.

Mr. Romano arrived with a loaded crossbow. Gilbert and Snpgrdxz had their M16s at the ready.

"Are you okay?" Mr. Romano asked.

I checked my throat for bite marks, but found none. "Yes."

Jennifer wiped her hands across her blue jeans. "Yes."

The young vampire flew out of the darkness so Mr. Romano shot it with an arrow. The vampire caught it with his bare hands and laughed. Gilbert and Snpgrdxz opened fire with their M16s.

Bullets sank into the vampire's chest. "What's this?"

"Lignum vitae bullets," said Mr. Romano. "It's the hardest wood known."

Chauncey fell back against the tunnel wall and slid to the floor. "Why did you shoot me?"

"You're a blood sucking vampire from long ago," said Mr. Romano.

"That's a real vampire?" Gilbert asked.

"Show them your mouth, Chauncey," Mr. Romano ordered.

Chauncey opened his mouth a good two feet to expose eighteen-inch fangs. He closed his mouth. With a normal shaped mouth he said, "I guess there's no way I can talk you into yanking these bullets out, is there?"

"Not today, Chauncey. You've needed your heart broken for a long time," said Mr. Romano.

"But my heart has been broken since, oh, I get it. Your little joke," said Chauncey.

"Why would someone from nineteen eighteen know me?" Jennifer asked.

"Because we met at your grandmother's house back before I was converted to the vampire cause. We were rather fond of each other then. Don't you remember?" Chauncey asked.

"Why would I remember nineteen eighteen?" Jennifer asked. "Besides, my grandmother wasn't even born until the nineteen fifties."

"Pity." Chauncey vanished into a puff of smoke as a half dozen lignum vitae slugs dropped to the ground where he had been sitting.

Fear gripped my throat as I slid to the ground. "Did we kill it or has it escaped?"

Mr. Romano rubbed his chin. "I'm not sure. Either way, it makes two vampires so far today. I've never seen two in one visit to the tunnels before. Something must be up so he's not the last monster we'll run into."

"He's not?" Jennifer asked.

CHAPTER 9

OUR SECRET WEAPON

Once I settled my bottom next to my backpack in an intersection of tunnels, I brought up our secret weapon. "Danny the Brick has something he wants to tell everyone."

"I do?" In the lamplight next to me, Daniel took on a sinister, angry appearance.

The air was cool and dank, but the dirt floor was dry in this classroom-sized space where we parked in a circle.

"Danny, they have to know what you're capable of. This mission has become too dangerous." I punched him on the arm.

"You promised, Bryan. I shared my secret the other night in strictest confidence." Daniel stood up.

"You screwed up and gave yourself away."

Jennifer placed the Bowie knife across her lap. "Why do I get the feeling this has something to do with that girl in your room the other night?"

"What were you doing in Bryan's bedroom with another girl?" Gilbert doubled over in laughter. "Somebody had a party and didn't tell his friends. His guy friends, that is."

"She visited me on Skype so keep your head out of the muck." I punched Gilbert on the shoulder. To Jennifer, I said, "Good guess and it wasn't a girl."

"Sure it was," Daniel said.

"How do you know?" Gilbert asked.

"Because he was there," I said.

"You were?" Jennifer asked.

Daniel stirred dust as he sat down with his head bowed. "If I tell you, will you promise to keep my secret?"

"Depends, Dude," Mr. Romano said.

"Sooner or later you'll find out anyway. We're headed into danger. The trolls, or whatever those creatures are, may turn us into hors d' oeuvres. No way we'll be back in time for dinner so what you need to know is I'm not from around here," said Daniel.

"Yeah, you have an accent, like from Philadelphia, right?" Gilbert asked.

"He's from a little farther away than Philly," I said.

"How far?" Mr. Romano straightened up and lost his pothead look. With his long hair and Roman nose, the idea of an ancient warrior popped into my head.

"Far." Daniel morphed into an Asian girl. Everybody backed away. In the darkness of the tunnels, enough light emitted from our helmets and lanterns for me to figure out this was the same Asian terrorist who invaded my bedroom the other night.

Gilbert screamed.

"Whoa, how'd you do that?" Jennifer asked.

"I'm a shape-shifting teenaged space alien." Snpgrdxz the Asian girl said. "But please promise never to tell anyone. If the feds find me, I'm done for."

"Seriously, how'd you do that?" Jennifer asked.

"I changed. It's what I do." Daniel turned his hair red and back to black.

"I change, too, but into a different blouse or shorts. You're like a whole new person." Jennifer gestured down Daniel's entire body.

Gilbert recovered. "Who are you, girl? You're cute."

Snpgrdxz shrugged. "I don't have a name for her yet, but I like Amelia."

"Not very Chinese," Gilbert said.

"I was thinking Chinese American. Short skirts. Sexy. Maybe a slut."

Jennifer slapped Snpgrdxz's face.

"Why did you hit me?" Snpgrdxz rubbed his cheek.

"For pretending to be me in Bryan's bedroom the other night and for calling yourself a slut. If you plan to girlify yourself, you need to know we are not sluts. We're good girls or you are not hanging with us. The last things we need on this road trip are boys dithering their ying-yangs with fake ding-dangs."

"Say what?" Snpgrdxz morphed back to Daniel.

"Daniel, I thought you told me you did not have your Amelia visit my bedroom the other night with Gilbert in tow, yet here you are. And this isn't the first time you two carried an M16, is it?" I asked. It can't hurt to bring this stuff up again.

"What are you talking about?" Gilbert asked.

"Daniel denied being the Asian girl when she visited me the other night. Remember I asked you about dating an Asian girl?" I retied my sneaks.

"Yeah, but I didn't," said Gilbert.

"Either she was in my room with you or I have ultra-realistic dreams. I could have sworn this Amelia the Asian girl visited my bedroom the other night." I glared at Gilbert until a punch from Jennifer smashed into my shoulder.

"What?" I asked.

"You had another woman in your bedroom and you didn't tell me?" Jennifer asked.

"Why would I tell you? You were there, too. Besides, it happened before we kissed."

"Oh, another one of your dreams?" Jennifer asked.

I tightened a strap on my backpack. "Yes, if you guys don't remember. But Amelia showed up days before Daniel shape-shifted into her. How could I know about her before he invented her?"

"I told you Jennifer was the Wild Thing." Mr. Romano rotated his head in Daniel's direction. "Let's not have any more dreams on this here outing, okay?"

Never order the impossible. The living dream began with a flicker of light from down in the tunnel ahead of us. It floated our way in a wavy motion like a butterfly.

As we stared, Gilbert said, "It's a cockroach with a butt light."

It wasn't of course. It was another fairy. Everyone knew that except Gilbert. The fairy flew right up to my face so I took a good gander at it with my minor's helmet light. It appeared as an attractive young lady with wings. She was no more than three inches tall and wore a short orange dress. She smiled in my face, and in the tiniest squeaky voice possible said, "Hi, Bryan, are you on your way to visit me again? It's been a long time, you know."

"The roach roared," said Gilbert.

The fairy glared at Gilbert. "Not making fun of Hyminia, Gilbert."

Jennifer sniggered earning a glower from tiny Hyminia.

"CJ? Kill her." The fairy flew into Jennifer's face and drew blood. I yanked the creature off Jennifer. The fairy wiggled in my hand so I threw her against the wall of the tunnel.

"Bryan not nice to Hyminia." The fairy flew back down the tunnel to vanish in the darkness.

"The cockroach attacked Jennifer," said Gilbert. "It knew my name and Bryan's, too. But it called Jennifer BJ or DJ. How do they know our names?"

I dabbed at Jennifer's face with my shirt tail to stop the bleeding. Mr. Romano pulled some goop out of his backpack and applied a dose to Jennifer's cheek. The bleeding stopped.

"You won't need bandages, Wild Thing. She didn't scratch deep enough. I doubt you'll have any scars either. This stuff helps prevent scaring and promotes healing."

"Why'd the fairy attack me?" Jennifer asked.

Gilbert placed his arm around Jennifer's shoulder. "The roach is jealous of you. You saw how she was hot for Bryan."

"Back to business." Mr. Romano placed a hand on Daniel's shoulder. "What's your real name, son?"

Daniel shrugged. "Snpgrdxz. And you promise not to reveal my secret, right?"

"We promise," Mr. Romano said. "Don't we, children?"

We each said a yes, except for Gilbert. He stalked off.

"Dude, where you off to?" Mr. Romano asked.

Gilbert peered over his shoulder. "I promise not to tell, okay? And you guys can call me a coward if you want to, but I'm returning home to my mother where I belong. I've had enough of Halloween in August to last me a lifetime." He turned around to face us. "How do you think your mothers will feel when you don't come back?"

"What about Maria? Doesn't she deserve to see her mom again?" Jennifer pointed the sheathed Bowie knife at Gilbert.

"Not my problem," Gilbert said.

"She's your friend," Jennifer said.

"She's just a kid at school. No. I admit it. I like her." Gilbert slouched in defeat.

Jennifer strode over to Gilbert. She placed a hand on his arm. "Like like her or truly, passionately love like her?"

Gilbert groaned. He stared at Jennifer. He gazed around at the rest of us in the dim lamplight. He sighed. "I like her like it would be fun to get to know her better and explore if I, or rather we, fall in love."

"Dude, how will you two fall in teenaged love with her cooked over an open troll fire?" Mr. Romano asked.

Gilbert glared at Mr. Romano. "Cooked?"

Mr. Romano said, "What do you think trolls do with people? Man, they come across the tunnels hunting dinner. They ain't after bed buddies. We're not their type."

Jennifer's voice cracked. "Do... do... you think they ate her already? She's been missing for days."

"Time is on our side, but let's move out pronto." Mr. Romano headed down the tunnel to the right of the way we had come without so much as a glance back to check who followed him.

***

"Never open strange boxes in the tunnels," Mr. Romano said.

Too late. Jennifer removed the lid from what appeared to be an old cardboard shoebox she had tripped over. "It's packed with fur."

"Close that lid," Mr. Romano shouted.

"It looks so soft." Jennifer knelt by the box and reached into it. She screamed as hundreds of mice clambered out of the box. The pests climbed over our shoes and up our jeans. I brushed some off my shoulders.

"Run!" Mr. Romano shouted. We followed him deeper into the tunnels.

The mice dropped off us and ran the other way.

"They're deserting," Gilbert said. "Why are they going the other way?"

"Rats abandon sinking ships," said Snpgrdxz. "Mice must do the same thing."

"We're not on a ship," Jennifer said.

"Unlike us, maybe they're smart enough to run away from danger," said Snpgrdxz.

***

Losing track of time was easy in the tunnels. We passed three more intersections, but I noticed Mr. Romano always turned right.

As the last one in line, I heard footsteps behind us in the dark when the others didn't. I stopped. "Hey everybody."

"What?" Mr. Romano asked.

"We're being followed again," I said.

"Don't hear nothing," Gilbert said.

"Sounds like water dripping," said Jennifer.

"I don't hear it now so they stopped when we stopped," I said.

"Your imagination can run wild down here, so let's keep on trucking," Mr. Romano said. "But keep alert. What you can't see can hurt you in these tunnels."

"No biggie. Bryan's imagination has been cooking in high gear for a week. But what do you mean by keep on trucking?" Gilbert asked.

"Sixties speak," said Daniel. "It means the same as keep on keeping on."

We stopped at an intersection where the lamplight revealed heavy wooden posts against one wall. Someone had painted them dark blue. The footsteps behind me stopped also.

Mr. Romano fumbled around the blue post on the right side of the beam structure. "Aha. Here it is." He yanked down a long wooden handle hidden by the blue beam.

A bright light blinded us as a door opened between two of the blue beams. The door pushed the tunnel wall aside and when our eyes adjusted, revealed a whatever that didn't make any sense to me. The best I can think of is it opened a doorway to another place.

"Listen up, children," Mr. Romano said.

How'd he get so serious and when did we turn into children? We didn't, of course. I was still sixteen and the others appeared the same age as always. Snpgrdxz looked like Daniel Brickmaster.

Mr. Romano continued, "This doorway leads to another place. But it's not just a place, a where. It's also a when. You can think of it as a different dimension or another part of our universe. The main thing is it is someplace other than here, and it's not some big tunnel. You will see a sky, but it ain't our sky. And you'll see mountains. Trolls love to live in the mountains."

"What do you mean it's a when?" Gilbert asked.

Mr. Romano shrugged. "When you go through this portal, you will arrive in that place you're gaping at but *when* you arrive won't be our present now. It won't be our *when*. It'll be a different when. The portal crosses time as well as place."

"So we could end up anywhere or anytime?" Jennifer backed away from the doorway.

Mr. Romano smiled like a good dad or a favorite teacher. "The *where* is always the same, but the *when* is always different. There's no telling if we'll end up in the same *when* Maria ended up in. We could miss her by a few minutes or a few years or a few lifetimes."

"Then why pass through?" Gilbert shook his head.

Mr. Romano sighed. "Dude, how else will you save your friend? She's in there sometime. We have to find her. If we don't the first time we jump in, we'll try again."

"What if we get trapped?" Gilbert asked.

Mr. Romano placed a hand on Gilbert's shoulder. "You return the same way. You enter the Wheaton When Portal and hope it's the same *when* when you return or close enough to it so no one will notice."

"How can we tell we'll end up back here? We could find ourselves in the middle ages or far in the future." Gilbert's voice rose an octave, and he breathed heavy.

"Calm yourself, young man. You'll come out okay. Trust me on this one. We'll get you children home in time for dinner even if we're gone a few hours or days." Mr. Romano let go of Gilbert's shoulder.

"How can you be so sure?" Gilbert asked.

"Because I know whereof I speak," said Mr. Romano.

Daniel Brickmaster attempted to settle the matter for us. "My people forbid time travel so I can't go."

"So, alien dude, when was the last time you spoke to your people?" Mr. Romano asked.

"About seventy years ago." Daniel shrugged.

"Then it's time to stop worrying about what your people might think. We're your people now."

Daniel's grin was about as big as you can get. "You're right. As long as I'm stuck in your world, I might as well live like I belong. This is the greatest opportunity to time travel ever invented. We shouldn't hesitate. We pop through the doorway and pop back. Ta-da, we're some when else. It'll be a blast. Come on."

From the darkness down the tunnels ahead of us we heard giggles and laughter. I shined a light in time to see a group of teens disappear deeper into the darkness. "They're headed in the wrong direction."

"They're okay," Mr. Romano said. "They better be for our sakes."

"Why our sakes?" Gilbert asked.

"You want to be lost down here forever?" Mr. Romano pointed a bony finger at Gilbert.

"Not really," Gilbert replied.

"Neither do they," said Mr. Romano.

"Okay, let's go then." Daniel Brickmaster headed for the portal opening.

Mr. Romano snagged Daniel before he could leap through. "Whoa, friend. We have to hold hands, or we could end up in different whens. Now let's grab hold, but before we go, it's time you people stopped calling me Mr. Romano. You will be putting your lives at risk today, and we shared a beer, so it's official. You're to be treated like adults as long as you act like adults. Please, call me Tony."

I wanted to think about this dive into the unknown land longer and discuss this trip we contemplated with "Tony" some more. Wouldn't we be better off if we never left home? That cold, tingly, scary feeling crept up the place my spine would have been if I had one. But the warmth of Jennifer's hand on mine and the tug that followed were all I needed to enter the Wheaton When Portal with the rest of our group.

CHAPTER 10

IN THE LAND OF THE TINY TROLLS

Despite the bright daylight, a giant white bat circled above us. The new place didn't feel like a different when or a different where. The sky was blue, the clouds white, the air hot and humid. The grass was as green as the trees. We could have been in Pennsylvania or upstate New York with the mountains around us.

"Is that a bat in the daytime?" Gilbert asked.

"You will see lots of stuff you're not used to, kids." Tony let go of Jennifer's hand which he held since crossing the Wheaton When Portal. "Turn around, Wild Thing. You have the stakes."

"I'm not hungry," Gilbert said.

Tony gave him a cold stare. "Good, because these stakes are made from vampire-penetrating oak."

"You mean?" I turned my attention to the white bat that circled above.

The others must have been staring up at the bat also, which explained why we didn't see the troll army attack.

The trolls were tiny but powerful. I watched the guys fight off three or four of them before a dozen more pinned me to the ground. For all of Tony's M16 rifles and ammunition, I didn't hear anyone get a shot off. Before everything went dark for me, I gawped as Jennifer hit the ground bleeding from her nose. One of the trolls positioned himself over her as he swung a large wooden mallet. I screamed before passing out.

***

Course rope bindings scratched against my wrists and ankles. I'd been dreaming about a beach. The tide washed in, but I was tied down and couldn't move. That's when the real bindings grabbed my attention.

Mr. Turpelator, the science teacher from Lincoln High, stood over me. He drank from an old-fashioned beer bottle. "Trolls make a great brew, gentlemen. Drink some before they cook you." His breath smelled of beer vomit which was better than the time his breath smelled of dead rat back in my bedroom when my crucifix saved me from the evil teacher.

Mr. Turpelator ambled out through a large sheet of leather that served as a door or cover for the teepee or whatever I was in.

The ropes were tied to pegs pounded into the ground. The pegs looked suspiciously like Tony's oak vampire stakes. As my head cleared, I realized I was in a primitive straw hut.

I moved my head around to check my bindings. The rope was thick but crude.

"You're awake?" The masculine voice came from my left.

I turned my head. A Wheaton fireman, still in his rubber coat, was staked out next to me.

"You're the reason Mr. Turpelator said 'gentlemen.' Can you get free?" I asked.

"I'm working on it. The rope is tight. What about you?"

I tugged and the rope gave way instead of tightening the way some knots do when you pull away from them. But I couldn't wiggle out. "Have you seen my friends?"

"I just got here."

"You arrived after me?" I rubbed my wrists.

"Yeah. You were passed out when they dragged me in and tied me to the ground."

"But I arrived in this place after one of the searchers went missing from the tunnels. You're still in your fireman raincoat, so I assume you're the one." I inhaled the aroma of a stew mixed with smoldering wood from a cook fire.

"How did I arrive here after you? Need I mention the trolls plan to eat us?" The fireman struggled against his bindings.

"You're certain?"

"Take a gander over there."

A stack of bones and a pile of black clothes stood next to wood crates filled with brown beer bottles. There was no mistaking Maria's Goth outfit.

"Maria Gonzalez," I said.

"The girl we searched for?"

"Yeah." I couldn't help it. I bawled.

***

By the time I freed my wrists, I learned the fireman's name was Frank. He didn't want me to call him "Mister Bronson" or "Fireman Bronson."

"Frank will do," he said. There must be something about near death calamities to put people on a first-name basis even if one of us is a teenager.

I sat up to loosen the ropes around my ankle when the hide covering the hut entrance wobbled. I lay back down and wrapped the ropes around my wrists. Three trolls ambled in. They were obviously Papa Troll, Mama Troll and wee baby Troll. All I needed was Goldilocks. Then the thought occurred to me that Frank and I were Goldilocks except we couldn't run anywhere as fast as our little tied-up legs would carry us.

Goldilocks Troll arrived. She was the biggest troll I had seen up until then so there must be big trolls and little trolls.

Bathing wasn't one of the more important habits of trolls. Mama Troll exuded an aroma of old sweat and overcooked meat. She spoke in grunts, moans, wails and hand gestures. Goldilocks Troll replied. They either argued or communicated. Either way, I did not want to be around when one of them became angry.

Papa Troll roared when Goldilocks Troll bopped Mama Troll on the head with a club. Papa charged Goldilocks Troll, but fell over when his turn came to eat a club sandwich. Wee Baby Troll giggled and remained seated on the floor playing with a bone. Not Maria's mind you, but another old bone she had brought into the hut with her.

Goldilocks drifted over to me, still holding the club in the swinging position. I wished I had a body part I could reach so I could kiss it goodbye. Goldilocks Troll swung the club.

**

Goldilocks Troll flung her club into a corner of the hut, not far from Wee Baby Troll. Goldilocks laughed.

I glared at Goldilocks Troll with question marks for eyes. Her guffaws subsided into a grin. Her body shook and the flesh wiggled, and shazzam, she turned into Daniel Brickmaster aka Snpgrdxz.

"What the..." Fireman Frank's jaw was located somewhere south of his left kneecap.

"Figures," I said. "Get us out of here."

"How, how..." Frank the fireman's jaw made its way up to the rest of his face while Snpgrdxz untied him.

I loosened my ankle bindings. "Frank, meet Daniel Brickmaster. As you have noticed, he changes his anatomical features. That's good news for us because he's on our side. But you must swear to never, ever tell anyone."

"Is this like *Star Trek*? I mean this guy was a troll for Pete's sake. How did you do it?"

Daniel stared at Frank for a moment. "I made a costume change like *Star Trek*."

"Yeah, but..."

"Don't ask questions. We don't have time, and you can't tell anyone so the less you know the better." Daniel poked his head out of the hut. "Let's go."

I glanced over to the black clothing and stack of human bones. "What about Maria?"

Daniel gave me an expression teens use when it's obvious they didn't listen when the teacher said something would be on the test. "She'll be okay."

"What do you mean she'll be okay?" I didn't mean to shout, but I did. "She's a pile of bones."

"Quiet. We're supposed to sneak out of here not parade." Daniel stepped outside.

I yanked a piece of shirt up to hold against my forehead. A scab had formed, but it broke while I untied my ropes. "Anyone have aspirins?"

Frank and I followed Daniel to the hut next door. The two suns dipped near the horizon, one ready to vanish into the coming night, the other behind it by about an hour of sky.

Inside the second hut, Gilbert Armstrong was strung out on the floor the same way Frank and I had been. A troll lady stirred a boiling pot of goop over a fire. Six stacks of beer cases filled with the brown bottles lined the wall along one area of the straw hut.

"Don't let her boil me," Gilbert begged.

I was about to ask why not as a joke, but Snpgrdxz shape shifted into a tall, bony troll. Instead of the regular tan and gray troll colors, Snpgrdxz turned pure white. When the troll lady spun around, she fell to her knees in front of Snpgrdxz. He spoke to her in the grunts and groans of trolldom. The troll plastered her face to the dirt floor of her hut.

"We need to leave now," Frank said.

I took the knife from the troll lady's hand and cut the rope binding Gilbert to the floor. We stormed out of the hut with Snpgrdxz. He remained in the white troll shape while leading us out of the troll village.

"What about the others?" Frank asked.

"They're waiting for us by the entrance to the tunnels." Snpgrdxz continued up the hill toward the location of our brief battle when we first arrived in this world.

"Anyone have any acetaminophen?" Gilbert dabbed at the lump on his head.

I'd known Maria Gonzalez since preschool. She wasn't much of a friend after she went imitation Goth in seventh grade, but she had been a pal in elementary school. I would miss her drugged out, starvation sculpted body at school.

Before the second sun dropped away leaving the land of tiny trolls dark, we found Tony at the top of the hill with Jennifer. She wore a good-sized bandage on her forehead. I hugged her.

"How did you guys get away?" I asked.

"You're bleeding," said Jennifer.

Tony shot a wayward glance my way. "We scared off the trolls." He dug into his backpack and pulled out a first aid kit. "Sit."

Tony stitched my head wound and bandaged it. "You and your girlfriend will have matching scars."

"Awesome," said Jennifer.

"Not if your dad thinks we did it to celebrate our love," I said.

"What, are you stupid? Who would injure themselves for love?" Jennifer asked.

"Romeo and Juliet," I said.

"Oh," said Jennifer.

"Does anyone have any ibuprofen?" Gilbert asked.

"So how did you guys fight off the trolls? Last I remember one was about to clobberbust Jennifer with a hammer," I said.

Jennifer chuckled. "I used my karate and jammed my fingers into that puppy's throat. When he dropped his hammer to grab his broken Adam's apple, I busted him with his own hammer."

"And that's when the vampires attacked," said Tony.

Jennifer punched my arm. "Yeah, Tony was great with the vampires. They know about crucifixes in this world and the vampires don't like them. The trolls don't like the vampires, so when the vamps showed up, the trolls took off. Unfortunately, they dragged you and Gilbert with them."

As if on cue, a white bat landed on my shoulder and went to work on my fresh bandage.

Snpgrdxz, aka Daniel, pulled the bat off me and flung the creature into the air. Tony shot it with a wooden arrow. He shot another one, but the third bat got away.

Frank checked the bat carcasses. "Through the heart. They're cold."

"They were cold before I shot them." Tony slung the bow over his shoulder.

"Unsling your bow, Mr. Romano, I mean Tony," I shouted.

"What's wrong? Oh." Tony opened fire with his bow. "Lignum vitae bullets, now!"

"Our stuff is scattered everywhere," Gilbert said.

"Then we're plasma pouches for blood suckers," Tony said.

The cloud of vampire bats descending on us included too many wing flappers to count, but I had no doubt my crazy days were about to end at the hands of the ultimate insanity.

***

My madness may have begun earlier than I thought. In literature class one time, Miss Throngbottom showed us *Nosferatu*, a movie from the silent film era. Why she showed a silent movie in a literature class was beyond me. Wasn't

English Literature about words? More likely, I wasn't the only one insane in Wheaton, Illinois. Sanity was not defined by Miss Throngbottom showing the nineteen twenty-two silent movie classic to our class.

I remembered that the subtitle was "a symphony of horror." Not many people knew that. I was not certain many kids of high school age knew that "nosferatu" was another name for vampire. I brought this up here not so much to talk about silent films, but to show you what the vampires looked like that at the moment carried me tied to a long sort of log or big stick like the kind the natives used to carry captured people in those long ago jungle action flicks. You know the kind. The hero was tied to the fat stick and hung down while two big hulking natives carried the ends of the thingie on their shoulders. I was spread out between them with my butt bouncing on the ground whenever they walked over a high spot in the earth. I would have preferred taller nosferatu.

As the too short vampires carried me along in a stick parade with my friends, it was easy to think about that silent movie *Nosferatu* because the creatures looked like Nosferatu from that movie. They had white skin, bald heads, long skinny faces, huge eyes, big noses, and wrinkled and grey lips. Their swollen tongues hung out and they displayed large needle-like fangs located in the front of their mouths rather than to either side like a Bela Lugosi vampire. Think how a rattle snake's fangs were positioned.

I learned this before the second sun set and the nighthawks tied me to one of their poles. I expected the vampires to light torches like the natives in the old movies, but vampires saw fine in the dark as it turned out.

From my horizontal, tied-up and carried position, I couldn't spot many vampires in the moonlight and starlight, but the ones I observed were all males. They wore raggedly old suits like they hadn't changed since the seventies or maybe the fifties. The clothes were old and out of fashion.

In the distance, a pack of wolves howled at the moon.

"So do you guys talk?" I asked just to be friendly.

The vampire walking in front of me with the log thingie on his shoulder turned around and glared at me with his red eyes. His neck zoomed out about three feet from his body in my direction. He opened his mouth about a foot and hissed. I figured these vampires weren't big on talking to their food.

What could I say at a tender moment like this? "Hey, I need a pee break here."

The wolves continued to howl. As if in answer, the nosferatu had their own roar I assumed they used to scare the wolves away. The next round of wolf howling put me in mind of werewolves.

***

The full moon sank behind a mountain. The stars vanished. The temperature dropped. We entered a cave. The nosferatu vampires stopped. They dropped me on the ground but did not untie me.

That certain urge became urgent. "Hey, a little help here. You can lead a guy to the tinkle zone but you have to untie him if you want him to relieve himself."

I heard nosferatu dropping the others in our group nearby. The nosferatu were not the brightest of vampires. Snpgrdxz slipped out of his bindings and morphed into a well-dressed nosferatu. He untied me in the dark. Together we untied the others.

Snpgrdxz led us to the cave entrance but we were stopped by a group of very tall and skinny nosferatu. We backed into the darkness of the cave.

Tony said, "The side wall of the cave is over here. I suggest we use it now while we can."

Jennifer said, "Use if for what?"

The guys had the urgency of purpose to not have to ask questions. Instead we each made a splashing noise.

"Oh, I'll wait over here." Jennifer's voice faded.

"Why haven't they blood-sucked us yet?" asked Frank.

"Maybe our blood is a bit tart until we have our morning coffee," said Tony.

"They have other plans for us," said Jennifer.

"Not to worry. These guys will be asleep as soon as the two suns come up." Gilbert patted me on the back.

Mr. Turpelator walked into the cave behind the little crowd of nosferatu guarding the entrance. The other nosferatu had vanished but we could see a veritable cloud of white bats in the darkness clinging to the ceiling of the cave. The cave itself was about fifty feet high.

"Hi, Mr. Turpelator. Are you here to negotiate our release from the vampires?" asked Gilbert.

Snpgrdxz punched Gilbert.

"Sorry to disappoint you, old boy, but your release is not my purpose. Quite the contrary, in fact. I'm here to facilitate your trade to a pack of werewolves."

"You can negotiate with werewolves?" Jennifer asked.

"Werewolves pack together?" Frank asked.

Mr. Turpelator waved an arm to silences us. "Patience, my children. We will wait for the werewolves to change back to their human form. I've required these nosferatu to, shall we say, stay awake long enough for the negotiations.

"How do you know which vampire is the leader," Jennifer asked.

Mr. Turpelator passed through the group of nosferatu to approach her. "My dear, your concern for proper leadership is admirable. I am their leader, and I will be your master. You may kneel before your king."

I pushed Mr. Turpelator back and stepped between him and Jennifer. Three Nosferatu dragged me off to the side and hissed at me. Just as they were about to sink their fangs in, Mr. Turpelator waved his arm at them and they backed off.

I brushed myself off. "She's only fifteen."

Turpelator glared at me. "You speak bravely for a coward, young Ganarski." He gazed upon Jennifer. "My dear, you will be the first one turned to a *teenage* (scowled at me for one word) werewolf where you will serve me in your slavery. The others will be turned when their time arrives. The only thing remaining is to negotiate the deal with the nosferatu. But since they, too, are my slaves, I foresee no major disputes in the negotiations."

Mr. Turpelator raised his eyes to the ceiling where his slave army of nosferatu bats slept. He smiled like the Buddha.

A group of men approached. For a moment, I thought they were our rescue party. Then I realized what they were – werewolves turned back to their human form.

"Greetings, Master," said one of the werewolves. "What is your wish?"

Why were monsters so predictable? You'd think one of the werewolves would offer a little resistance, but no, these puppies obeyed their master's every command. Was this my future?

Mr. Turpelator said, "My child, I wish you to negotiate with the nosferatu for their reward for delivering this token of wolfly affection."

"We shall, oh master. How much blood do you demand?"

"That's up to you to decide, my son. Speak now with Glimtuckmucker and be at peace." Mr. Turpelator said.

A large white bat descended from the cave ceiling. It landed at Mr. Turpelator's feet as it morphed into one of those ugly nosferatu. By ugly, I mean the king of ugly. This nosferatu was so ugly he could have been a rock star. Maybe he was a rock star. We had no idea where these creatures came from originally and I'm not a big fan of sixties rock n' rollers. Did these creatures start out as humans on the other side of the Wheaton When Portal? How many students had Lincoln High lost over the years?

"Ve vant your blut," said the nosferatu in his best eastern Euro accent. Why was it that adults, even undead ones, insisted so much on stating the obvious? What would you expect a nosferatu to want from a negotiation with a werewolf tribal leader, even an enslaved werewolf?

"No shit, Glimtuckmucker" said the werewolf. "Ve know zat already. How much blood sucking do you want for your five weakling slaves?"

"Veakling slaves? They are well-fed Americans, Growlpucket. And we captured six of them for you."

Did you like the way I stopped with the accents after Veakling? I found accents annoying, but I wanted enough so you got the idea these folks weren't from around here. Well, we weren't from around there either, but you got the idea.

I gaped about the cave and noticed the rest of us did the same thing. We took stock of our group. No one said a word, but we all knew Daniel Brickmaster Snpgrdxz had vanished. He could be that rock over in the corner or a stalagmite cropping up from the floor. Or he could be long gone. Either he abandoned us or headed back to the fort to round up the cavalry for our rescue, assuming there was a cavalry this side of the portal.

I didn't expect much in the way of military support since I had no idea if there was a fort filled with anti-vampire, anti-werewolf good guys nearby. The Wheaton When Portal was not to be predicted if you believed Tony, and why would we not believe our beloved art teacher? Our situation appeared to be a case of not *if* we would become hideous monsters, but *when*.

CHAPTER 11

WEREWOLVES SUCK

"We want to suck five hundred werewolves," said Glimtuckmucker, the nosferatu leader.

"Our tiny village doesn't have five hundred werewolves, you idiot," Growlpucket growled.

"He's right, you know, old boy," said Mr. Turpelator.

"Then you will find them," said Glimtuckmucker.

"We'll let you suck one werewolf for each new slave, but only one liter. No more," Growlpucket barked.

"No, we want more. Give us one hundred werewolves to suck on. We will take a full quart." Apparently math was not Glimtuckmucker's strong suit.

"We don't want your slaves, Glimtuckmucker. You keep them. Suck them dry for all I care." Growlpucket headed for the cave exit.

"Wait," said Mr. Turpelator. "You must negotiate a deal."

Growlpucket turned toward Mr. Turpelator. "Yes, Master." He continued his march out of the cave.

Mr. Turpelator smiled. He turned to Glimtuckmucker. "Negotiate, you fool."

"Yes, Master." Glimtuckmucker flew to the mouth of the cave to prevent Growlpucket from leaving.

"Yes?" asked Growlpucket.

"The slaves are yours. I give them to you as a gift in exchange for sucking your blood." Judging from the smoke rising from behind Glimtuckmucker's back, which at the moment stood in the bright sunlight of a new day, I felt the negotiations would end soon.

"We take them. You may suck one quart from my neck." Growlpucket cocked his head to one side to expose his neck.

"Oh, but we need one more thing," said Glimtuckmucker.

"What?" asked Growlpucket.

"Five of my nosferatu will suck one quart each from five werewolves."

"Deal," said Growlpucket.

Glimtuckmucker spiked Growlpucket's neck to drain his quart of blood.

***

"This one will be my sex slave." Growlpucket snatched Jennifer.

Jennifer screamed.

"Touch her and I'll kill you." Where had my courage come from? Somehow my guts had disconnected from my brain but not my heart. My feelings for Jennifer added up to lust, love, and true affection, what you would expect for a guy who had a crush on her since seventh grade, but this was nuts. You don't threaten a werewolf even if the full moon cycle has passed.

"Don't worry, Bryan, I'll kill him myself if he so much as tries to touch me." Jennifer gazed my way with her face scrunched up into a killer pose. Better she should face the werewolf with that look.

Growlpucket laughed. "I make you both my sex slaves. Bring them to my cabin. Tie them to the bed."

Three werewolf men stepped forward and dragged us off, two on me and one on Jennifer. Keep in mind, these bozos were not in their werewolf mode. One of them looked like a junior accountant from a Bible college, no offense to junior accountants or Bible colleges, but the guy was a wimp. The other two were bigger, but only slightly. I'd say five-four, five-five tops.

Jennifer waited until we were in the cabin before she judo flipped her Bible college accountant to the floor. While the guy checked the view of Jennifer's jean-covered butt from down on the floor, Jennifer kicked-started his brains with the best heel stomp ever. The guy's skull cracked into pieces as she flattened his head on the floor. My head hurt just thinking about receiving a crack like that.

I yanked on my guys, but they were too strong for me. Jennifer ripped her blouse open sending buttons flying, but the little plastic pills missed the werewolf men. One hit me on my cut which made me wince. Just as I had thought, Jennifer's cup size was larger this year. You notice things like that when a girl performs a strip tease right before the werewolf Bible college accountants attempt to kill you.

I about passed out as did the other guys. This gave her the split second she needed to knee-kick both of them in the groin. While they were bent over in agony, I punched one in the back of the head while Jennifer dispatched the other using the same technique.

"We have to chop their heads off." Daniel Brickmaster burst through the backdoor of the cabin. He carried our backpacks and M16s on a pair of extra wide shoulders. He dropped the equipment to the floor and morphed into his usual Daniel Brickmaster body except for his right hand and arm which he transformed into an axe. Jennifer squealed as he dispatched the werewolves by removing their heads.

"The nosferatu will be delighted to help clean that floor," Snpgrdxz said.

"Silver bullets?" Jennifer tugged at her blouse to cover herself.

"Already locked and loaded." Snpgrdxz gave us each an M16 and ammunition belt lined with loaded clips. Three grenades dangled from the front. We wore the straps over our right shoulder. Mine was heavy enough that I worried about Jennifer. "Are you okay with this weight?"

Jennifer giggled as she attempted to close her blouse under the belt. "I'll lighten it soon."

"Ready?" asked Snpgrdxz.

"Move fast because we don't know if and when they will scatter the rest of the gang."

"Wait," said Jennifer.

"What?" asked Snpgrdxz.

"What if we run into nosferatu?" Jennifer asked.

"Right. I forgot." Snpgrdxz reached into one of the backpacks and yanked out three Glocks. "Lignum vitae bullets. You have to hit them in the heart."

I tucked my Glock into my waistband. "Let's go."

"Wait," said Jennifer.

"What?" asked Snpgrdxz.

"My waistband is too tight," she said.

"There's a hook on the ammo belt," Snpgrdxz yanked Jennifer's blouse wide open with one hand and yanked on her ammo belt.

Snpgrdxz smiled.

"Here?" Jennifer pointed the pistol where Snpgrdxz held the ammo belt.

"Naw, I just wanted a peek. Put it over here." Snpgrdxz tugged on a fold out leather strap that clipped to the trigger guard on Jennifer's weapon.

Jennifer slapped Snpgrdxz on the face. She rearranged her blouse for limited privacy. "Okay, I'm ready."

"Don't do that, man," I said to Snpgrdxz.

We charged out the door to free our comrades. Our mistake was not knowing where they were. The good news is the werewolves, while brighter than the nosferatu, weren't all that bright. They must have assumed we were performing our tasks as werewolf slaves. Why wouldn't they? Bullets couldn't hurt them unless they were silver. Protected by Mr.

Turpelator in the troll world, they may not even know about how silver is poison to them.

Ever notice how men never ask for directions, but women do? I know it's a cliché and asking for directions is the right thing to do when you're lost, but it never occurred to me to ask where our comrades were. Snpgrdxz never asked, but Jennifer did. Even werewolves in their normal human-like form become happy when a pretty teenage girl asked where they stashed her friends.

"This way," she said.

We found Tony, Gilbert and Fireman Frank yanking weeds in a cornfield outside the village of the damned werewolves.

"About time you three showed up," said a guy who must have been a supervisor judging from the long whip he carried. He began to swing the whip at Jennifer when she plugged him with a burst from her M16.

Snpgrdxz distributed M16s and backpacks to our friends.

"We're out of here," said Tony.

"Don't you want to know how we escaped?" I asked.

"Not now. I'm sure Buttsmacker over there isn't the only dead werewolf in this village. We have to evacuate the premises before they become wise to us." Tony jogged along a path that led around the werewolf village towards the path that would take us back to the troll territory and the Wheaton When Portal.

***

Mr. Turpelator blocked the way to the Wheaton When Portal when we arrived later that day. "Going somewhere, slaves?"

"Out of the way, Turpelator," said Tony.

"I can't do that, old boy. Turns out there are werewolves on the prowl, even if they are stuck in human form until the next full moon. Lay down your weapons and – "

Jennifer had enough of Mr. Turpelator. As a sophomore, she wasn't in his class anyway, so she didn't have to worry about receiving a lower grade or detention. She fired her M16 at point blank range at our physics teacher.

Mr. Turpelator fell back almost into the Wheaton When Portal. He stood back up with three bullet holes bloodying his chest. "You've ruined my shirt, my dear. I shall take yours despite your lack of buttons."

"Like hell." Jennifer stepped back with her M16 pointed at Mr. Turpelator's head. The rest of us stepped in close to Jennifer with our M16s locked and loaded.

Mr. Turpelator curled his lip at us. His eyes flared. "You fools. Don't you know you can't kill me?"

Jennifer didn't know. She fired a burst that splattered Mr. Turpelator's head. Blood sprayed around him like a red halo. Then something weird happened.

Mr. Turpelator vanished.

***

Jennifer glanced around at our little group. She whispered in my ear, "I need your help."

"What's wrong?" I asked.

"Shh! Look down."

Her pants had a big wet stain from the crotch area down to her knees. The ground was wet around her.

"Want to borrow my pants?" I knew I had asked a dumb question as soon as I spoke, but there was no way to take it back.

"It happened when Turpelator's head exploded. Give me your shirt." Jennifer's red cheeks held tiny tear drops. I couldn't help myself. I kissed her nose. She smiled. I stripped off my t-shirt and handed it over.

"Let's skedaddle," said Tony.

"Wait a sec." Jennifer headed around a large rock to switch out of her peed on pants and into my shirt.

"Bryan, you're too skinny to go bare-chested," Daniel Snpgrdxz Brickmaster said.

"I gave my shirt up for a worthy cause." I folded my arms across my chest.

"Here, take mine." Snpgrdxz unbuttoned his short-sleeve dress shirt. He wore a white t-shirt underneath.

As I buttoned the shirt, Jennifer returned with a face as red as a teenage girl can muster in her time of highest embarrassment. She dragged her blue jeans behind her back with her left hand and carried her sneaks in her right. My t-shirt converted into a longer mini-dress than I expected but not enough to cover her birthmark reverse map of Italy.

"Carry these in your backpack for me." Jennifer handed her pants to me as the gang gawped.

My mind contemplated the meaning of "these" because she gave me one pair of pants. I peeked inside her waistband and spotted her still damp undies. I placed her items in my backpack without another word.

Jennifer smiled and kissed my lips a quick one. I stopped contemplating her pants and thought about how a beautiful teenager wearing only a bra and my t-shirt had kissed me, her bare bottom inches away under my shirt.

"So we're like a couple now, right?" I asked.

"Shut up." Jennifer slipped her sneaks back on while leaning against me.

"Don't I get a kiss for lending you my shirt?" Snpgrdxz floated in close to my face.

Jennifer pushed Snpgrdxz away. "Any boy kissing happens around here, I'll do it, Shapeshifter."

"Maria's dead." I couldn't think of a reason not to tell everyone. Besides, changing the subject before the guys invited Jennifer to kiss more than this boy seemed like the right thing to do. "Let's go home."

"Dude." Tony said. Then he gawked at Jennifer like a man who was not a drug-crazed old pothead high school art teacher. "Wild Thing, you look wild today."

Jennifer's whole body went red.

"Leave her alone," Gilbert moved between Tony and Jennifer.

"Don't mind him," Jennifer said. "He's harmless."

"Bait's bait, Dude," Tony said as if that ended the matter for everyone. "Time to collect Maria and go home."

"Tony's right," Frank stormed off towards the troll village.

"Whoa, cowboy." Tony yanked the fireman back. "Wrong way."

"But her bones are down there." Frank held his hands out palms up.

"We don't want her bones, Dude. We want her whole self." Tony grinned ear to ear.

I yanked on Tony's arm. "I saw Maria's bones. There is no putting her back together."

"Not now," Tony said. "But if we head out for a different when, we may find her alive and well. We need to leave now and return in a before when. And we need to go now before the werewolves find us."

Fireman Frank asked, "You want us to go out through the portal and come back into this place?"

"Precisely," said Tony.

"What if we come back to the same time and find ourselves here. That'll make two of each of us." The fireman smiled.

"Dude, if we could do that, we could make an army and overrun this place. Odds are you always come back to a different when whenever you cross the Wheaton When Portal." Tony grabbed the fireman's hand and pulled him to standing position. "Time to go now."

"Why now?" Gilbert asked.

Tony pointed towards a crowd of very ashen people staggering up the hill in our direction. "Zombies."

"What now?" Jennifer asked.

"Grab hands and jump through the portal," Tony shouted.

CHAPTER 12

WHEN ARE WE?

I blinked several times to adjust to the blackness of the tunnels after the bright sunlight of the troll world. "We have no idea when we are."

Gilbert said, "But we were gone overnight. That makes it Sunday or is it Monday? I lost track."

"Mr. Romano, I mean Tony, you promised we'd be home for dinner and now it's Sunday. I'll be grounded forever." Jennifer stamped her foot.

Tony led the way into the tunnel system maze. "We have no idea what year it is let alone what day. I'll show you the way out so we can find out."

"How long were we among the trolls?" Snpgrdxz asked.

Tony stopped. "Not sure, but it was overnight in their world like Bryan said so you raise a good point. We've been gone two days. Let's keep track of the time we're away. It may prove important later depending on how protracted our journey becomes."

"Uhm, Tony, did we forget someone?" Fireman Frank asked.

"Who?" Tony asked. "Oh, you mean Maria Gonzalez. Yeah, we could turn around and jump back in, but we have to check out what when we landed in first."

"Is it important to calculating our return to our proper time?" Frank asked.

"Nope." Tony's response echoed off the tunnel walls.

"Then why do we need to go up top?" Gilbert asked.

"Aren't you curious? If the time is right, I might not return to your time," Tony said.

"Our time?" Jennifer asked.

"Wild Thing, how many sixties radical hippies do you think run around Wheaton at the age of thirty-eight in the early part of the twenty-first century?"

"Not many, Tony. You'd have to be in your seventies." Jennifer was a whiz at math.

"As I said, this may be a better when for me. We have to check it out." Tony tugged us deeper into the darkness.

We heard scampering noises, a few screams and passed a couple of rats feasting on something dead that we didn't want to know about. But we didn't come across any living or undead creatures. The ghosts scared the crap out of us with their howling. We stumbled upon two of them singing the blues in that rest area we stopped at on our way to the Wheaton When Portal. One was short and stubby while the other was tall and less stubby. They both wore black suits and ties. The lapels on the suits were ultra thin the way they made suits in the sixties. The ties matched. Both singers wore black hats and dark sunglasses despite the darkness of the cave. We heard their band playing but we didn't see any backup musicians, ghosts or regular.

"Tony, we better be home because I don't think I can return to these tunnels again. They're too creepy and dangerous," Gilbert said.

"It's like a Halloween haunted house, Gilbert. Get over it." Jennifer punched Gilbert a good one on the upper arm.

I tried dancing with Jennifer to the blues music, but it didn't work with the backpacks and weapons we carried. I liked the way my shirt flapped around while Jennifer danced, but in the darkness I wasn't sure the other guys noticed.

"Way to hop, girl," Gilbert's powers of observation were still strong.

"Oh." Jennifer stopped and smoothed down her t-shirt.

Snpgrdxz punched Gilbert on the arm.

The outside light, when it came, hit us sooner than I expected. We exited into the oldest part of Lincoln High School and climbed an ancient staircase to the first floor landing. Frank, to his credit, wrapped his firefighter's coat around Jennifer to provide more coverage when we arrived at the steps. The jacket's shoulders were way too wide for her, but it made a longer skirt than my shirt did.

"I don't remember this staircase," Gilbert said.

"It's plastered behind a wall in your time," Tony said. "This is the first time you've seen it."

"I hear footsteps," Jennifer stopped.

"Let's hightail out," said Tony.

We raced through the empty building, empty except for the person whose footsteps echoed behind us. I kept spinning around to spot the person but all I saw was the darkest of dark shadows.

We stepped outside into a large field where more building used to be.

"Where are the building additions?" Frank asked.

"Not built yet," Tony said. "We came out before World War Two when the first addition was built."

"When are we? Is this like the Great Depression?" Gilbert asked.

"Let's head downtown and find out," Tony said.

"Wait, isn't that Mr. Turpelator?" asked Gilbert.

We turned back towards the front entrance of Lincoln High. A man stood on the front steps. He ducked back inside when he noticed us.

"How could it be?" asked Tony. "Mr. Turpelator lives in the future."

"He was in the troll village," I said. "Jennifer dispatched him."

"His being here is not good," Tony said.

We strolled north on Main Street toward downtown Wheaton. The air was hot and sticky and I guessed midsummer, late afternoon by the position of the sun in the western sky. Summer explained why the school building was empty, except for our mysterious follower.

"Check out the cars," Gilbert said.

"Most of them are Ford Model Ts," said Frank. "Any color you want as long as it's black. That car has a LaSalle name plate. And there's an old Buick. If we squeezed any one of them through the tunnels to take back home, we could be rich."

The women shopping downtown wore long skirts below their knees.

"I'd guess we're in the late teens or early twenties rather than the thirties," Tony said.

"I need to buy a longer skirt before I wind up in trouble," said Jennifer.

"You have money suitable for the nineteen twenties?" Tony asked.

"That would be a problem, but I can't earn any dressed like this, can I?" Jennifer glared when the guys laughed except me.

"You're dressed for a certain kind of work, but I don't think you had that profession in mind, did you?" Gilbert asked.

"Oh." Jennifer's neck turned red and then the redness rose up her face to her hairline. "You boys are so mean."

The police officer carried a billy club. He had a gun in a holster on his leather belt. He wore a large hat with lots of sides. It matched the dark blue of his old-fashioned uniform. The uniform included a long jacket with brass buttons up the front and a high collar like a priest, except it was blue.

"Hey, what's the meaning of this?" The officer grabbed Jennifer. "You can't go around Wheaton dressed like that. We don't allow your kind in a Christian community."

"Officer, please," I said. "We've had an accident and my friend Jennifer Hawkins here had her clothes ripped in an explosion. I gave her my shirt to wear and Frank gave her his jacket."

The policeman gawped at us. "Her skirt ain't long enough for public decency and you're all dressed funny. What's going on here?"

"We're in a play at the college, officer." Gilbert stepped forward.

The officer glared at Gilbert. He turned to me. "Tell me the truth. There's no way his kind would act in a play at the college. You let a few coloreds in and they'll take over the place. Besides, they ain't smart enough for college."

"Officer, please, Gilbert is with us. We recruited him for the part in our play. He's a student from the mission fields in Africa. He's studying for the ministry before returning to his homeland to save the souls of the heathens. We needed a Negro for one of the parts, so we asked him to join us." I was mighty proud of remembering to say "Negro." I learned it in history class as part of the Civil Rights Movement of the fifties and sixties. I figured an occasional lie may be the price of travel in time. No sense confusing the natives even if it technically was wrong.

The policeman glared at me like I was crazy. "Darnn fools, you could have blackfaced a student. Now tell me about the explosion. Where did you say it happened?"

"In the tunnels under the high school," I replied. "It was a little gas pocket, but Jennifer Hawkins was closest to the explosion and the results embarrassed her. You wouldn't want your daughter standing around town in her all together. We need to find her clothes fast."

"Did you say Hawkins? You mean the Hawkins who live in the old Hawkins house over on Washington Street?"

"That's right," Jennifer jumped in. I wish she hadn't. Her family was decades in the future.

"I better escort you home." We followed the police officer to Jennifer Hawkins' house. It was the same house she grew up in, but it wasn't Jennifer's home in this when, as Tony would say.

Did Jennifer's ancestors live here this far back in time? Jennifer said her family had owned the land since the eighteen thirties, so her clan must live here in the nineteen twenties. But they wouldn't know Jennifer.

The officer marched us up to the front door and thumped an antique brass knocker. It was missing from Jennifer's house in our day. Would the police throw us in jail or let us off with a warning when the current day Hawkins family rejected us?

The front door creaked open to reveal a young woman about college age. She could have been Jennifer's older sister, if she had one.

"My goodness, you're here at last. And you found something to wear this time. Clever." The woman grabbed Jennifer by the arm and yanked her into the house. She slammed the door behind her.

CHAPTER 13

NINETEEN TWENTY-THREE

"Head back to campus before you get into any more trouble. And keep away from loose women. Young girls have no place performing on stage. Good Christian girls shouldn't show their legs and what-not in public," the officer said.

"Wild Thing has nice little what-nots," Tony said.

The front door opened as the officer headed back to the sidewalk. An elderly woman dressed in a long pink dress from before the First World War glared at us. She smelled of cake flour and vanilla. Her apron carried a heavy dusting of white. "Jennifer said you may come in, except for you." She pointed at me and led the others into the house before slamming the door.

Standing on the front porch alone didn't make sense so I banged on the funny brass knocker to see what would happen. The old lady came back to the door.

"Is it okay if I join the others now?" I asked.

"Jennifer said to slap your face and send you away, but you seem like a nice enough young man, and I'm sure Jennifer forgave you years ago. And you'll want a glass of my lemonade."

"Homemade lemonade?" I asked.

The old lady laughed. "Where else would you make it? Come in, boy." She let me pass into the house.

The entrance alcove or hallway had a doorway left and a set of stairs in front. The little hallway was missing from

Jennifer's house in our time, I mean the twenty-first century. You saunter right into the living room or up the stairs.

In the living room, the others sat on one of two frilly, high-backed sofas placed on opposite walls. The aroma of fried chicken wafted in from Great Grandma's kitchen.

"Take a seat on the chesterfield, young man." The old lady passed into the dining room.

"Chesterfield? I'll sit here on the couch instead," I said.

The old lady popped back into the room laughing. "You young people make the funniest jokes. Always playing with words. Now, I have to see to your dinner. Jennifer said to expect you but she must have miscounted because there is one more of you than we expected. It's no problem because I purchased lots of chicken at the market today." She headed back into the dining room.

"Where's Jennifer," I asked the group.

Gilbert said. "She be looking for blackface so she pretty for you, Massa Bryan."

I slugged Gilbert on the shoulder. He ducked the blow and laughed.

"We haven't seen her," said Frank.

"Wild Thing!" Tony bellowed up the stairs.

Two voices shouted back, "Coming."

"Sounds like Wild Thing has a wild friend," Tony said.

"Yeah and a nice set of what nots," said Daniel.

As I wrapped my mind around the idea of two Wild Things, I punched Daniel, but my fist sank into his shoulder like it was made of Jell-O.

The college-aged girl ambled down the steps followed by Jennifer. I figured the college girl for a Hawkins because she looked like an older version of Jennifer. Same face, same brunette hair, but shorter with finger-sized waves through it. She had the same pale complexion. Even her green eyes matched Jennifer's.

The college girl wore a long navy blue blouse that came down below her hips and same color pleated skirt. The top had long sleeves and a pattern that looked like she wore a vest, but the vest was printed on the blouse. The part that seemed a vest was light gray. The blouse did not have a collar. The neckline came down to a point below her neck so it didn't reveal much skin. Colorful stripes in red and white completed the outfit. The stripes were repeated at the bottom of the skirt. The skirt came below her knees. The whole thing appeared to be silk or a combination of silk and soft cotton. It was pretty except the skirt was too long for my twenty-first century boy's eyes.

"You guys like my twenties image?" the older girl twirled around.

Jennifer had changed back into the pants she wore before her little accident with the pee-pee, so she was decent. The outfit was clean, but showed fold lines like it had sat in a bureau drawer for a long time. Her top had a folded flat appearance like it had been pulled from a long sit in a drawer as well, although she wore it when we jumped into the Wheaton When Portal to find Maria.

The college girl meandered up to me. I smiled while contemplating the pleasure of a hearty chicken dinner. She slapped my face hard.

Jennifer said, "You deserved it. We're not talking to you."

***

Tony shook his head. "Two Wild Things?"

"Shut up, Tony," said the college girl.

"How'd you know his name?" Gilbert stared at the college girl.

"I waited five years for you people to show up so don't pretend you don't know me, Gilbert Armstrong." The college girl was beet red with eyes as cold as a smart phone with a dead battery. "And who's the new guy? You didn't bring him the other times."

Gilbert's eyes formed black question marks. "You better fill us in, lady. You look like you could be Jennifer's big sister, but she doesn't have a sister. We don't know who you are or what you're talking about."

"I'm Frank, by the way." Frank offered his hand. The college girl smiled and took it.

The old lady strolled in with a small wooden cart with two big wheels and two little wheels. A large glass pitcher sat on top. It was filled with lemonade. A half-dozen cut glass tumblers surrounded the pitcher. A china sugar bowl was nestled against a stack of cloth napkins. A dozen or so teaspoons sat there also. They were real silver rather than stainless steel.

A second shelf under the top held a chocolate cake, a stack of dessert plates made of fancy painted china with lots of little flowers. The forks were real silver also.

The college girl said, "Thank you, Great Grandma. This should tide us over until dinner. I'll need time alone with my friends now. You don't want to hear about this."

The old lady smiled at the college girl, "Oh, Jennifer, you have no need to worry. I don't want to spoil your party with your time-travelling friends." She sashayed out of the room.

"Time-traveling friends?" Frank asked.

***

"You're not from around here, are you?" Gilbert asked.

The college girl smiled at my Jennifer. Well, she was my Jennifer until the college girl slapped me. My former Jennifer smiled back at her. Gilbert was right. They could be sisters. The college girl could be Jennifer's great grandmother as a young woman.

The college girl sat on the arm of one of the chesterfields, across the room from me. "You don't recognize me, do you? I'm Jennifer. Your Jennifer plus five years."

I smiled. She was my Jennifer again.

My Jennifer giggled. "This is what I'll look like in five years, Bryan. What do you think?"

"Wild," Tony jumped in.

I tugged at my backpack, which reminded me that the pants covering my Jennifer's butt right now were still in the backpack. I was under attack from another bout of the insanity I thought I had left behind back in the twenty-first century, but the chicken smelled tempting. "Are those the same pants I have here in the backpack?"

College kid Jennifer patted younger Jennifer's leg and hauled my backpack towards the entrance hallway. "Yes, and please don't say another word about them. It's embarrassing. Great Grandma washed them for me five years ago when I arrived, and I saved them for today. It's not like I can wear wrinkle resistant blue jeans in nineteen twenty-three."

Frank the fireman asked, "You have two pairs of the same pants?"

"Yes," said the older Jennifer. "And two mes to wear them."

"Two yous?" I asked. A special joy surged through me because I no longer was the only one experiencing the craziness. Misery may love company, but insanity likes it better.

"Yes. I'm you're Jennifer, darling, except I'm a bit mature for you now, don't you think?" the older Jennifer asked.

"One Jennifer should be enough for him," Gilbert said.

"Wow, we broke one of Mr. Turpelator's rules of time travel," said Daniel. "Rule three states you can't meet yourself or your ancestors."

"So much for his rules," said Tony.

Older Jennifer said, "You never liked Mr. Turpelator, did you, Tony?"

"What's to like?" Tony replied.

Frank said, "I understand we did a time travel thing through the Wheaton When Portal, but why do we have two

Jennifers? And one of you is five years older than the other? Shouldn't you at least be twins?"

"It's complicated," younger Jennifer said. "I better let my older self explain. Rest assured she is me and vice versa."

Older Jennifer hugged her self... sister... whatever... the other Jennifer. The universe didn't collapse. The time-space continuum didn't explode. The room stayed together and the earth continued outdoors with no disruption in space-time. And the chicken cooking in the kitchen still smelled delicious. So much for not coming into contact with yourself in a time travel road trip.

"Explain how you arrived ahead of us while aging five years, won't you, old-type Jennifer? And by the way, your boobies have aged nicely along with the rest of you. Where'd you get that butt, girl?" Gilbert grinned big enough for the both of us.

"Okay, I'll explain," said Jennifer the elder. "I knew you guys would show up today because I'm here with you as my younger self, aren't I?" She glanced at her younger self. "This is not the first time I have lived on this day. While you're taking that in, consider this little tip – after you leave here, you... we... whatever... will return to our search for Maria Gonzalez – "

"Do we find her?" Gilbert exploded the words out of his smiling mouth. He might admire the elder Jennifer, but his heart belonged to Maria.

"How would I know? I've been stuck here waiting for you guys. Listen to me because this is important. When you go through the tunnels to the troll world, zombies will attack you. You'll fight them off at first, but then large numbers of them will overwhelm you. You'll join hands to jump back across the Wheaton When Portal to escape. That's when numbnuts over here will let go of my hand. I'll be in mid-leap and not able to stop myself. I'll land in nineteen eighteen in time to settle in before catching the great flu epidemic and waiting five years for you guys to show up again."

My Jennifer jumped in. "Jen, I don't think we should say 'numbnuts.' It's not Christian."

Elder Jennifer glared at my Jennifer like she was the numbnuts. "Spend five years in this lifetime, honey, and numbnuts ain't all the shit you'll say."

Younger Jennifer turned beet red. She stormed over to me and slapped my face. She hugged elder Jennifer with no fear of destroying the universe.

***

The front door flew open with a bang against the wall. I jumped off the chesterfield fearing we'd been busted, but I didn't know who would bust us or why. I stared at the hall to the front door and waited.

A little girl entered. She was about the same size as my twelve-year-old sister Katie. Behind her a woman entered carrying packages.

"We have the clothes you asked me to buy," the new woman said.

"We bought yucky men's underwear," said the girl. "Oh, your friends are here, Cousin Jennifer."

The older college age girl returned from the kitchen. "Time for introductions. I know everyone except the guy holding the fireman's jacket."

"Is that a real fireman's coat?" asked the girl.

Fireman Frank held his coat up so the girl could see it better. "It's the kind they use where I come from. We call it 'turnout gear.'"

"These are for you then," said the woman.

"No, I wasn't expecting any Franks to show up," said college age Jennifer. "I guessed at most of your sizes, but I knew you'd be more comfortable dressed in, uhm, the latest attire. We'll get clothes for Frank after everyone has bathed and changed."

"Great because we need a shower anyway," I said.

"What's a shower?" the little girl asked.

"It's a type of bath where somebody has to pour water on your head," said college age Jennifer.

"Oh, you mean like when Mom shampoos my hair on Saturday night," said the girl.

"Exactly," said college age Jennifer. "Now, let's do introductions. This young lady is my cousin Chrissie, short for Christine McNaughton. She's eleven years old. And this is her mother, Cousin Laura McNaughton. Mr. McNaughton is no longer with us as he was lost in the war. The McNaughton inheritance was sufficient to provide for our needs, including Laura's generosity in allowing me to live here with them. So we have much to be thankful for, and we owe Laura a great debt of gratitude which I hope one day to repay."

My Jennifer embraced Laura. "Thank you for keeping her off the streets for so many years. What would she do without you?"

"I couldn't turn away my young cousin, could I? She arrived a penniless teenager without a home. I accepted her as I would a prodigal sister come home. Now, we love each other dearly."

"And for Laura and Chrissie, may I present my friends Tony Romano, Gilbert Armstrong, Daniel Brickmaster and Bryan Ganarski? And this is my younger sister Jennifer. And this gentleman I have met for the first time, and he is a huge surprise to me and a pleasant one. His name is Frank. What's your last name, Frank, if you don't mind my asking?" the college aged Jennifer took Frank's arm.

"Frank Bronson. And I am also happy to make your acquaintance."

"How come Jennifer and Jennifer have the same names if they're sisters?" Chrissie asked.

"Good question," young Jennifer said.

"Don't you want to tell them, little sister?" college age Jennifer folded her arms across her chest and flashed a big grin.

"You tell it so much better than I ever could," said my young Jennifer.

College age Jennifer said, "You see, Chrissie and Laura, Mom and Dad loved the name Jennifer so much that when my little sister came along, they couldn't think of any better name for her so they called her Jennifer."

"Cousin Jennifer, how come I've known you since I was little, but this is the first time in my whole entire life I heard you had a sister?" Cousin Chrissie asked.

Great Grandma returned to change the subject and save the day. "Dinner's ready."

The food was what my mom might serve any night of the week, if she had time to cook, which she didn't because she worked, but anyway we had breaded chicken, lemonade, summer squash, boiled potatoes, and homemade bread with farm fresh butter. For desert, we could have more of the chocolate cake or cherry-flavored Jell-O. Okay, so mom would not have made the bread herself and she'd lose the squash and buy the chicken at a fast food joint, but when you think about it, folks in nineteen twenty-three ate pretty much what we eat today, except the stuff they made tasted better.

After dinner, elder Jennifer kicked us out of the dining room back into the living room while she and Great Grandma did the dishes.

A burst of machine gun fire silenced our discussion minutes after it began. Bullets shattered the living room window and made popping noises against the wood siding of the house.

CHAPTER 14

BLOW MY HEAD OFF WHY DON'T YOU

Chrissie and Laura hit the floor with the first volley of bullets. I dove with the sound of grunts and oomphs as my companions landed on the living room carpet. I couldn't help but think the ladies of the house had experience with drive-by shootings.

College Jennifer ran into the living room with a shotgun. She joined us on the floor as another volley of shooting began. The smoke and aroma of hot lead and gun powder permeated the house to compete with the lingering smell of fried chicken.

Most of the bullets splatted against the house next door but that didn't stop me from wishing I wore a diaper and hoping my time travelling companions thought I chose that moment to dance the Crocodile Rock while on my back on the floor rather than assume my shaking somehow had something to do with fear.

Despite my long sentences and natural inclination towards cowardice, I poked my head up enough to take a gander out the big hole where the front window used to be before the bullets destroyed it. Four men stood around a maroon LaSalle stopped in the middle of the street so it wasn't a drive by shooting so much as a drive by and park attack. Two outlaws fired Thompson submachine guns, the kind you see in the old gangster movies with the round canisters attached to them. The other two fired pistols. One of them was our nineteen twenty-three version of Mr. Turpelator.

Mr. Turpelator took aim in our direction. Based on where he pointed his gun, I realized my Jennifer was about to lose her head. She had stood up to point her M16 out the window hole. I rose off my butt with the intention of pushing Jennifer out of danger, but instead I heard a pistol shot and felt a burning sting across one side of my head.

The blast spun me around, but I don't remember hitting the carpet. I opened my eyes, not remembering when I shut them. My head was fuzzy, and I couldn't remember where I was for a moment. Spots danced in front of my eyes and the room moved in circles.

My skull hurt on the left side where the bullet struck me so I placed my hand over the wound. When I yanked it away, my hand was covered with blood. My nose hurt so I placed my clean right hand over it, and it came away wet with blood. I must have smashed my nose when I hit the floor. I raised my head again and noticed the blood on my shirt from the nose bleed.

I sat up with my back against the wall under the window. My eyes insisted on remaining in the shut position while my brain buzzed. Bullets whizzed by.

I opened my eyes long enough to notice Tony step up to the window frame with his M16 and open fire. I rose up to see what kind of damage he accomplished. I poked at my right eye to keep it popped open. The trick worked in time to spot one of the bad guys with the machine gun by the car. He fell on his face. Mr. Turpelator fell on the ground with a pistol in one hand and his free hand pressed to his wounded shoulder. The other two gunmen fired in our direction.

I closed my eyes but opened them again to the sound of a loud whoosh. A giant American bald eagle dove out of the sky. Its wingspan was a good thirty feet. It snagged Mr.

Turpelator while he sat with his shoulder wound and pistol. The raptor dragged him into a tree across the street.

By this time, Gilbert had his M16 locked and loaded. He opened fire and may have killed as many as two dozen roses across the street.

Was this action in slow motion? I couldn't tell because my head was so buzzy, but it happened faster than I can write it here because it wasn't until this point that young Jennifer screamed, "You bastards shot my boyfriend."

While I smiled, bled, fought off a fainting spell, and thought about how I was her boyfriend again, my Jennifer fired a short burst with her M16. I peeked through the bouncing spots in front of my eyes. She dropped the other guy who held a pistol. The back of his head exploded and blood spilled out from under his chest area. The pistol guy must not have noticed Jennifer shoot at him because he was busy aiming at the eagle when she killed him.

Jennifer blasted another round at the remaining machine gun guy, splattering bullet holes across his chest as he bounced off the front fender of the car and his face met pavement.

When the eagle dropped Mr. Turpelator, he abandoned his pistol and scrambled for the driver's door to the LaSalle. The vehicle sped away.

"I got two of 'em," my Jennifer shrieked.

"Nice shooting," said little Chrissie. "Anyone hurt?"

Laura lay on her stomach not moving while the rest of the group stood up except me.

"You okay, Laura?" I felt funny calling an adult by her first name, especially with a faint voice, but Tony got us started. If you find yourself in the wrong century, it's okay for kids to use first names.

Laura rolled over. Her upper arm appeared to have a red gash with heavy bleeding.

"Mommy!" Chrissie ran to her mother and hugged her.

Great Grandma carried a tin white box into the room. It had a red cross painted on it. "I'll take care of this. Anyone else hurt?"

The others indicated they were not injured. My world turned black as the brain fuzz increased. I pointed my bloody face in the direction of my beloved with what must have been enough wounded puppy sadness that my Jennifer's heart broke.

"Bryan!" She dropped at my side, but College Jennifer beat her to me. By this time, my shirt front was red and wet from my nose bleed. My bullet graze wound gushed enough blood that my ear and shoulder felt wet.

The older Jennifer shed tears as she hugged me. "Darling, they never shot you before." She backed away to allow her little sister to kiss me on my forehead which was my only face spot where I didn't feel wet blood.

"You're bleeding," my Jennifer wiped the blood off my face with her handkerchief.

"No shit." Why mince words when you're dying and the love of your life can't say more than the obvious. Give her a break because she killed two men after witnessing her boyfriend shot in the head. Did you notice she called me her "boyfriend?" I wasn't about to argue with her. And College Jennifer called me "darling." What was that about?

I fell into a black void for I don't know how long, but I popped back into reality when Chrissie yelled, "Hey, where'd this pile of clothes come from?"

"Daniel will need these." Gilbert snagged the clothes and headed upstairs with them.

I don't remember hitting the floor again, but I didn't have far to go because I was already sitting. I dreamed about Jennifer shooting Jesus on the cross above my head back in my bedroom in the twenty-first century. Little plastic Jesus took the shot like another sin added to his burden. He writhed in pain and shed a tear for Jennifer.

When I popped awake, I was still on the floor. Great Grandma bandaged my head. My Jennifer held a cloth bag stuffed with ice cubes on my nose. The bag had a small, screw top lid so it was something they must have sold in those days. I learned later it was called an ice bag and most people kept one around as a cure for headaches or other aches and pains. Dump in the ice and apply it wherever it hurt. You could use it to cure a hangover. The cloth on this ice bag had a grey plaid design.

Everyone stared at me, including Daniel who had returned to the living room fully dressed from his adventures as a giant bald eagle. The expressions on their faces showed their fear for my life. I felt so loved in that moment.

A new guy with an old-fashioned bolt rifle flew through the opening where the front window hung before the shooting began. His feet missed my head and succeeded in brushing against Great Grandma's hair. In the distance, I heard sirens.

"Repack," Tony shouted. He placed his M16 next to his backpack. The rest of the twenty-first century crew followed suit.

"Upstairs," the older Jennifer ordered. Tony and Gilbert snagged our bags and headed for the bedrooms.

The new arrival on the floor wore a white collarless dress shirt and navy blue linen slacks. He sported high-button shoes or boots on his feet. He gazed about the room. "Two casualties. Anyone else hurt?"

The older Jennifer sighed as if she was bored. "No, Ernie, except for Laura and Bryan,"

"A piece of flying glass caught me unawares," said Laura.

Ernie stood up. "I see you have visitors. I'll schedule a social call with you later, Jennifer."

"You will?" young Jennifer asked. Tears streamed down her cheeks.

"He means me," said the older Jennifer. "Ernie, we could use your help. Can you house our male guests for us?"

Ernie brushed back his brown hair. He wore it cut short on the sides and back, but long on top. "Of course, Jennifer. You have but to ask, and I am at your service unless you happen to be engaged or married to one of them."

"You know I'm a free woman," said the older Jennifer.

"Free, white and twenty-one," said Ernie. "No offense to your Negro."

"And I'm not twenty-one yet," said the older Jennifer.

Gilbert closed to within an inch of nose-to-nose with Ernie. "Her Negro takes offense at racial prejudice, Ernie. I'm free, Black and proud."

"Yes, uhm, I see. Of course." Ernie backed up three feet and raised his rifle to the port arms position. "Will you join the others as guests in my home, sir?"

Gilbert smiled. He stuck out his hand. "It would be my pleasure, Ernie. I'm Gilbert Armstrong. Pleased to meet you."

Ernie shook hands. "May I call you Gilbert?"

"But of course, Ernie" Gilbert said.

Ernie was half-way through the broken window when the police arrived. My Jennifer continued to sob while I bled.

***

"What did Chrissie do this time?" Police sergeant O'Malley asked.

"She didn't do anything," Laura shouted.

"Then why'd you people call the police," asked the sergeant.

"Officer, we didn't call about Chrissie. We needed help with those mobsters who shot up the place," the older Jennifer said.

"I can see that. But wasn't your Miss Chrissie behind it. She always is," said the police sergeant.

"Don't speak about my daughter like that. She may be a bit strong-headed but she is a good girl," said Laura.

"Right." The police sergeant took our statements concerning how the drive-by shooters blasted away at the Hawkins' house by mistake while aiming for Ernie's house next door. I couldn't speak because I kept passing out and waking up. On one of my more coherent awakenings, I noticed Great Grandma had finished bandaging my head. My nose still dribbled a little blood.

Ernie said he had no idea why anyone would want to shoot at his house. I heard some of the statements but my eyes remained shut.

"They must have been a group of high school students invigorated by bootleg gin," Ernie suggested. "They staggered out of their machine before they opened fire."

When the police sergeant asked how students could get their hands on submachine guns, Ernie didn't remember machineguns.

"They had machineguns? Could be, I suppose. They fired their weapons in rapid form. Perhaps their parents are involved in the illegal gin trade," Ernie said.

I opened my eyes at this curious statement.

Ernie pulled a pipe from his pants pocket to gesture to the outside. "Why, if that large bird hadn't dropped out of the sky, we may all have been wounded by the scalawags. As it was, we have two injured on our side. Has someone sent for a physician?"

"Oh my," said Great Grandma.

"I'll call." College aged Jennifer headed to a table in the corner.

The police sergeant asked the rest of us about the bird. Tony assured him there indeed was an eagle involved in chasing off the gunmen.

"What's wrong with her?" The sergeant gestured towards my Jennifer.

"They shot my boyfriend. I didn't mean to hurt them," my Jennifer sobbed.

"Hurt who?" the sergeant asked.

"Whom. Hurt whom," Ernie corrected.

"The dead men, the one where the side of the car used to be and the other one with the missing parts to his head," my Jennifer cried. I reached up to hug her, but my arms were too weak to hold her. Jennifer noticed and cried louder. She lay across my chest while sobs racked her body.

"Oh my, was that your handy work, Miss?" the sergeant asked.

"It was self-defense," Tony said. "You can still see the gun in the man's hand." I couldn't see, but I assumed Tony was right.

"So it was," said the sergeant. "We'll have no more crying now, Miss. We can see they were ruthless gangsters out to shoot you and yours. You did our fair town a favor by killing them. Now, now, my dear, no need for tears." The sergeant patted Jennifer on the shoulder.

Before leaving, the sergeant said, "We don't see any evidence to point to the other guilty party. There are blood stains, a few tire tracks and used shell casings out on the street, but nothing useful."

My head slipped into a deeper shade of fuzzy. Why didn't anyone mention Mr. Turpelator? Maybe they did and I missed it. Before my eyes stopped working, I spied a guy dressed in black robes in the corner of the room. He didn't seem to notice me taking a gander at him as he stood waiting for my death. I think my eyes were still open at this point, and I had no idea why the creepy fellow in the corner made me think of my death. I was about to blurt something to comfort Jennifer, but my brain picked that moment to shut down.

CHAPTER 15

THE PATIENT AND THE NURSE

My Jennifer held a small coffee can with a bottom full of blood under my nose when I woke up during the night. I was propped up with pillows. I spied a pile of blood-soaked toilet paper around the bed. The bed sheets and pillow cases had blood smears on them.

"Hi," Jennifer said.

Something cold draped off the top of my head and clung down to the swollen side with the bullet wound. "Why am I still alive?"

Hallucinations are part of the fractured skull experience, I suppose. I glared at the dark shadowy creature waiting in the corner for me to croak. I heard the growl of a large jungle cat outside my window. "What's that?"

"What's what?" Jennifer asked.

"Some kind of jungle cat."

"Like a lion?"

"Smaller. Maybe a mountain lion or panther."

"The bullet fractured your skull so you're probably hearing things. You have a concussion. We tried to keep you awake, but you passed out and –" Jennifer lowered her head and sobbed. "I... I... thought... I lost you."

I snagged her hand. "Jennifer, we Ganarskis are a hard-headed clan. I'll be fine." Except I wasn't. "Why am I still bleeding?" I closed my eyes.

When I opened my eyes again, the sun shone in the room. Tony smiled as he parked on the side of the bed with a bottle of medicine in his hand. He pushed one of the capsules into my mouth. "Penicillin from my private stash. Follow the directions on the label every day for two weeks. Don't tell the doc because these things ain't invented yet."

I swallowed my medicine with water. I took a gander about the room. No dark shadow guy and no panther calls.

The college-age Jennifer entered the room carrying a tray with toast and a cup of tea. She appeared worried. "Keep your strength up, Bryan."

"Water, okay?" I asked.

Tony refilled my glass from a pitcher on the night stand. He held it to my lips.

"Jennifer?" I bubbled.

"Yes?" the older Jennifer asked.

"My Jennifer?"

"Oh, we made her go to bed. She stayed up two nights and days with you. She'll return when she wakes up. To tell us apart, Bryan, the rest of us now call me College Jennifer or CJ. Try it. Your teenage Jennifer is now your Jennifer. We gave her to you." College Jennifer bowed her head. "I'm sorry, Bryan. I promised myself I would smile around you." She slathered my toast with her tears softening the butter.

I ate half the toast and sipped a little of the tea. My head ached too much to give much thought to CJ's tears. I was dizzy, but at least my nose had stopped bleeding. I went back to sleep with CJ holding my hand.

I woke up in the dark with someone next to me on the bed. I was afraid it was the dark shadowy guy, but he stood vigil in the corner. The person sharing the bed with me was either my Jennifer or my dream. Either way she squeezed my hand before I sank back into the darkness. The last thing I heard that night was the growl of a jungle cat.

The next time I awoke, the sun shone through the window, but I didn't know if it was the next day or the next week. Police Sergeant O'Malley visited me with my sleepy-headed Jennifer, Tony, Daniel, Gilbert and CJ squeezed into the room.

Sergeant O'Malley said, "We interviewed James Turpelator about the shooting because you said you recognized him."

"You arrested him, right?" CJ asked.

"Couldn't." Sergeant O'Malley said.

"Why not?" Tony asked.

"He was giving a speech at the Cicero Police Benevolent Association at the time of the shooting. There must be at least twenty or thirty police officers ready to testify that he was with them that day."

"But we saw him," my Jennifer said.

"It's your word against theirs, isn't it? Maybe you saw a gangster as looks like your Mr. Turpelator," said Sergeant O'Malley.

"We know he was there," my Jennifer said. "I shot him. He bled. He fell to the ground. Doesn't the bullet prove he was involved?"

"See, there's the issue, ain't it ma'am? I mean you folks says you shot a gentleman in your street who got away, and I've no doubt you did for there was blood enough on the street, but James Turpelator never had no such wound. He ain't hurt since I interviewed him and he showed me his shoulder, both of them mind you, and neither was wounded nor scarred. I'm afraid you folks recognized the wrong man."

"I know it was him," I whispered on my way back to sleep.

When next I woke up, a heavy set man in a business suit fumbled about with a small black bag. I tried to clobberbust the intruder with my pillow, but the force of my swing knocked me down on the bed. I tried to scream, but no noise would come out of my dry mouth. I wasn't so much afraid as parched. Oh, all right. I was scared crapless.

The rotund man must have heard me swing and fall. He turned in my direction. "Now, now, son, you have to stay in bed. No trying to get up."

He introduced himself as Doctor McCully and gave me the diagnosis he had given the others earlier. He said I had a fractured skull to go with the grazing wound from the bullet. Apparently the gang had dragged me to the hospital for the x-ray and then dragged me back home against the doctor's wishes. Doctor McCully was quite upset about it and so his bedside manner was not the best.

"You had no business leaving the hospital, young man."

"I wasn't there in person, only my body."

"Still you may have fallen into a coma and died. You are a most uncooperative patient."

"How is it my fault? I didn't exist at the time. My brain was dead so maybe I was in a coma."

"Perhaps, but you are here now and in very bad shape. Your wound will become infected if I don't take you back to the hospital, but you will die if I move you. See the situation you have placed me in?"

"Aren't I the one in the situation, doctor? I mean I'm the one who will die either way." I gazed about for the black-robed guy who haunted my corners.

"Do not speak of dying. You are young and strong. You will fight off the fever and live. I wish you were in the hospital where I could monitor your progress and control your diet. Everything must be scientific for you to survive this terrible wound you have received. I hate to see another hero die needlessly."

"Hero? How did I become a hero?" I asked.

The black-robed guy in the corner must have taken a lunch break.

"Don't be modest, Bryan. Your friends described how you jumped in front of your girlfriend and saved her life by taking the bullet yourself. That was the bravest thing I have heard since the Great War. Yes, whether you consider yourself a hero or not, you are one."

Gilbert brought in a fresh pitcher of water. He asked the doctor if he didn't worry about patients suing him if he didn't do enough tests and x-rays to establish a clear record of diagnosis and treatment. Doctor McCully laughed and asked Gilbert why anyone in their right mind would sue a doctor for healing them.

The doctor visited most days and insisted I have a registered nurse visit me during the day. Apparently the doctor and nurse had been visiting me every day but I hadn't noticed. Young Jennifer became my nurse at night and the joy of my life during my recovery. Doctor McCully ordered me to stay in bed for eight weeks. He and that nurse he sent yelled at me and the gang every time they caught me out of bed which was every time they came after my fourth week.

We settled the issue by firing the nurse Doctor McCully sent. Instead, we retained the services of Nurse Nora, aka Snpgrdxz. His advanced alien technology first aid skills exceeded Doctor McCully's physician skills but he lacked the tools to properly serve as our group's medical officer. Even so, he brought me the blessing of advanced nursing care. The best thing, of course, was Tony's supply of penicillin, which seemed to keep the guy in the corner at bay.

Medicine in the nineteen twenties may have wanted patients to remain inactive long enough for bedsores and pneumonia to set in, but I was committed to a quick recovery. So was my Jennifer and the rest of my twenty-first century friends. I was now the holdup preventing the search for Maria Gonzalez and our return to our home time.

***

Ernie caught me and Jennifer in bed together one night. She slept in my arms while I read a new novel by F. Scott Fitzgerald.

"Ho-ho, what goes on here?" Ernie asked.

I startled so I must have been half asleep or deeper. "It's after midnight, Ernie. Shouldn't you be home in bed?"

"I'm talking about the half-naked jail bait in your bed, my friend."

I gawped down at my Jennifer, still asleep. I had to rise up in the bed to notice she had stripped off her pants. She wore a t-shirt and panties. Ernie, at the foot of the bed, had the better view. I flipped my blanket over Jennifer.

"Why did you do that?" Ernie asked.

Jennifer opened her eyes before I could answer. She smiled at me and rolled over. "Oh," she gasped.

"No need to answer the question," Ernie said.

Jennifer must have become unwrapped again in rolling over. She snagged more blanket off me to cover herself. "What's he doing here?"

"I don't know. What are you doing here, Ernie?"

Ernie grimaced. "To tell the truth, I snuck in to pay a midnight visit to Jennifer, the other Jennifer. I saw the light on in your room. I guessed it was her room but guess what? I was wrong. Nice legs, by the way."

"Thank you," I said.

My Jennifer punched me. "Did you let him peek at me?"

"No, but I think you may have not been quite covered to your satisfaction when he first arrived."

"Boys!"

Ernie's eyes lit up inspired by the sight of my Jennifer and me in bed together. "Two love birds. One of you suffered a bullet wound. The other is his nurse. Yes, I see this working. I may use you two in one of my novels. I see it as a tale of the Great War, but the western front was so boring with everyone sitting about in trenches for years. I may move the adventure to Italy where they fought in mountains and along rivers. Yes, that will work. We'll put you in a hospital in a beautiful Italian city like Milan. This will work. I'm so glad I met you people."

Jennifer said, "I think it's time for you to go, Ernie."

"Okay."

Jennifer smiled at Ernie as he opened the bedroom door. "And Ernie, if you ever sneak into this room again, I will personally remove your male thingie and feed it to that loud cat we hear every night."

"Painful, but what an idea for another novel. Soldier suffers war wound. He has all the urge his testosterone can muster but his, uhm, thingie, as you call it has been shot off in the war so he can't perform. He's in love with a girl. She loves him. But they can't consummate the relationship so she sleeps around with other men to satisfy her urges. I think I can work with that. Thanks for the idea, Jennifer."

The big cat roared.

"Sounds like it's in the yard," I said.

"You hear the cat, too? I think it's a lion or some other big critter," said Ernie. "I've been tempted to hunt it down. I could use a trophy for the living room."

"Ernie!" my Jennifer protested.

"Goodnight." Ernie meandered down the hall. We heard him knock on Laura's door. Her door squeaked open and Ernie asked for CJ. I fell asleep to the sound of a twelve-gauge being snapped into shooting position.

***

Fear rode my spine like a cowboy bucking a bronco the day CJ showed up in my bedroom with another young man. I was still in that wake-up-and-wonder-how-long-I-was-out phase. My Jennifer sat on my bed and held my hand. She appeared rumpled like she had been lying next to me.

CJ's new friend scared me almost as much as the shadow man who stood silent in the corner and invisible to the others.

The brave die but once or so they say, but I saw death every time I stared into a dark corner.

CJ introduced her other "beau" as Chauncey Chadsworth.

"Your name sounds familiar. Have we met before?" My voice quaked.

"I don't believe we have. I'm a member of the Lincoln High class of nineteen eighteen so I was quite a few years before your time," said Chauncey.

It took me a moment to figure out Chauncey meant some years before nineteen twenty-three rather than the twenty-first century, but in that moment I felt dread slither up my backbone.

I went through a mental dive into my list of Facebook friends and high school connections. As far as I could recall I didn't know anyone named Chauncey but I knew the name from somewhere. It sounded old-fashioned and Brit. "Are you from England?" I asked.

"Do I sound English?" Chauncey asked.

"He's from Wheaton, Illinois, Bryan. Same as the rest of us," said CJ.

"You have to forgive Bryan. He's been wounded," said my Jennifer.

"Of course, I can see that." Chauncey smiled the way an in-crowd quarterback smiles at a nerd with no respect intended. I picked that moment to drop off into my afternoon nap.

Chauncey Chadsworth stopped in most afternoons while Ernie worked. What amazed me was the way he took over my daily care. He and I soon became friends as my fear of him faded away like the shadow guy in the corner. Chauncy joined Tony, Gilbert and Daniel in taking turns regarding my manly needs such as potty breaks and bathing, the things that caused my Jennifer to blush whenever CJ teased her about nursing "her man." The guys dumped me in the bathtub at a time when that nurse we later fired insisted I remain in bed and have sponge baths and use the bedpan. Who was she kidding?

Chauncey taught me to play chess apparently to have someone to destroy on the chessboard and to have an excuse to spend more time with CJ.

"How long have you known CJ?" I asked one afternoon while setting up the chess board. We were alone because my Jennifer had the night shift and needed a nap. She slept in the morning but needed extra sleep. During the day, she snoozed in what the ladies laughingly called "her room" next door. Thinking about her in bed so close by about drove me up the wall in a manly sort of way.

"Who is CJ?" Chauncey asked.

"Your girlfriend. You know, Jennifer?"

"Oh, of course. Why do you call her CJ?"

"Short for College Jennifer. I have to tell her apart from my Jennifer."

"They're sisters, but Jennifer, that is my Jennifer, is clearly the older girl and hasn't' been to college as far as I know," said Chauncey.

I was still fuzzy enough not to remember if it was that day or another afternoon that Chauncey saw the shadow man.

**

Chauncey screamed. He had asked, "What's that?" He turned around, opened his mouth and let out a blood-curdling noise heard up and down the street, I'm sure.

He backed up, bumped into my bed and landed on top of me. He cowered against the wall, leaving me to face the monster in the corner.

"What is that?" Chauncey pointed at the shadow creature.

The creature pointed back but I couldn't tell if it pointed at me, Chauncey or both of us. It's not a good thing when death points a finger at you.

"Death in the shadows," I answered. I don't know why I said it that way. It sounded poetical but this was no time for beauty, yet beauty is what we received as CJ popped into the room.

"I hope I'm not disturbing you boys."

"N-no," said Chauncey.

"Funny you don't sound gay," said CJ.

"What's that thing?" Chauncey asked.

"What thing?" CJ asked.

"In the corner."

CJ checked out the corner where Chauncey had indicated. "Just some spider webs. I'll have Bryan's nurse clean up in here." She passed her hand through the shadow man without seeing him. Shadow man faded away.

CJ parked in the chair by my bed. "You're still in bed together. Are you gay because if you're gay, Chauncey, this is the first I've seen or heard of it?"

"Do I look gay?" Chauncey asked. "That thing scared me out of my wits."

"Do gay guys often share each other's hallucinations?" CJ asked.

"We're not gay," I said.

"Why would we be happy?" Chauncey asked.

I glared at Chauncey. "Oh, you think CJ means 'happy' when she says 'gay.' Gay has a different meaning where we come from."

"You come from Wheaton," Chauncey said.

CJ, bless her heart, came up with a great cover for our gaff. "We mean Europe. Bryan's family spent years in Europe where gay is a reference to homosexuals. I just picked it up here since Bryan's family moved back to Wheaton."

Chauncey peered up at the ceiling in thought. "That's why I haven't met anyone named Ganarski before. Your people were overseas for years."

"Since after the Great War," I said.

***

126

"I peed my pants," said CJ.

I had asked CJ how she and Chauncey met. I was still spending most of my days in bed. CJ's answer startled me and Chauncey both.

Chauncey was established in the chair by my bed one afternoon while CJ knelt next to him and latched onto his arm. My Jennifer slept in her bed in the other room.

"What happened?" I asked.

"You will recall how you guys arrived in Wheaton this time, right?" CJ asked.

"Yes, of course." I also realized she did not want to alert Chauncey to our time traveling ways.

"Well, my pants had the same problem your Jennifer's pants had when she arrived, except I still had my pants on at the time."

"Oh, that would be embarrassing," I said.

"Like you guys, I arrived in summer, but that was back in nineteen eighteen. Somehow by passing through, I mean entering, no, arriving in Wheaton – "

"We know what you mean," said Chauncey.

"You do?" I asked.

Chauncey chuckled. "Certainly. It could happen to anyone. The excitement of arriving in a strange town where you don't know anyone but you think you have family, and you don't know if they'll take you in, and you were what, fifteen at the time? It's frightening to be an orphan in a strange place and traveling on hope that a distant relative will take you in. What if they said no? Then where would you go? What would you do? A teenaged girl alone on the streets usually ends up in prostitution or worse."

"Worse?" CJ asked.

"Murder, rape, etc." Chauncey explained.

"Etc?" CJ asked.

"You know," Chauncey said.

"I do?" CJ asked.

I whispered in CJ's ear, "Porno films, nudie magazines, strip joints, drugs and alcohol. That kind of etc."

"Oh, my." CJ placed her hand over her mouth. "I never thought of those."

"You must have thought of them at the time, at least some of those things, because they are the only reasons a girl would pee her pants on the train to Wheaton."

"You're right," I said.

"Yeah," said CJ. "Funny I don't remember."

"We tend not to remember the things that scare the piss out of us. While the reason CJ had her little accident is interesting, especially for us boys, you haven't told the story of how you guys met as yet." I grabbed my shoulder after CJ punched me on the word "boys."

"You boys are creeps making me tell about the most embarrassing moment of my life. I had an accident. Let's just leave it at that. When I arrived in Wheaton, I didn't know what to do so I headed home, except of course, I didn't know if I would be welcomed home in nineteen eighteen but where else could I go dressed in wet pants? So, I plodded through downtown Wheaton on my way north from Lincoln High School hoping no one would notice and that it would dry quickly in the summer heat. Everyone did notice, of course. How can you miss a young girl wearing wet blue jeans and a t-shirt in nineteen eighteen at a time when women simply didn't wear pants?"

"That was so strange," Chauncey said.

"If you will recall, Chauncey, that's almost exactly what you said when you found me waiting for that freight train to pass."

"I meant why would you walk north from Lincoln High School when it's south of the train station? Your great grandmother lives north of the train station. How did you end up at Lincoln High?"

And it was strange. Jennifer told her tale as though she had experienced it one time, but in fact, she passed through her time loop twenty-seven times and was now on loop twenty-eight. She had the same accident twenty-seven times. You'd think she would be better prepared after the first time around, but what could I say?

CJ knew during every time loop, except the first, that she would be welcomed home by Great Grandma Hawkins and Laura. But she went along with the idea that she experienced everything for the first time so as to not reveal herself as a time traveler to her friends and family. And I suppose this was the twenty-eighth time she dated Chauncey, and she still liked him so they were close even if it was Chauncey's first time around with CJ.

CJ said, "I went the wrong way. What can I say? It was my first trip to Wheaton. You found me when I arrived back at the train tracks after figuring out I had gone the wrong way."

"I joined you on the sidewalk waiting to cross. You were so pretty and your pants so sexy. I could see the entire outline of your wet ass. What a turn on."

CJ chuckled. "I can laugh now, but then I was crying. Chauncey, you placed your suit jacket around my shoulders to cover what you considered my nakedness, remember?"

"Yes, and I asked you if you needed help?"

"I said no and continued on my way because the train had passed."

"I followed her home," Chauncey said.

"He stalked me," CJ said.

"I wanted my jacket back," Chauncey said.

"I returned the jacket when I arrived at Great Grandma's house. Remember, I was only fifteen at the time so I was bawling my head off. I never felt so alone and scared and embarrassed. And you, Chauncey, tried your best to be nice to me, but I was too freaked out to appreciate it."

Chauncey's eyes screwed into question marks. "There you go with your unusual slang. What does 'freaked out' mean? Did you turn into an extremely ugly person on the outside?"

CJ laughed. "You were so sweet to me. I never thanked you enough for coming to my rescue that day. Fortunately for me, Great Grandma and Laura took me in. Even though I was a stranger, they recognized me as distant family."

Chauncey leaned over to kiss CJ on the lips. She let him. She smiled after the kiss. She leaned her head into his lap. There's a look my Jennifer gets sometimes when I know she is thinking about me or showing me she loves me like right after we kiss. She even showed it that first time we kissed back at Lincoln High. CJ had that look of love on her face for Chauncey.

CHAPTER 16

PANTHER

The jungle cat burst through my bedroom window one night in late August. With Jennifer wrapped in my arms, I pulled her back from the side of the tiny twin bed facing the black panther. The big cat roared.

My love for Jennifer Hawkins grew during my recovery as her love for me increased. We were faithful churchgoers back home, and we stayed good during my down time, but not that good. I mean Jennifer took to spending the "nightshift" with me on my bed where we cuddled and kissed the night away. That's how the cat found us that night.

Jennifer jumped up to stand on the bed in her short, low cut summer night gown, the one she began wearing after Ernie had barged in on us to catch her in her skivvies. "Shoo!" she shouted.

The panther backed off to the window where it circled. I think the panther wasn't sure if it was safe to attack or if it should bolt. Jennifer came across as pretty aggressive at times.

Jennifer took advantage of the confused panther by jumping off the bed and running out of the room. She slammed the door behind her. I was proud of her for making her escape. There was no reason for both of us to turn into panther fodder.

"Hello, panther." My voice shook. In the darkness, I noticed a darker area in that corner where death waited my soul to take. With death merely standing and watching, the panther became the action so I turned my attention to it.

The panther had question marks for eyes. I'm serious. It appeared confused at my talking to it. At some deep place in my mind, I must have prepared for my own death by panther because I thought I saw the panther morph into a naked woman down on all fours.

The shadow man appeared behind the panther where I could see it more clearly. The angel of death never showed its face. You couldn't tell if was male or female because of its long, flowing black robes. I assumed angels were sexless but you never knew for certain.

The panther made a feminine growl at me that was sexy. Was I about to be eaten by an erotic time-traveling fugitive from the futuristic play *Cats* or was I facing an escaped zoo creature about to devour me without regard to my overactive imagination, the angel of death or my general insanity? Whichever it was, I had just enough time to kiss my butt goodbye.

***

Jennifer barged back into the room with a shotgun. Don't ask me where the weapon came from. Tony's bottomless backpack most likely. Or maybe it was the one CJ had used when those gangsters opened fire on the house.

The panther appeared to recognize both the shotgun for what it was and Jennifer for what she was, a fearless warrior. Cats are known for wisdom, at least as compared to dogs, and that panther had enough smarts to bolt through the window just as Jennifer opened up with the twelve-gauge. The cat screeched in pain before hitting the ground.

Jennifer and I ran to the window in time to see the big cat head over the fence for the back alley behind the Hawkins house. Well, Jennifer ran with her shotgun in hand. I meandered in a daze towards the window and slapped my hands on the wall to keep from falling over. Jennifer snagged my arm to hold me up.

Everyone barged into my room in Hawkins House which meant all the ladies. The menfolk, other than me, bunked next door at Ernie's house. CJ asked what had happened.

"I shot a panther that leapt into our bedroom," my Jennifer said. The room was still dark so you couldn't see if her face turned red, but I bet it did. This room was now "our" bedroom. A guy can't overlook a comment like that. No one else did either. I became dizzy and had to sit down so I made my way back to bed.

"I thought 'your bedroom' was the room down the hall, young lady," said Great Grandma Hawkins. "And why are you dressed in a skimpy night gown when you are supposed to be his nurse?"

"You know what I meant," said my Jennifer. "And I was in the middle of getting ready for bed when the panther attacked. My bed. Next door."

"Yes, we do know what you meant and why you were out of your street clothes," said Laura.

"You know I'm the night shift nurse for Bryan so I spend my evenings with him here and sleep days in my room," said my Jennifer. "He seemed well enough tonight for me to sleep in my own bed."

"Who shot who?" asked a sleepy Chrissie.

"Go back to bed, Chrissie. There's nothing for you to see here," said Laura.

"Is young Jennifer sleeping with Bryan? I didn't know they were married," said Chrissie.

"To bed," yelled Laura.

Chrissie left.

"Maybe we should all go back to bed," said CJ.

In the darkness I doubt many of them saw her, but from my angle, there was enough moonlight to notice my Jennifer mouth "Thank you" to CJ.

"Come, Jennifer, both of you," said Great Grandma Hawkins. The ladies returned to their rooms. On the way out, Great Grandma said, "I don't know why you fired that weapon, but you can come up with something more creative than a jungle cat, my dear. Next time, try a burglar. I always told my husband it was a burglar."

"Great Grandma!" Jennifer said.

She waited all of about ten minutes before tip-toeing back to my bed while still in her summer nightgown. Mosquitoes buzzed through the broken window and screen so we abandoned the bedroom for the chesterfields down in the living room.

***

I spotted the dark stranger in the shadows of one corner of the front porch of Hawkins House. My Jennifer and I reclined on the glider while CJ, Laura and Chrissie relaxed in the kitchen chairs around a table sipping their lemonade on the afternoon following the panther attack. My Jennifer and I held hands, something that had become a constant during my recovery as did our smiles and love-glazed eyes. The others noticed of course.

What they didn't seem to notice was the mysterious shadow creature. How long would death pursue me? If death was near, did he intend my death or someone close to me? The scar from the bullet itched and a headache formed under my scar. I blinked against the pain. When I opened my eyes, the shadow creature I called death had vanished.

"What's wrong, Bryan?" CJ asked.

"Headache."

"You look as though you've seen a ghost," Laura said.

"He looks pale as ghost." My Jennifer ran her hand down the side of my face. I kissed her hand and took it into my own.

CJ said. "In twenty-seven times through this infernal time loop, Bryan and I never grew close. Bryan, you were always the first boy I liked, the one who got away. I'm amazed at you two, and I'm happy for you. But I'm worried about you, little sister. At fifteen, I don't think I was ready to handle a serious relationship."

My Jennifer answered for me. "What can I say, big sister? Does age matter when we're so happy together? I can't wait for Bryan to get better so we can spend serious time doing boyfriend-girlfriend stuff."

CJ laughed at her younger twin. "I don't think it's possible for you to spend more time with Bryan, dear heart. And what you guys do at night... well, I'm sure at least some of it is boyfriend-girlfriend stuff."

Laura said, "Jennifer!"

My Jennifer said, "We didn't do anything, honest."

Laura turned to my Jennifer with a quizzical expression. "I meant your big sister, dear, the one who accused you and Bryan of fornicating under my roof."

"What's fornicating mean?" Chrissie asked.

"Never mind, Chrissie. It's time for you to run along and play."

"But I want to know what fornicating means so I can do it too."

A young lady limped on a cane along the sidewalk at that moment. "Chrissie, you're not ready for boys."

"Oh, it's a yucky boy thing. I didn't know that, Aunt Lilly." Chrissie ran down to the sidewalk and hugged Aunt Lilly.

"Ow!" said Aunt Lilly.

"Did you hurt yourself, Aunt Lilly?" asked Chrissie.

"Just a little, dear. You run along and play."

"What happened to you?" CJ asked.

"Rather embarrassing, I'm afraid. The story will cost you one of Great Grandma Hawkins's lemonades." Lilly wore a summer dress with a hat that covered her light brown hair.

Her bangs came to just above her brown eyes. Her thin lips had an unusual sensuality about them. Her nose extended beyond perky but less than bulbous, a nondescript schnozzle. Her chin fell and faded under her mouth, making for a weak jawline but a beautiful young lady of college age with small breasts and that boyish figure you see in old photos from the twenties.

"Come sit with us and I'll fetch one," said CJ.

"Aren't you going to introduce your friends?" Lilly asked.

"No, I'm busy plying you with spiked lemonades. Everyone please introduce yourselves to my dear friend Lilly Blackstone while I'm gone." CJ sauntered into the house.

After a round of introductions in which Lilly informed us that she was a lady of independent means from a good family who enjoyed golf, tennis, skeet shooting and sex, CJ returned with a pitcher of off-color lemonade. "None for you, Bryan."

"My head isn't ready for anything stronger than iced tea or Great Grandma's lemonade without the extra spike." While I felt the temperature rise on my face for being the only nondrinker, CJ came to my rescue by changing the subject.

"Give. We want to know what happened to your butt," said CJ.

Lilly turned beet red. "What makes you think my limping has anything to do with my butt?"

Laura laughed. "The careful way you parked it and the way you keep adjusting your position. Would you like another pillow?"

"Yes, I would." Lilly lifted off the chair while Laura stuffed a pillow from the glider on the seat. "Thank you, Laura. Okay, I'll tell this story once, and it must never leave your lips or surely I will eat you all. The short answer is skeet shooting."

"Give. We want more." CJ winked at me while she poured a spiked lemonade for my Jennifer.

My Jennifer sipped her lemonade and then winked at me using exactly the same wink style her older twin used. I believe CJ's wink meant she intended for my Jennifer to become high so she would put out for me later. And my Jennifer's wink meant she drank hard stuff now so we could have a good time later. The only problem I foresaw was how I would have to explain to a drunken girlfriend that tonight wasn't possible because I had a splitting headache thanks to that gangster who had planted a bullet up the side of my bean.

Lilly rolled her pretty head from side to side, gazed to the ceiling of the porch perhaps to check with the gods for story inspiration. She lowered her head to meet my Jennifer in the eye. "My friend shot me in the ass. Can you imagine? We were walking out to the skeet range with me in the lead. It was a big mistake, by the way. Always be the follower when carrying your weapon loaded." Lilly turned to me. "Is your weapon loaded, Bryan?"

"Huh?" I asked.

My Jennifer turned beet red while CJ and Laura roared with laughter.

Lilly shook her beautiful light brown hair. "Apparently that's a personal question not fitting for a group conversation. Perhaps you will permit me to ask it again sometime. Say up in your bedroom alone this evening?"

CJ and Laura laughed until my Jennifer jumped out of her seat.

CJ said, "Easy, Jen. She's just teasing."

Laura said, "Lilly, please. Jennifer and Bryan are a couple. Didn't you see them holding hands?"

Lilly laughed. "Oh, dear, I'm so sorry. I wasn't thinking. Please, young Jennifer, accept my apology. I'm a constant tease. I don't jump into the sack and eat all the boys I meet."

CJ laughed. "Lilly is very particular about her beaus. As for the bed hopping thing, well, I wouldn't know about that, but it does seem out of character for a good Christian lady."

"I'm so sorry," said Lilly. "I'll make it up to you in some way, okay?"

My Jennifer sat back down without a word. She snagged my hand onto her lap. I gazed at her while steam rose from her ears and eyeballs.

"So who shot you in the ass?" I asked to change the conversation and lighten the mood. It worked because my Jennifer tittered.

"A dear friend. I don't want to mention her name. No need to embarrass her more than she already is. Of course, her embarrassment is nothing compared to my own as I attempt to continue sitting here. Lucky for me she loaded bird shot and was some distance behind me when she tripped. Otherwise I wouldn't be here to sip spiked lemonade and tell lies."

"What about your young man?" CJ asked.

Lilly eased her butt from the chair and lowered it ever so gently back down. Either her butt still hurt or she farted, maybe both. "Jennifer and I like to compare our young gentlemen. That's how I'm not surprised to finally meet Bryan. But Jennifer, I thought Bryan was your age. You're robbing the cradle with this one. He's more fit for your younger sister, who by the way, you never mentioned in all the years we've known each other. What gives?"

"I attend school in Switzerland. This is my first trip home in years," said my Jennifer.

"Yes, but that doesn't explain you two having the same name, does it? But never mind. Jennifer has too many beaus as it is without the addition of Bryan. You may have him, little school girl from Europe." Lilly poured spiked lemonade from the pitcher on the table.

CJ said, "You're not jealous of my beaus, are you, Lilly?"

"Of course not, but the polite thing to do is to marry one and donate the rest to me."

"Maybe I'll do that. Which one should I marry?" CJ asked.

Lilly said, "Frank, of course. He's the one not from around here. He doesn't appear to have money, but he has brawn enough to please a woman."

***

That jungle cat continued meowing at night, or more precisely, growling. The thing wanted in. I figured it detected me as weakling meat ready for the slaughter, but the new window in my room discouraged an attack. A wounded animal is the more dangerous, according to legend, especially for those who are the weakest members of the herd or tribe.

I spent eight weeks listening to that jungle cat and watching the dog days of a hot August fade into a milder Midwest Autumn. September became October. Chauncey returned to Urbana for college despite tears from CJ at his departure. Lilly stopped limping in time.

The cat attacked again in late September. I woke to the big bang of something flung against the side of the house below my window. My Jennifer and I stepped to the glass as a large panther clawed its way up the side of the house to the glass. The creature growled before losing its grip and dropping to the lawn below.

The cat gave up after that evening, but I worried about the neighborhood, especially the children. The police expressed their concern by organizing a hunt for the cat, but nothing came of it. Through October the cat had vanished.

Meanwhile, the backyard that had been packed with greenery and tomato plants under the protection of old oak trees all summer faded to yellow-green leaves and dead or dying flowers.

Observing nature through my bedroom window and on my escapades into the backyard depressed me as the summer wore down. But as the fall season with its warm days and cold nights marked the death of summer, my strength returned like an apple ripe for the harvest. In the first week of

October, I was ready to take on the world so long as I didn't stand too fast to make myself dizzy or let my daily battles with headaches get me down.

Doctor McCully expressed amazement at my quick recovery and surprise at how no infection had set in. After eight weeks of "bed rest," he gave me a clean bill of health despite the lingering headaches and occasional dizziness. "They will diminish over time, my young friend," he said.

During my recovery the guys found jobs. When he wasn't busy with my care as Nurse Nora, Daniel worked as a waiter in a Chinese restaurant in Chicago's China Town so he could practice his new hobby of oriental shape shifting. He said he wasn't sure if he wanted to become a Buddhist monk or a Japanese Geisha so he worked on both which necessitated a budget for the proper apparel.

With the doctor's pronouncement that I was fit for duty, my Jennifer and I stepped out for the evening to celebrate.

"We're going with you," Gilbert said.

It wasn't what I had in mind, but when Gilbert said "we" he meant everyone. "It's always best to share the good news, isn't it?" he asked.

***

No one seemed bothered with teenagers drinking gin at a Chicago speakeasy or gazing at the scantily-clad chorus girls performing to the jazz band. Young Jennifer smacked me on the leg under the table a few times when I enjoyed my view more than she deemed appropriate, but she held my hand between smacks.

Frank and CJ danced a Charleston. She got it right away while Frank gave up and relied on our modern hop up and down basic dance step. He stopped when the other dance couples glared at him.

We drank our choice of gin or beer in the backroom of the 226 Club in Chicago. We entered the speakeasy after

Ernie treated us to a steak dinner in the restaurant that served as a front. The location was south Wabash Avenue a block off the State Street shopping area.

Heavy smoke and tobacco aroma mixed with the smell of meat. Like the rest of Chicago in the nineteen twenties, this place was about steaks whether you sat in the front or back room. And smoking produced a hazy atmosphere that cut the visibility and gave us modern types a headache, especially me.

Ernie's friend Scarface joined us. He listened to Ernie's tale of the hit men and the eagle. Scarface patted CJ's hand. "Such that you should not have to worry about violence in yous peaceful neighborhood, I shall look into this thing that has happened to yous and yous neighbors. And Ernie here shall join my organization now that his former employer has met with a sad end." He left on "ergent bizdness wid the mayor" while we enjoyed more of the floor show.

Killing those two men left my Jennifer sad at times. Our growing affection for each other cheered her whenever she felt down. I hesitated to call it depression as it sounded too clinical. She was in mourning and passing through phases on her way back to the full joy of our love. The beer and party atmosphere cheered her up. She placed her hand on the back of my neck. "It was self-defense, wasn't it?"

"Yes, you saved my life, Jennifer. You're my hero or heroine, I should say. And the best nurse ever." Next, I totally screwed up. "Besides you killed a couple of werewolves back in the troll world so it's not like these guys were your first kills."

My Jennifer bawled with her hands covering her face. I knew her makeup must be running down her face, so I leaned in, pulled one of her hands away and kissed her on the lips. She responded with passion. As we broke off, I noticed a Mr. Turpelator approach our table.

"Good evening, old boy," Mr Turpelator said to Ernie. Unlike our modern Mr. Turpelator physics teacher back home, this Mr. Turpelator wore his hair slicked down with enough oil for an engine overhaul atop his otherwise square-jawed, rugged face. I considered poking young Jennifer to take her eyes off him.

"What?" she asked when I worked up the gumption to tap her on the arm. "He looks like Mr. Turpelator back at school. Maybe he's related."

"He is Mr. Turpelator, the one who shot at us," I whispered.

Ernie unbuttoned his suit jacket to reveal a pistol in a shoulder holster like you see in the movies. "What do you want?"

"I want you, old boy. I hear you work with discretion and as I can see now, you carry yourself well in a fight, including a gun battle. You could be useful to me and Scarface in the suburbs."

"I work for Tommy Lutherman," Ernie said.

"Oh, you haven't heard the news, old boy."

"I heard Scarface offer me a job because my old boss was deceased. Is that your news?"

"Tommy and six of his boys passed away quite unexpectedly earlier this evening. I believe the cause of death was lead poisoning as they had a large quantity of lead in their bodies. The cause of death also could have been due to a large number of holes in their bodies that leaked quite a quantity of blood on the concrete floor of a garage on the southside."

"Why you dirty —"

"Don't display your anger here, old boy. I'm offering you a job. Scarface likes you despite our past differences. But there are others in the organization concerned about you contracting a bad case of instant lead poisoning."

"What kind of money are we talking about?"

"Triple what Tommy Lutherman paid you. Of course more will be expected of you since your employment on my team will involve a promotion as well as a pay raise."

"In that case, I'm your man as long as this isn't a setup." Ernie stuck out his hand for Turpelator to shake.

"It's not a setup, old boy. The deal is quite simple. You may choose to work for me for increased wages or you will be dead within the week. Do you have any questions?" Turpelator shook Ernie's hand.

"Given the options, I'll take the job, Mr. Turpelator."

"I knew you'd see the wisdom of my offer, Ernie. Welcome aboard." Turpelator placed his other hand over Ernie's as the handshake continued.

Ernie invited Mr. Turpelator to join us at the table. Mr. Turpelator took the seat vacated by Scarface. Ernie introduced the man as James Turpelator, his new boss.

Young Jennifer flashed a "told-you-so" grin at me.

Despite CJ's obvious interest in Chauncey and Fireman Frank, and despite the attention given her by Ernie, James Turpelator made it apparent he was attracted to her. CJ didn't complain and no one mentioned her dear away-at-college friend Chauncey.

James purchased a round of drinks for everyone. This was our third or fourth cocktail on the first night of drinks for me since the shooting. I'm not sure of the drink count, but the time to stop had arrived if we planned to make the train back to Wheaton without appearing drunk and disorderly. It may have been too late. I wasn't sure in my current condition, but at least my head didn't hurt.

Our crew at the table spent an inordinate amount of time laughing so it was time to bring our little party to an end. Snpgrdxz, aka Daniel Brickmaster, told a bunch of travel jokes but otherwise seemed fit, except for the joke about the travelling salesman whose ship broke down as he passed through the rings of Saturn and had to spend the night with the space miner's daughter.

Young Jennifer snuggled closer to me as James Turpelator flirted with CJ. When Ernie finished his drink, he gazed about, "Time to head out, gang. We've a long train ride to Wheaton. James, why don't you join us?"

"Good idea, old boy, but I've got the machine outside. We can squeeze everyone in." James headed for the door.

Outside, we didn't all fit. James, CJ, Ernie, Gilbert, Tony, Frank and Daniel managed to squeeze into the big LaSalle with the aid of the jump seat and Daniel's flexibility. Young Jennifer and I strolled arm-in-arm around the block to the Palmer House Hotel on State Street. The rest of the gang seemed pleased to see us snuggle together.

Chicago in nineteen twenty-three was far more polluted than our time. This evening was the first time I appreciated the clean air act. The cool October night smelled of hot steel, coal, industrial chemicals and dead meat. The pollution coated our faces with dirty oil.

At the Palmer House, we picked up a taxi to take us to the train station. Some things never change in a hundred years, like the best place to hail a taxi in the Loop or the yellow color of the cars.

"Do you have money to pay for the taxi?" Jennifer asked.

"Yes."

"I mean current currency, darling."

"Yes, Ernie helped me out with funds."

"Good." Jennifer closed her eyes and leaned her head on my shoulder as I placed my arm around hers.

Jennifer Hawkins, the most beautiful girl in the tenth grade at Lincoln High School in Wheaton, Illinois, in the first part of the twenty-first century, called me "darling" in nineteen twenty three. I was in love, dizzy and carsick from the drinks.

And I didn't feel better later when I discovered Chrissie had short-sheeted my bed.

CHAPTER 17

HUNG OVER

With my arm wrapped around young Jennifer's shoulder, I sipped a bubbling glass of Bromo-Seltzer while leaning into the corner of a nook in the Hawkins kitchen. The little out cove contained a wooden table painted white with two white wooden benches. A window centered against the outside wall.

"We can't leave yet." CJ sat across from me. She dumped a tablespoon of Bromo-Seltzer from a blue bottle into a glass of water.

"Why not?" Tony stood by the wood stove where he poured a cup of coffee.

"Bryan needs more time to recuperate before he returns to the troll world. It'll give you more time to explore this time period." CJ sipped her bubbling headache relief formula.

"CJ wants to get into James Turpelator's pants." Gilbert held his coffee cup out for Tony to fill.

"I'd like to get to know him, sure, but he's only part of the reason. After all, I have several beaus." CJ turned her red face away from Gilbert to take a gander out the window.

Gilbert said, "Yeah, she wants James to get into her panties. And she's the one who shot Turpelator back in the troll world. He hasn't forgotten the M16 blast to the head, I'm sure."

Young Jennifer sipped from her steaming cup of black coffee and rested her cup on her lap. "Cool it, Gilbert. We're not in a big hurry because CJ is right. Bryan hasn't regained his full strength yet. And for the record, I shot Mr. Turpelator."

"Actually, we both did. Twenty-seven times," said CJ.

My Jennifer patted my knee. "And in this time period, we're treated like adults, although I drank too much last night at the speakeasy and said something I shouldn't have."

My face heated. What had my Jennifer said that was out of line? I leaned in close, took her hand in my free hand and whispered, "What did you say wrong?"

"I may have called you 'darling,'" she said aloud.

"You did?" Daniel asked. He sat on the other side of young Jennifer.

CJ swallowed a mouthful of Bromo-Seltzer bubbles. "I don't remember ever calling Bryan 'darling,' though I would have welcomed the opportunity had we the time to get to know each other before I slipped into nineteen eighteen. But the way you two make googly eyes at each other, it's like that Barney Google song that came out this year."

"You called me darling when I was shot," I said.

CJ appeared puzzled. "I did, didn't I? It must have been the old Jennifer sneaking out of my brain. But honey, I can assure you that you are too young to be one of my darlings. I bequeath you body and soul to my younger self."

"Thanks, I'll take him." My Jennifer kissed me on the cheek.

"And I'll keep her," I said.

Tony sat down next to Daniel. "I don't think you two should fall in love. We have work to do, and we don't need teenage romance complications. Write it off to the Florence Nightingale effect or save it for when we get home, okay?"

"Too late, Tony, or haven't you noticed the way those two snuggle?" Gilbert parked next to Frank who was next to CJ.

At this point, young Jennifer was about two thousand shades redder than she had been.

I squeezed her hand. "You did call me 'darling,' but you didn't say anything wrong."

Young Jennifer gazed into my eyes. "I love you, too," she said in a loud voice. She choked up, dropped my hand, climbed over Daniel and Tony, and ran out of the kitchen.

Great Grandma fried bacon in a cast iron skillet on the wood stove. The aroma stirred my headache so I opened the window.

Frank rested his head in his hand.

"Good, we have that settled, don't we?" asked Tony.

"No," CJ and I both shouted.

***

"I could fall in love with James or Frank except for one thing," CJ sat in the chair in my bedroom. My Jennifer and I shared a seat on the bed.

"What's that?" my Jennifer asked.

"I'm hopelessly in love with Chauncey." CJ lowered her head and sniffled.

"Hey, it's okay. Chauncey is good people and he has lots of money," I said.

"I love him so much. I didn't realize how much until he went back to school this term. He's been asking me to become his girlfriend for years and now I'm afraid I may have lost him." CJ's shoulders rose and fell as she wept.

My Jennifer hugged her older twin self. "You haven't lost him. He's away at school. Why don't you write him a letter?"

"Because email would be faster." CJ's voice faltered.

"Have you tried calling him?" I asked.

"You don't know what it's like to place a long distance call in nineteen twenty-three, do you? Or how much you would have to pay. It would be cheaper to hop on a train and visit him in Urbana."

"Road trip!" I said.

"No, I'd have to go by myself."

"Why?" my Jennifer asked.

"So I could cry all the way down because I miss him so and then cry tears of happiness when I get there. Oh, and I would cry all the way home because I would miss him so. I don't want to impose a crybaby on anyone."

"We'd be there to support you," my Jennifer said.

"What if he doesn't want me?" CJ asked.

"He'd be a fool," I said.

"He wouldn't. He loves you," said my romantic Jennifer.

***

CJ left for Champaign-Urbana on the afternoon train on Friday. That evening, Chauncey showed up on our doorstep.

"Where's CJ?" he asked.

"Visiting you in Urbana," Daniel said.

"What?" Chauncey asked.

"You guys have to communicate a little better," said my Jennifer.

"I wanted to surprise her," Chauncey said.

"Surprise," said Daniel.

"I'll head home to call my frat brothers and let them know to send her home. They'd do that anyway, but I'll feel better if I call so there's no question." Chauncey drove off in his Stutz Bearcat.

Ernie stopped by while we were parked on the front porch to enjoy a fall evening. "Is Jennifer around?"

My Jennifer giggled. "I'm right here."

"No, I meant your older sister," Ernie said.

"We know," I said.

"She's on a weekend getaway," Daniel said.

"Getaway? Did she rob a bank" Ernie asked.

"No, silly. She's out of town for a few days. She'll be back," said my Jennifer.

"I'll be back then," Ernie said.

"Why don't you join us," I said. "We're sipping hot spiked cider."

"Don't mind if I do," said Ernie.

Ernie no sooner parked on a chair and sipped alcoholic cider when James Turpelator stopped by. "I say, is Jennifer Hawkins about, the elder version?"

"No, sir," said Ernie. "She's out of town."

"Oh, too bad. I so wanted to speak with her," said James.

"Want to join us? We're drinking cider spiked with some of your booze," Gilbert said.

"Why, I'd be delighted." James parked on the front steps leading up to the porch.

Frank strolled over from Ernie's house. "Ah, so this is where everyone is hanging out."

"Hanging out?" James asked.

Frank said, "Where we're gathered. Except I don't see CJ. Is she in the house?"

"She's on a road trip," said my Jennifer.

"In that case, what are we drinking?" Frank poured a glass of cider for himself and one for James.

The evening went well despite our not knowing for sure if James Turpelator was somehow connected to the evil high school physics teacher from our future who traded us to the werewolves in the troll world. While James Turpelator participated in the illegal booze trade, he behaved like a wealthy businessman bachelor without a hint of vampires or werewolves.

The air cooled around ten o'clock to the point where a sweater wasn't warm enough even though we had loaded up on antifreeze in the form of spiked cider. Just as my Jennifer and I were about to turn in, Ernie made a general comment about manhood and the various sizes of things and the advanced knowledge of the Greeks and French people. Somehow, most likely due to the amount of spiked cider consumed, Frank took exception to the comment. So did James. Since I also had a few spiked ciders teasing at my fuzzy but insane brain cells, I don't remember which of them threw the first punch, but indeed it was thrown. As was the second and third and so on and so forth.

Tony remained sober throughout the evening despite his leadership in cider consumption. He stepped between James and the others after James threw Ernie ten feet down the street and Frank at least twenty-five feet away. He roared while making the tosses, and if I had consumed fewer glasses of cider, I might not have seen his mouth open about two feet and those eighteen-inch incisors drop down from his upper gums.

While Tony and James engaged in a discussion in which Tony backed James up the street one-half block, Ernie and Frank continued their antics.

Full grown men fight pretty much the way boys fight in the schoolyard. You begin with punches, but you soon realize that hitting does as much or more damage to your fists than to the other fellow's jaw. Once you reach that conclusion, the wrestling moves take over. Soon, you are on the ground, or in this case, the sidewalk, rolling about picking up leaves and twigs on your clothing and in your hair.

Sure enough, the final step in a brawl is when you come to the realization that the other fellow isn't so bad after all. He throws a mean punch, and he's your equal or better at wrestling. You have worked up a great thirst by this time. Thirst replaces anger as the primary motivator to action.

At this point, Frank and Ernie marched arm in arm in search of a drink to celebrate as a new-found band of brothers. The alcoholic cider on the Hawkins front porch had somehow been forgotten during the battle. And they forgot the nearest speakeasy was two or three towns away. But they hadn't strolled far when they caught up with Turpelator who joined them in the band or should I say the a cappella street singing group. They sang something that almost sounded like *Bill Bailey*.

James Turpelator had the final word of the evening. "Not to worry, old boys, I've plenty of troll beer in the basement."

***

"They had a knocked-down, dragged-out-on-the-sidewalk punch fest," said my Jennifer.

"Who were they?" CJ asked as we strolled home from the Wheaton train station on Saturday afternoon.

"James Turpelator, Ernie and Frank," I said.

"You didn't get involved?" CJ asked.

"No, I'm in love with my Jennifer. No need to do battle for your affections."

"What about Chauncey?" CJ asked.

"Nowhere to be found, the coward," my Jennifer said.

"He's not a coward. Takes a man to back away from a fight," said CJ.

"He wasn't there," said my Jennifer. "Besides it was over quickly. They threw a few punches, wrestled a bit and then decided you weren't worth the trouble so they headed off arm-in-arm in search of beer and song."

We strolled in silence for another block when CJ said, "O'Henry would be proud."

"Because you went to Urbana to surprise Chauncey while he came here to surprise you?" asked my Jennifer.

"Chauncey will be at the house this evening," I said.

"Did he tell you that?" CJ asked.

Chauncey caught up to us from behind. "Jennifer."

CJ leaped into Chauncey's waiting arms. They kissed.

My Jennifer and I deserted the two lovers.

Daniel asked where CJ was when my Jennifer and I arrived back at the house.

"She's with Chauncey. Last we saw of them, they were making out on the corner by the church. Better prepare for wedding bells," my Jennifer teased.

***

151

Chauncey returned to Urbana Sunday afternoon without presenting an engagement ring to CJ. On Monday, Snpgrdxz and I became bootleggers.

"We were so close," said CJ. "With more time, I'd be on my way to becoming Mrs. Chauncey Chadsworth. He might want to wait until Christmas now, but I so love that man. Sorry, Bryan."

"Don't be sorry for me. Feel sorry for Ernie and Frank. They both have a crush on you. And worry about yourself because you don't yet know what Chauncey's intentions are."

"He'll come around. He loves me. I know he does." CJ and her red face headed off for a shopping trip with my Jennifer.

Laura's injured arm had healed better than my dizzy head. She and Chrissie tagged along with them. CJ had money saved from a job she took as a sales clerk in one of the local dress shops.

With no modern shopping malls to venture upon, shopping in nineteen twenty-three involved a visit to the local merchants in town or a ride on the train to another community along the line to Chicago. The train station in Chicago was a half dozen blocks west of the State Street shops, making Marshall Fields and other stores within range of CJ's small resources. In those days, the Magnificent Mile wasn't magnificent yet. The action was on State Street south of the Chicago River.

Gilbert hired out to help a local carpenter fix up houses. He had a knack for hand tools and loved working with wood without power tools.

To assist with finances, Daniel Brickmaster volunteered to quit his waiter job to assist Ernie in one of his "projects." Daniel and I hopped into the front seat of a black one-ton Ford delivery truck. Ernie drove despite a face full of bruises from the fist fight. The sides of the enclosed truck displayed the Meyers Moving and Storage Company name with a phone number and the city of Cicero, Illinois.

We drove south along Main Street in Wheaton and then turned east on Illinois, the first street on the north side of Lincoln High School, the same as our day. We pulled in front of Tony's house at the corner of Illinois and Naperville. Well, in our day it would be Tony's house. Ernie said James Turpelator owned it at present.

The front room of the bungalow contained the usual living room furniture you would expect to find in a small suburban home built in the first decade of the twentieth century. The furniture was dusty like no one had plopped down in years, despite its young age. The house possessed an unhealthy musty smell to complement the dust bunnies.

Two men barged in through the open front door, one in a suit and the other in a police uniform.

I envisioned hard time in an early twentieth-century chain gang even though I knew Illinois didn't have chain gangs. Or did they? It wasn't like I had access to Wikipedia.

"Hello, Hanratty, Officer Phillips," Ernie said. "Are you boys thirsty?"

"Been watching for you, Ernie," said the guy in a business suit I took to be Hanratty.

Maybe we could post bail and skedaddle through the Wheaton When Portal. Ernie could come with us.

A set of heavy oak double doors cut the front room off from the rest of the house. Ernie, who appeared calm despite our pending arrest on bootlegging charges, pulled a set of keys from his pocket and opened the doors to reveal the aroma of beer and a dining room filled with wooden crates labeled "Troll Beer."

Any when but this when sounded good to me and we were close to the high school and the Wheaton When Portal.

On top of one of the four-foot high stacks of beer cases sat two standard business-size white envelopes stuffed thick. They weren't addressed to anyone, but a return address listed "Turpelator and Company."

Ernie distributed the envelopes to Hanratty and Officer Phillips. "You boys have time for a brewski?"

Hanratty and Phillips each took a beer from one of the crates. A bottle opener on a string attached to one of the door hinges served to pop the bottle caps. After the pop, fizz and guzzle, Officer Phillips asked, "You will join us, gentlemen?"

"Of course we will." Daniel opened three beers and passed them around, keeping one for himself.

Hanratty and Phillips finished their beers without a word. They each picked up a wooden box of beer and left. I relaxed.

"Liquor tax is paid, boys, so let's load up." Ernie grabbed a case and headed for the door.

"I don't think this is legal," I said.

Ernie clapped a hand against my shoulder. "Too late. You already drank the beer."

The house served as a warehouse for Troll Beer with the rooms filled with stacks of cases three-to-five feet high. A narrow path meandered through the rooms to make it easy to get at the cases.

"Are you sure you're ready to work?" Ernie asked me.

My head hurt. I felt dizzy but not too dizzy. My back hurt and my arms and legs felt stiff. "Yeah, I've been lazy long enough."

We loaded beer from the upstairs bedrooms first. "We move out the older inventory first, boys," Ernie explained.

We spent the rest of the day hauling beer to suburban Chicago speakeasies. I felt good hauling the cases of beer until I tired in midafternoon. I dragged my way to day's end. And yes, I know where all the speakeasies were located in the western suburbs of Chicago. If you need a tour of illegal beer joints, just let me or Jennifer know.

At the end of the day, Ernie handed Daniel and I a tiny pouch filled with coins. As I thought what a rip off, Daniel emptied his into the palm to reveal eight silver quarters and six gold coins.

"They're ten-dollar gold pieces," Daniel said. "Thanks, Ernie."

Ernie nodded. "We pay for your hard labor in the form of eight silver quarters for a day's work. The gold coins are to keep your mouth shut. You won't get those every day, but on a good day, you never know."

"Thanks," I said. "This will allow us to look good tonight at Turpelator's party."

"We work for him, now, boys. He'll expect to see you tonight. And he expects his bootleg drivers to dress for success. It makes it easier to recruit new crew members."

"Business is growing, then?" I asked.

"Yes, and crew members are constantly terminated."

"They can't handle the work?" I asked.

"They can't handle the lead. Turpelator and Scarface have enemies with machine guns. And you always have to watch for the Feds."

"I know about the Feds," said Daniel. "Do your Feds wear black suits?"

"All the time," said Ernie.

After parking the Ford truck in the backyard of the house where the beer was stashed, we strode home.

Daniel and I talked Frank, Gilbert and Tony into a visit downtown to purchase fancy dress suits, shoes, shirts, ties, underwear, the "whole kit and caboodle" as Ernie said. We arrived at a men's clothing shop with enough time to make our purchases and have the suits tailored before the store closed.

We were ready for Turpelator's party but was Turpelator's party ready for us?

CHAPTER 18

PARTY TIME

The creature that opened the great front door to Turpelator's home wore a long red hat that came to a point above the quiver of arrows hung upon his back. To accompany the quiver, he carried a bow in a leather holster hung on his belt. He carried a sword as tall as he. A tiny knife hung from his belt along with an assortment of pouches. His outfit appeared medieval. He stood two and one half feet tall. His lengthy nose spilled out of his face in a downward angle for a good eight or nine inches. Two fangs pointed up from his closed lips. He wore side whiskers but kept his chin clean-shaven perhaps to better display his many moles, cysts and boils. The kindest thing I could say about his aroma was he had neglected to take his Saturday night bath for a period of years.

"Hail and greetings to ye. Welcome to the castle of James Turpelator. Robin the hobgoblin at your service."

The "castle" Robin referred to was a Victorian on the north side of Wheaton three blocks north of the Hawkins home and several blocks west of Main Street. The house was large, but not so big as to qualify as a mansion. It was more like an oversized version of our modern mini-mansions. The grand home was lighted outside and inside. It stood out against its neighbors on a September evening when the sun had not yet set.

Robin the hobgoblin led us into the dining room which was decked out with an array of food enough to satisfy an army of aristocrats. Champaign sat in ice buckets along one wall while bottles of Troll Beer filled several tubs of ice. Two bartenders worked the bar along another wall.

"I'm thirsty," said Gilbert. Daniel agreed.

I snagged a sandwich. "Food looks tasty."

"Let's eat," said Tony.

"Let's check this place out, little sister." CJ led young Jennifer away from the food and into the depths of the house. Laura and Chrissie tagged along.

Frank and Ernie built sandwiches while the rest of the guys snacked on cookies and chocolates from the big Marshall Fields department store in Chicago.

Food in the nineteen twenties tasted better than ours as I mentioned before about Great Grandma Hawkins's cooking. While that may not surprise you, it astonished me. I thought modern food preparation and storage kept our food fresher and tastier. But food from the old days was plain, simple and delicious. And it was non-GMO, unwaxed and pesticide free.

While the girls toured the house, the guys progressed from chocolates to cold cuts and cheese sandwiches washed down with Troll beer. The sandwiches featured tasty pickles and mustard. The tomato slices seemed a bit off color and misshapen, but they were sweeter than any I'd tasted back home. The food aromas formed a sweet mixture of herbs, cold meats, bread and spices.

When the trolls made beer, they didn't worry about future federal or state regulations regarding the amount of alcohol in their swill. They brewed until it was done, and then they bottled and sold the stuff. As a result, the beer had a rich syrupy flavor, and you became dizzy faster than with our twenty-first century brewskis which Gilbert called "panther piss" whenever we talked about the merits of various types of beers.

"I don't think we're supposed to drink beer, fellow church members," said Gilbert.

"It's okay," I explained. "We're in the era of Prohibition. There are no laws regulating the age of drink."

"What about Prohibition?" asked Gilbert.

"Stupid law. It gets repealed. We can ignore it." I sipped another beer.

"It's like weed?" Daniel asked.

"Exactlly. If a law is immoral why would you obey it?" I drank more beer.

The party passed by us instead of our having to find it. Scarface stopped accompanied by a group of "perfezzionals" as he called the women with him. He offered to have the painted ladies entertain us, but Tony suggested we wait for another time, like when we were ten years older. Gilbert kicked him on the ankle, but Tony insisted we were not ready for participatory adult entertainment what with all the lovely Wheaton young ladies for us to choose from. I allowed as how I had already made my choice. Gilbert socked me on the shoulder and told me to speak for myself.

Robin the hobgoblin wandered by accompanied by a three-foot tall troll. Robin pulled the troll away from our group. "They're not the food," he insisted.

The troll grunted in the troll language, shrugged his hairy shoulders and moved on. Robin said, "You boys were between Glupnooger and the food. You may want to relocate before he or one of his troll friends returns."

We moved closer to the beer.

James Turpelator stopped by our group. "Are you gentleman enjoying the evening?"

Tony said, "Yes. Thanks for inviting us."

"My pleasure," said James. "I host these parties so my friends may enjoy themselves. And if we do a little business? Well, so much the better. And if I fall in love, or you fall in love..." Here he glanced my way. "...what's that to anyone except us, eh?" Turpelator laughed and moved on with a couple of his lieutenants at his heels. The hangers on approached seven feet tall with shoulders the width of your average doorway.

"Speaking of falling in love," said Gilbert, here comes Lilly Blackstone."

Lilly snagged Gilbert's arm. "Hello, boys. Ready for fresh meat?"

"You're not limping," I said.

"I'm healed and would appreciate your not mentioning my little escapade." Lilly plopped several slices of ham into her mouth.

Gilbert said, "Are you enjoying the party?"

"I am now that you're here. How about showing me around this museum of nineteenth century whoredom?"

"Whoredom?" Daniel asked.

"I don't know my way around. It's my first visit," said Gilbert.

"Then we can explore it together starting upstairs with the bedrooms. We'll only need one." Lilly tugged Gilbert into the crowd.

"Not to worry. He will return a man," said Daniel.

"That's what I'm worried about," I said.

Another hour went by when Tony asked, "Where are the ladies?"

"I'll find them." I headed out of the room.

Daniel called after me, "Good because we're busy eating and drinking. You can roll us home when you find the girls. And don't forget Gilbert."

I didn't see our women on the first floor, but a young lady caught my eye in the crowded kitchen. She had long curly blond hair around a face that could launch more ships than Helen of Troy. Her gown was what you would expect to see a woman wear around the First World War with a longer, almost Victorian cut with the skirt down to her ankles. She caught my eye and smiled. I returned the grin and took another peek around for Jennifer. When I returned to introduce myself to the girl, she had vanished. She reminded me of the blond I met back in the tunnels at the beginning of our journey, the one no one else had noticed.

***

On the stairway to the second floor, I spotted Laura and Chrissie coming down. "Enjoying the party?" I asked.

Laura sighed. "We were."

"What happened?" I asked.

"It's not my fault," said Chrissie. "I just wanted to see what was in that room upstairs where there was nothing, and then I saw the ghost so I screamed, and that's when I ran out of the room which was okay until I ran slam bang into Mr. Turpelator and knocked him into Mr. Scarface, and they tumbled to the floor, but I didn't mean to hurt them. Why did they get so pokey angry anyway? It was just an accident. Besides Mr. Scarface only looked angry. He's my friend, you know. He wants to give me a contract and has a baseball bat he wants to introduce me to. He wants me to play with the fishes but I have to cement on my galoshes first. I don't think it's a good idea to cement your galoshes to your feet, do you?"

"Needless to say, we're twenty-three skidoo." Laura snagged Chrissie's hand and hurried her down the remaining steps. They headed out the front door without stopping.

"Twenty-three skidoo?" I asked no one in particular.

On the second floor, I discovered the Asian girl who killed Jennifer Hawkins that time in my bedroom a few days before school started back when my sanity had gone south for the winter despite it being August.

***

The young Asian lady terrorist parked on a davenport in a sitting room.

She waved a cocktail when I entered. "Hello, Bryan," she said.

"How do you... oh, it's you, Snpgrdxz."

"My name is Amelia for the moment. I found the dress in a closet in one of the bedrooms. Skirt could be shorter, but I like the fringe." Snpgrdxz slid the skirt up a few inches.

"You can call yourself Amelia all day long, Snpgrdxz, but you're still Daniel Brickmaster to me. But thanks for not pretending to be Jennifer Hawkins."

"I keep my promises. I wish you'd let me turn you on. You make me want to snuggle female close to you." Snpgrdxz crossed her legs in a most provocative way.

"Have you seen the Jennifers on this floor?"

"Not for a while."

"That reminds me, weren't you just in the dining room?"

"I get around."

A young lady waltzed into the room. She held a glass of root beer. "Hey, I have a dress like yours in my closet upstairs."

***

Gilbert and Lilly formed one of a pair of couples making out on a long couch in a third floor sitting room with a piano-playing voyeur gawping at them.

Lilly stood when I entered. "Bryan, so lovely to eat... I mean greet you. Will you excuse me, darling, while I powder my nose?"

Gilbert watched the spring in Lilly's caboose bounce up and down as she left the room.

"Better wipe that grin off your face. She's too old for you and not that into you, is she?"

"Don't know, don't care as long as she takes me on a midnight adventure." Gilbert grinned enough to light up the room.

The roar of the beast was deep but feminine. We heard it just before the jungle cat burst on the scene. It was my panther from Hawkins House. It leaped for my throat as I stepped back in a futile attempt at self-defense.

Robin the Hobgoblin appeared out of who knew where. He snagged the cat around the neck and wrestled it to the floor. Glupnooger the bridge troll leaped on the cat and jabbed it with a knife into its front paw.

The giant cat squirmed its way free and bolted for the door despite its injury.

"What was that about?" Gilbert asked.

"I don't think that critter likes me," I said.

"It may be jealous of you and Jennifer Hawkins. Who do you know is most upset about you guys being together?" asked Gilbert.

I checked around the room to watch the other couch couple make out. They didn't seem to notice the invasion of the cat creature. "Probably the same dude that owns a big, black cat."

"You know that thing crossed your path, right, Bryan?" asked Gilbert.

The most interesting room in the house had no furniture. Wall paper depicting large yellow flowers on an off-white background covered the walls. Two closed and shuttered windows peeked out from behind a set of large Kelly green curtains. The curtains went with the flowered wallpaper and a green Asian carpet that covered the floor to within about eighteen inches of the wall.

I gazed around at the empty space before opening the closet door. It was filled with dresses, hat boxes, shoes and other feminine things.

"Find what you're searching for?"

I turned around to spot the blonde from the kitchen. She smiled but crossed her arms.

"I'm sorry," I said.

The girl startled and stepped back like I was the one surprising her. She recovered fast. "It's okay. I'm glad you came up to see me."

"I'm Bryan Ganarski."

"Hi, Bryan. There's something strange about you."

"Yeah, everybody tells me that."

"Your aura is all wrong. You don't belong here, do you?"

"I have an aura?"

"When did you die?"

***

"There you are," young Jennifer said.

I turned away from the blonde to glance at the two Jennifers as they entered the room.

"We searched for you, Bryan. Your girlfriend missed you." CJ said. "Are you blushing?"

"I am? I'm embarrassed talking to this young lady alone in an upstairs bedroom. We didn't do anything, honest."

"What girl?" young Jennifer asked.

I turned back to the blonde, but she wasn't there. "Now, where did she go?"

"Didn't sneak past us," CJ said. "We didn't see anyone when we came in."

"How many drinks have you had, Bryan?" my Jennifer asked.

"More than I should? I had the loveliest conversation with a young lady until you guys came along."

"Sorry to interrupt your fantasy," CJ said.

I rubbed my chin. "She asked me when I died. What do you think?"

"Too much Troll beer, but if you cheat on me, your death will be arranged," young Jennifer said.

***

I didn't see the blonde in the dining room, but that didn't stop her from whispering in my ear. "Meet me back upstairs."

I had followed the girls downstairs to the dining room. They ate while the guys added a few more beers to our evening.

My head cleared a bit as I made my way to the third floor. I bumped into a tall version of Robin the hobgoblin on the steps between the second and third floors. "Hello, Snpgrdxz."

"Shhh! Never say that word in public."

"It's not like the Feds are on your tail this year."

"You never know, Bryan." Big Robin or Daniel or whoever Snpgrdxz was pretending to be made his way down as I climbed up. Where did he find the hobgoblin suit?

I passed the sitting room with Gilbert and the other make out artists with the lonesome piano player. Gilbert kissed the girl who previously made out with the other guy in the room. They must have switched. The other guy snuggled with a new girl in this center of lovemaking. The gentlemen's hands were higher up under the skirts than before, but otherwise all seemed normal in the room.

Back in the empty bedroom, the blonde waited for me. "Thank you for returning. We need to talk."

"We don't know each other," I said. "Why do we need to speak?"

The blonde placed a hand on my sleeve as she moved into kissing range. "Because we can."

"What about James? You're staying at his house. Doesn't he listen?"

"He did once, but not anymore. I have no one else to turn to. I know the hour is late, and you've been drinking, but if you come back tomorrow, I'm sure you'll see me."

"Yeah, I am a little out of sorts what with the beer. I'll come by after lunch."

"Wonderful."

"Who should I ask for?"

"My name is Brigitta Wurzburger, but don't ask for me. I prefer you not tell anyone you met me. I'll answer the door when you come."

"So if you have a problem meeting here, we could hook up at a restaurant downtown for lunch." I wanted to ask her if she was the girl in the tunnels in the twenty-first century, but I would give away our group's little time travel secret if it wasn't her.

"That's not a good idea. I have difficulty traveling beyond the house."

"Good because I have a girlfriend." And Brigitte had the ability to walk the tunnels so she may have difficulty but it's not impossible.

"I saw you two together. I'm sorry. I wouldn't ask for your help except it's necessary and for your benefit as well as mine."

"Is that why you asked when I died?"

"I was mistaken, but you have something wrong with you. It's like you don't belong here, but you're here anyway. I don't understand. You can explain tomorrow, okay?"

CHAPTER 19

THE RANSOM OF CHRISSIE

Instead of shooting us, the rival bootleg gangsters kidnapped Chrissie from the Hawkins home Saturday morning. The guys found out when the Jennifers pounded on Ernie's front door to wake us up. Yes, I now lived at Ernie's house with the rest of the men since recovering from my head trauma. My Jennifer and I no longer shared midnight visits in which we mostly slept in each other's arms while preserving our youthful innocence.

I joined the guys as we headed over to Hawkins House.

"They came in with sawed-off shotguns. There was nothing we could do," said young Jennifer.

"They said to bring a hundred Gs to Rhinelander by Tuesday night or we'll never see Chrissie again," said CJ.

"What's a G?" Gilbert asked.

"You need to watch more old Cagney movies," Tony said.

"What's a Cagney?" asked Great Grandma Hawkins.

Chrissie's mom, Laura McNaughton, wept on the chesterfield in the Hawkins House living room.

"How will we find one hundred thousand dollars on short notice?" I asked.

"Is that how much a hundred Gs cost?" Gilbert asked.

Daniel punched Gilbert on the arm. "A G is one thousand dollars. Short for grand. Now all we have to do is come up with a hundred of them."

"If we wait long enough, they'll bring her back," said CJ.

Ernie stared out the window as though he'd find the one hundred Gs ensconced on the porch. "James will help. And we can always borrow the money from our friend Scarface."

Frank placed an arm around CJ's shoulders. "We'll get your little cousin back."

Ernie and Frank left to visit James Turpelator at his beer repository across from the high school. He was supposed to take inventory today and Ernie planned to join him after breakfast.

Laura called the police to report her missing daughter. She used what Gilbert called a "phone on a stick." It had a tall column with a base. The top of the column held a microphone or speaking device. The listening end was attached to a hook on the side of the mini-pole. You planted the ear piece against your ear. Releasing the hook opened the line so you could speak with an operator who made the connection for you to the person you wished to call. Phone numbers were local like Wheaton 123. Or you spoke to the operator like this: "Hildie, connect me with the Ericsons, please." It was old-fashioned, small town stuff.

Snpgrdxz and I cleaned the upstairs bedrooms to make Ernie's house presentable to the police in the event they wished to search it for the missing Chrissie. The police never did. It was a silly idea, but the place was a wreck so cleaning up didn't hurt anything.

Snpgrdxz stripped off his shirt and waved four arms and hands around the room for cleanup.

"So you can turn into any shape you want, right?" I asked.

Snpgrdxz chuckled. "There are limits. I have internal organs like you. Well, sort of like yours. And I can't squish them or move them around too much. So I can be a boy or girl, no problem. But I can't turn into a broom. The handle is too skinny. I can morph into a dog or cat, but you have to keep in mind I weigh one hundred sixty pounds so I have to hide the weight or become a big version of a cat or dog or whatever."

"So where do you stick the extra you?"

"People don't pay much attention to your feet so I bump up the shoe size a bit. For girls, I might increase the boob size and add an inch to her waist and hips. I stretch my head and neck a tad and lengthen my arms a bit. I add a touch more muscle to my arms and legs. And I do stuff internally, bigger bones, that sort of thing. No one notices these differences. If I'm making up a girl persona for myself, than I add height to take up the weight. If I'm planning to stay feminine for an extended period of time, I have a way to reduce my size and weight but it can be painful for a few days while my body sloughs off blood, muscle and bone tissue. It makes for interesting menstrual flow."

"I didn't need to hear that." I stuffed my dirty underwear back in the bureau to get it off the floor. "But when you pretend to be a girl, you're actually a boy shape shifter, right? You don't lose who you are as a person, but it kind of makes you a gay space alien?"

"My parents would get a kick out of your comment. We don't share your earther concept of gay and straight. We just are." Snpgrdxz used a four-handed flip to snap the comforter back on the bed.

"You have parents?"

"Of course. You think I was created in a lab?"

"Well…"

Snpgrdxz placed his four hands on his two hips, which was a bit awkward as the hands were in each other's way. "I was born. I had a mother and father."

"Where are you from? I mean are you a Russian experiment or a NASA space adventure gone rogue?"

"I'm both."

I hung a couple of dead shirts in my closet. "Russian experiment and NASA? How can that be?"

"No, I'm both. You know. A girl and a boy. With my people it's not one or the other. We're always both. That's why my people don't have your concept of gay and straight."

I dropped a hanger. "Your people? You mean there are more of you?"

"Not around here."

"Around where?" I nearly peed my pants. Okay, don't tell anyone, but a little may have leaked out. You'd have done the same thing if you spotted four-armed Daniel Brickmaster morph into one of those space aliens. The scary ones. They're gray and have a teeny, tiny slit for a mouth and have a triangular-shaped head and no hair. Their eyes are super large and twisted at an angle down from their oversized brains. They communicate by mental telepathy. You know the kind?

They kidnap weird people to conduct experiments like sticking long needles into their bellies and stealing their mojo before returning them to the world like a fisherman playing catch and release. Their victims then travel anywhere they can find listeners willing to hear about their alien abduction, but nobody believes them. Would you? Well, Daniel turned into one of those aliens.

"This is what we look like, Bryan. Now, if you don't mind, I'll try never to appear like this again because I can tell you're not too keen on this image. At least now you know it's okay to think of me as a girl sometimes."

"Did you just speak to me without moving your lips? Are you inside my brain?"

***

The front entrance of James's mini-mansion screeched open on rusty hinges the way doors always open in horror flicks, but no one answered. I stepped into the hall. "Hello?"

No response except the door slammed behind me. A cold breeze rustled my damp hair from my bath. Saturday meant "bath day" in nineteen twenty-three.

"Hello?" I repeated.

"This way." The feminine voice barely reached above a whisper. A whiff of rose petals accompanied the sound.

I turned. Brigitte Wurzburger leaned against the doorjamb to the dining room. She wore the same out-of-style dress from the party. Her blonde hair still featured the long, beautiful curls. She waved her hand at me to indicate I should approach her. When I did, she glided through the dining room. I followed her into the kitchen. In the corner by the backdoor was another door. It opened to reveal a dark staircase to the basement.

James Turpelator's home was a true Victorian constructed around eighteen forty or fifty. Stone walls and a dirt floor gave an eerie appearance to the basement. The musty smell and cobwebs added to the macabre effect. This could have been the basement to Edgar Allen Poe's home.

The furnace and boiler were near the front wall. The rest of the basement floor contained stacks of Troll Beer cases and piles of containers of Hobgoblin Ale. A path wandered through the stacks.

Brigitte took my hand and dragged me through the maze of beer and ale cases.

A chill ran through my spine. "Your hand is freezing. Would you like me to wait here while you run upstairs for a sweater?"

"No need." Brigitte stopped by a stack of empty Hobgoblin ale cases. "Here."

From the steps hidden by the maze of beer and ale cases we had traversed, a commanding male voice shouted, "Who's down here?"

"We are," I replied.

"What are you doing?" called the disembodied male voice.

"Visiting the basement," I said.

Robin the hobgoblin stepped around a stack of cases. "What are you up to?"

170

"We're on a tour of the basement," I said.

"Who are 'we'?" Robin asked.

I turned around to snag Brigitte's hand, but she was gone. "Brigitte was here a moment ago."

"I don't think James wants you snooping around his basement, do you?" Robin folded his arms across his chest.

"Guess not. I didn't think. But Brigitte wanted to show me something."

"Brigitte?"

"Yes, James's houseguest."

"Did you say 'Brigitte'?"

"Yes."

"James doesn't have a house guest. There is no Brigitte, not since, well, I won't go into it. But you're welcome to stay if you wish. The party doesn't begin until James returns at dinner time with the funds to free your young friend so you'll be alone. And if you don't mind, the basement is the one part of the house James considers off limits to his guests."

"No Brigitte?"

***

James Turpelator provided two cars for the trip to Rhinelander, Wisconsin, the next morning. Laura, Tony, Gilbert, Daniel, young Jennifer and I piled into the automobiles along with James. Fireman Frank and CJ elected to remain behind with Great Grandma Hawkins.

"You guys want alone time, right?" young Jennifer asked.

"Ernie will be here, little sis, but don't hurry home. Frank has the key to Ernie's house and we plan to spend a lot of time there while Ernie delivers booze."

"Oh, so you'll clean up the mess the guys made of my home?" Ernie asked.

"Nope. We'll check out your art paintings," said Frank.

"But I don't have any works of art." Ernie said.

Frank smiled.

CJ smiled.

Gilbert chuckled, "What about Chauncey?"

"If you can't be with the one you love, honey, love the one you're with." CJ leaned against Frank.

Young Jennifer shook her head and followed Laura into the first car in our little parade. "A girl's supposed to wait for the wedding ring from her main man."

Wedding ring? What a scary thought. "Hey, does anyone else want to take a potty break before we drive off?" I asked.

We left on Sunday morning after church and stayed over in a hotel in downtown Madison. That evening, we gathered for dinner in the hotel restaurant. We enjoyed pot roast with all the trimmings. Tony asked about beer.

The waiter appeared aghast. "I'm sorry, sir, but alcoholic beverages are illegal. We are a law-abiding establishment.

"Of course. Coffee will be fine," said Tony.

The waiter wrote something on his pad. "Just out of curiosity, sir, what kind of beer would you choose if it wasn't against the law to sell beer and if we sold beer, which of course we don't?"

"I do believe a light lager would have been my choice," Tony said. "The rest of us would want the same, that is, if you served beer, which I understand you do not."

Gilbert said, "I agree with my friend. A light lager would be our choice assuming alcoholic beverages were available."

"Might I suggest the root beer soda for your party? It arrives in a superb brown glass bottle and the flavor is light with just the right hint of hops, I mean, roots." The waiter stopped writing.

"A round of root beer it is," said Tony.

Within minutes, the beers showed up on our table, but they weren't all that showed up. Lilly Blackstone approached. "May I join you?"

"Of course," said Jennifer.

Gilbert flashed a grin.

"Wipe that smile off your face, Gilbert. We didn't get far enough for you to smile so much." Lilly's right hand was bandaged.

"What happened to your hand?" Jennifer asked.

"A little accident when a friend slipped with a knife." Lilly rubbed her injured hand.

"It looks serious," Tony said.

"It's deep, unfortunately. The doctor sewed a half dozen internal stitches plus seven more to close the wound. It's a knife stab wound that went almost through my hand." Lilly smiled but a tear dropped down her cheek. She wiped it away.

"You'll need to be more careful in the future. You seem accident prone," said Daniel.

"Oh, I am. I mean accident prone. I'm never careful. That's why I no sooner heal my butt than I suffer a knife wound. I can't help but find trouble," said Lilly.

"You must be part cat with all the lives you have gone through with accidents," said Tony.

"It's only been two lives, Tony. I have plenty more left with which to make trouble." Lilly smiled and headed out of the restaurant.

After dinner, James served booze from a stash he kept in his trunk.

November in Madison meant the nights were cold. We wore sweaters and sipped whiskey to keep warm in the suite James rented.

I held hands with young Jennifer on a small couch. Gilbert and Daniel parked on the radiator cover in front of the window. Tony and Laura sat in padded lounge chairs. James paced the room.

"How will we ever pay those horrible men one hundred thousand dollars?" asked Laura.

"No need, old girl," said James. "I know your daughter. The brutes will discount her ransom."

"I hope so," said Laura.

"James, do you have a houseguest?" I asked.

"Not at the moment," he said.

"What about Brigitte? I met her last night and thought she boarded with you."

James slammed his glass down, spilling whiskey. He backed away from the table. He glared at me for a few seconds before smiling. The smile faded to a flat line of lips under his nose. "The Brigitte I know is still in Europe with her parents, old boy. She's a student in Austria. No, I doubt you encountered sweet Brigitte last night."

"Short, cute blonde with the loveliest curly hair. She asked me to visit her after lunch yesterday. She took me on a tour of your basement," I said.

"The basement is off limits, chum. The rest of the house is open. Did you say blond curls?"

"Yes," I said.

"I don't know who you thought you ran into, old boy, but it couldn't have been Brigitte. Perhaps you met another blonde named Brigitte. Of course, I should have thought of that. There must be more than one Brigitte with blond curls in Wheaton."

CHAPTER 20

NORTHWOODS FRIGHTENED

Dark and lonesome pines lined the road as we sped north to Rhinelander. We left right after breakfast. Young Jennifer and I sat together on the ride up. Jennifer held my hand on her lap.

One surprise on the trip was our gas stop at a country crossroads. The station had a big sign that read "Last Gas for Miles."

James pulled in. "We better have a full tank if there are no gas stations for a while."

Two attendants came out to the pumps and filled the tanks of both cars, checked the tires and oil, and washed the windows. One of the attendants brought out a couple of five-gallon containers and a length of rope. He filled the cans with gasoline and tied them on the rear bumper of both cars.

"What are the gas cans for, old boy?" James asked.

"You'll need this if you're headed north. The next gas station ain't for a long time up that road. In fact, there ain't nothing but trees between here and Rhinelander."

***

The waitress never mentioned zombies that evening. We arrived late in Rhinelander with an empty gas can tied to each car. At one of the local restaurants, we met a friendly waitress who informed us about a tourist house that would put us up for the night. We were in the North Woods hunting season now that the fall color was past. Most tourist houses were booked, but the waitress knew the people who ran a place and some of their guests for this week had cancelled at the last minute.

"Could you call to make sure they can take us in?" Daniel asked.

The waitress laughed. "You better drive out there. Imagine wanting to make a telephone call out to the country." She laughed again before sauntering away. She shouted into the kitchen, "Hey, Herb, wait until you hear what these Chicago people wanted me to do."

The waitress should have mentioned the zombies so we would have been prepared in the lead car when a living dead person slammed into our windshield. The creature flew off as James skidded to a stop. Our other car bumped into us before Tony was able to stop.

In the headlamps we watched four zombies meander out of the woods. When night settled in the North Woods, the world went black. You only saw what came within the range of your lights. The zombies had skin the color of fresh cut onions, white with yellow and green around the edges.

The zombies pounded on the cars. We knew what they wanted but we didn't like the idea of them sucking out our brains.

"Move forward slowly," Jennifer suggested.

James placed the car in gear and lurched forward. The zombies pounded on the cars as we pulled away from them. I turned around and could make the four of them out in the lights from Tony's car.

Before we could increase speed, we had to traverse a sharp turn in front of us, but as James approached it, a crowd of zombies rounded the curve.

"Now what do we do?" James asked.

"We have to fight," said Jennifer. I would have said that, but I was already on the floor trying to hide under the seat. I didn't fit. I heard the zombies pound on the car so I sat back up in the seat to protect Jennifer.

Jennifer yanked a Glock out of her handbag. She rolled down the window. A zombie picked that moment to poke his hand into the car and grab Jennifer by the neck. Jennifer planted a bullet between its eyes. The dead zombie, that is, the newly permanent dead zombie, fell away as one of his friends stepped up and reached into the car.

The zombies were big men dressed in lumberjack outfits including flannel shirt, blue jeans and leather boots. I never thought about what happened to all the lumberjacks once the trees in Wisconsin were chopped down, but now I knew.

I heard gunfire from Tony's car as James and Jennifer fired their pistols in our car.

"This isn't going to work. There are too many of them." Snpgrdxz bolted from his seat by the passenger side back window. He morphed his hands into large axe heads and grew about a foot taller. His first axe swing took off a zombie's head.

The zombies stopped, made an ungh noise, and moved towards Snpgrdxz. He continued removing zombie heads by swinging both arms furiously as a buzzsaw.

Tony climbed out of his car and opened fire with his M16. I slid over to the window seat from my place in the middle. I snagged my Glock but I couldn't get the clip in. For some strange reason, my hand picked that moment to shake. Jennifer snatched a second pistol from her handbag. She replaced the clip on the Glock. When she stepped out of the car, she opened fire with both guns. For a girl with no target practice experience, she took down at least a dozen zombies.

I heard additional gunmen firing from the second car and assumed Gilbert and Frank had joined the fray. Laura cowered in the front seat. I managed to fire three times into the darkness without seeing or aiming at anything. You never knew.

Jennifer and Gilbert hugged Snpgrdxz.

Tony said, "Thanks, Snpgrdxz. We may find you useful on this time trip yet. And Jennifer, Wild Thing, you're a two-fisted sharp shooter, girl."

Gilbert said, "Hey, I got a couple and so did Frank and Bryan."

Jennifer chuckled. "Bryan? Why he wimped out in the backseat. I did all the shooting."

"Not to worry, children. You did well. James Turpelator shot at some of the zombies, too." Tony herded the gang back to the cars.

"What do we do with all the zombie bodies?" Jennifer asked.

"Nothing, old girl," said James. "They are the county's problem. They'll clean up the mess when they find it."

We found the tourist house by following the directions the waitress in Rhinelander had given us. The big farmhouse was outside of town about ten miles through the darkest woods any zombie ever crawled from. For part of the drive we passed through land that had been devastated by the logging industry. The new growth of trees was underway, but even in the dark, you could see the damage.

We weren't sure if the kidnappers would find us here in the middle of nowhere, but they did.

CHAPTER 21

NEGOTIATING WITH KIDNAPPERS

Two men dressed in torn flannel shirts pointed sawed-off shotguns at James, Jennifer, Tony, Laura, Gilbert and me. We sat at a large, round table chomping on pancakes, bacon, eggs and other good stuff in the tourist house. Several other guests ate breakfast in the large dining room.

One of the shotgun toting strangers had a single black eye while the other had two to go with a puffed out lower lip. They seemed nervous which was not a good thing when negotiating for the life of a little girl, especially because both men were a trigger squeeze away from killing us.

The guy with one black eye said, "You people bring the money?"

James dabbed at his mouth with his napkin and dropped it onto his lap. "We wish to see the girl first, old boy."

"Cost you one hundred Gs to see the brat." The man with two black eyes spoke with a shaky voice. His khaki trousers were torn at the knee.

"Return the girl to us before you get into big trouble," said James. His face had a sour, mean appearance that scared me.

Jennifer must have been afraid also because she leaned in close and held my arm with both hands.

"We'll shoot the brat and be done with her," said the man with two black eyes.

179

"Take us to her now," James stood up and approached the two men like he meant to paint their eyes a deeper shade of purple and black.

"Hold on, mister," said the man with one black eye. "We'll take you to her, but you have to pay us first. You have the money, right?"

"I'll not pay you one hundred G's to have to put up with that girl again," said James.

Laura suppressed a scream.

"You don't want her back?" asked the man with two black eyes.

"Would you want her back?" James asked.

The man with one black eye said, "I see your point, mister, but you have to take her back. We want our money."

James paced around in front of the two windows along the dining room wall. As I watched him rub his chin, I noticed several folks at the oversized table observed him, too. Our private negotiation with the kidnappers had gone public. It wasn't exactly Facebook in nineteen-twenty-three, but it was out there for the other five guests to see.

"Tell you what, boys," said James. "I'll take her back for twenty-five thousand dollars."

The five other guests laughed while Laura gasped. Jennifer squeezed my upper arm tighter.

"What!" the man with the two black eyes said. "Mister, are you out of your brain?"

"It's a fair price," James said. "She was worth one hundred Gs to you when you kidnapped her. Why, I have extended you a seventy-five percent discount, old boy."

"Mister, you have a lot of nerve asking for money to take her back. We kidnapped her fair and square. We put up with the little monster all weekend. You take her back now, and if any money changes hands, it'll be you who pays me. And the price is still one hundred grand." The man with one black eye stomped back and forth while waving his sawed off shotgun.

The other folks at the table by this time stood in a circle around us. I noticed several side bets. I remembered I still had a ten-dollar gold piece in my pocket so I offered to bet that James would get the girl back without a ransom. No one wanted to take my bet.

One of the customers scratched at his whiskers and whispered into my ear. "Them Jackson boys ain't what you call the brightest candles in the kitchen, son. We're betting on how long it takes the city feller to whittle them Jacksons down to zero."

"Tell you what," James said. "You bring the girl here to this house in five minutes, and we'll forget the whole thing ever happened. You'll save twenty-five thousand dollars plus you won't have to feed her."

The man with two black eyes scratched at his unshaven face near a long, thin cut that ran from his left ear to within half an inch of his nose. "He's got a point, Darrell. The little critter about ate everything not locked down yesterday, as you may recall."

While Darrell contemplated his brother's point, the critter in question burst through the front door and plowed her way into the dining room. Despite her wild appearance, she wasn't the one who snagged our attention while the other customers bolted out of the room.

If you're not familiar with the hodag, it's a creature with a giant frog's face, except meaner than any amphibian you ever saw. Picture a frog in Marine basic for meanness. Or a Marine drill instructor. Now stick the face on a black furry thing the size of a black bear and as mean, except it has dinosaur ridges along its back that about cut you just by staring at them. Its thick, shaggy tail is lined with foot-long sharp spikes. And don't mess with its razor sharp claws. The hodag is a sight to behold, and if you didn't know Snpgrdxz, you'd skedaddle out of the room, too.

I thought Daniel Brickmaster, aka Snpgrdxz, had slept in. I should have realized he wouldn't miss a country breakfast. Instead, he had gone on a scouting expedition.

"Hey, Darrell and Jeffrey, don't you want to play no more?" Chrissie screamed as the Jackson brothers fired their shotguns at the dining room windows. They leaped through the openings they had created.

Laura ran to Chrissie, "Darling, you're safe."

"Course I am, Mama. I was playing with Darrell and Jeffrey. They wanted to tie me up, but I wouldn't let them. And then they wanted to feed me mush for dinner, but I made them cook the ham and eggs. They made stew for themselves, but I ate it all because I was so hungry. After supper, I chopped down a big post they used to have in their cabin before the roof fell down on top of them. Then Darrel and Jeffrey ran away this morning when Wally showed up. That's what I named my new friend. May I keep him, Mama? I think he's housebroken. And may I have my pancakes now? I'm starved."

Snpgrdxz the hodag tore off upstairs. He once again proved he knew the best time to skedaddle.

James Turpelator picked that moment to prove what a total animal he was by grabbing my Jennifer by the back of the neck and planting one huge kiss on her lips. He dropped his hand along her back and gave her derriere a big squeeze. It was the same move Mr. Turpelator the physics teacher put on her back at Lincoln High.

Jennifer slapped James across the face hard enough to draw blood.

He laughed and strolled upstairs.

"Are you okay?" I asked.

Jennifer slapped me hard enough to make my mouth bleed. At least I didn't land on the floor.

***

The Jackson brothers ended up a bloody mess scattered across a half block of Stevens Street, Rhinelander's main thoroughfare as though attacked by a real hodag.

"They received full payment for the way they served me, chums." James refused to explain further or answer our questions about what had happened to the Jacksons.

Tony told James Turpelator to keep his hands off his friends. He insisted James apologize to Jennifer for his rude and inappropriate actions. James mumbled an apology to Tony and then hid in his room for the rest of the day.

At breakfast the next morning, James apologized to Jennifer. "Entirely my fault, my dear. I find you Jennifers attractive and all the more so because there are two of you. But I now realize my interests lie with your sister rather than you. My ill manners will never be repeated with you, old girl."

Without waiting for a reply, James left Rhinelander in one of the cars. He flipped the keys to the second car to Tony on his way out. We remained in Rhinelander for a few days to enjoy what little remained of the fall color.

Trees weren't the only thing we spotted the morning we left Rhinelander. Two hours into the drive south, Tony pulled over when he noticed a huge column of smoke rising in the trees.

"Is that a forest fire?" Laura asked.

"It could be," said Tony.

We climbed out of the car for a better view. Gilbert spotted a rough trail made when something crushed and broke the trees as it pushed through the forest. Without a word, we followed the path in the direction of the smoke.

"Isn't it dangerous to walk toward the fire?" Jennifer asked.

I snagged her hand. "Yes."

Jennifer slapped my hand and moved forward toward the smoke column. It became smaller until it disappeared in one last flume of black smoke.

"Did it go out?" Chrissie asked.

"What's that smell?" Laura asked.

"Smells like what the bull left behind," said Daniel.

We climbed a small rise in the land. On the other side, we came upon a cow plop the size of a small house.

"This can't be good," said Tony.

The earth shook.

We heard a loud pounding as though someone were attempting to drive a log into the ground, except the sound didn't stay in one place. It approached us.

"Up there," Daniel yelled. We took a gander at the tree tops in front of us as a giant set of horns in the range of twenty-five feet wide burst through the trees headed for us. The horns were attached to a giant ox head. The fur on the ox included a white splotch surrounded by the prettiest gray-blue I had ever seen.

As the ox strolled out of the woods, we realized it packed solid muscle and wasn't about to get out of our way.

"It's Babe," Jennifer said.

"It's massive," said Daniel.

A deep voice as loud as thunder called, "Halt, Babe." A giant lumberjack walked up to the animal. The man was at least twelve feet tall. "Oh, I see we have company, Babe." The man turned his attention to us, "Howdy, folks."

"Howdy," said Daniel. The rest of us nodded.

"Are you lost?" the lumberjack asked.

"We noticed the fire and thought we'd better check it out," said Tony.

The giant laughed. "I know a hungry lumberjack when I see one. How about some flap jacks, folks?"

"Are you him?" Jennifer asked.

"Him? Why I'm none other than Paul Bunyan at your service, ma'am. And this is Babe, my big blue ox."

"You're real?" I asked.

"Of course I am." Paul Bunyan pulled his backpack off his back and yanked a huge stack of pancakes out. They were wrapped in waxed paper. He pulled a giant plate out along with a humongous bottle of maple syrup. "Reckon you folks can share one of these. It's hot off the campfire."

"We always have time for elevenses," said Tony.

"We do?" Jennifer asked.

The giant pancake had a smoky fresh flavor that mixed with the maple syrup for the best elevenses snack I ever ate, despite the time which was closer to noon.

"Where are you folks headed?" Paul asked.

"Chicago," Jennifer said.

"A right fine toddling town. Best pancakes south of Baraboo," said Paul.

"And you?" Tony asked.

"I'm headed west. Trees in these parts are chopped. No need here for the likes of Paul and Babe. Out yonder West they'll be needing folks handy with an axe, I'm thinking. There are big fir trees and plenty of them. Oregon is my heading."

Jennifer's expression turned quizzical. "Stories about you have been told for a long time, Paul. How old are you anyway?"

Paul roared with laughter. I never met a giant who laughed so much. "You may be thinking of my dad and grandfather. Why, I'm not the first Paul Bunyan as roved the North Country. I'm what you call Paul Bunyan the third. And this here Babe is about the tenth in his line. Seems a man sometimes comes up short on grub, especially when the snow falls. Babe performs one last service those times. Ox ain't the best eating unless you're starving. Then it tastes as fine as one of those Delmonico's New York steaks."

A black panther ran across the field into the woods. Its front right paw appeared injured causing it to favor that side.

"Did you see that," I asked.

"See what?" Gilbert asked.

Babe mooed as he turned in the direction of the panther and pounded his front hoof into the ground.

"Easy, Babe," said Paul.

The panther must have stalked us the way cats hunt where they keep low and sneak up on you by hiding behind bushes and tall grass. Despite its injured paw, the beast burst into the air headed towards Jennifer. Paul flicked his arm out at bullet speed to grab the giant cat by the neck. He hurled it back into the forest where it slammed against a tree trunk about twenty feet off the ground before sliding down the trunk.

We heard the cat roar a few times, but each time it was farther away.

"That was one angry cat," said Paul.

"I don't think he appreciated bouncing off a tree," said Gilbert.

"It's a female," said Paul. "She had that look of an angry woman."

After we polished off the pancake, Paul repacked his bag. "I'm pointed in the direction of the golden sunset even if it is just coming up on noon."

"Goodbye," Jennifer said. We waved as Paul and Babe lumbered back along the broken trail we had followed.

Back at the cars, we had to maneuver around a fresh Babe plop.

"Tony, can you drive faster than the speed of smell?" Gilbert asked.

***

To pass time on the rest of the drive back, Chrissie regaled us with her story of the kidnapping. She squeezed in the backseat between her mom and Gilbert. Daniel stuffed himself in the backseat where he took advantage of his shape shifting abilities. I rode shotgun next to Jennifer, but she ignored me. Tony drove. That Jennifer sat next to me I took as a major indication our relationship wasn't over despite her anger at me for not clobberbusting Turpelator. I should have shot him or punched his lights out, but it happened too fast for me to respond. It's a good thing I'm not a police officer. I don't move into action fast enough.

We were about two hours north of Madison when Chrissie changed the topic after we had stopped for dinner in Baraboo.

"Time for a ghost story," Chrissie said.

"I know one," said Gilbert.

"No, let me tell you one," said Chrissie. "It's about the ghost in Mr. Turpelator's house."

"He has a ghost?" asked Daniel.

Chrissie pointed a finger to the sky. "Once upon a time there was a girl named..."

"We shouldn't tell ghost stories while driving," said Daniel. "You might cause Tony to have an accident by scaring him to death."

Chrissie laughed. "If I scare you to death, Mr. Romano, you won't have to worry about an accident. She was a nice girl, and the man who lived in the house loved her very much."

"You mean Mr. Turpelator?" asked Daniel.

"I don't know," said Chrissie. "It was a long, long time ago before I was born. Anyway, the girl had beautiful long blond hair and pretty blue eyes."

"Or were they green?" I asked.

"I don't know that either, Bryan. But she had pretty eyes. She was a beautiful girl. That's why the man liked her so much. One day the man asked her to marry him, but she said no. And he said pretty please so she said yes although she didn't want to marry him because deep down inside he was a warlock, a man who is a witch. But don't ever call him a witch. Man witches are warlocks."

"Manwitches?" young Jennifer asked. "Do you mean sandwiches?"

I smiled at Jennifer's first words on the drive.

Chrissie laughed. "No. That's silly."

When Jennifer turned her head to face Chrissie in the backseat, she leaned against me. I placed my arm around her shoulder. She didn't bother to move it. "I'll bet he kissed her when she didn't want him to ever touch her again or she would shoot him even if her boyfriend was afraid to pull the trigger." Jennifer smiled at Chrissie.

Chrissie said, "Huh?" She gazed at the forest and hills out the window and then settled back down in her seat. "So one day the man who liked to eat sandwiches asked the girl to run away to Europe and get married. But the girl didn't want to marry a sandwich man, so she said no. The man became very angry and conked the girl on the nose and killed her dead. He hid the body where no one would ever find her."

"Where?" Daniel asked.

Chrissie crossed her arms. "If I had any idea, then I'd tell the police so they could arrest the man and find the body, but nobody knows, not even me."

"And that's how come she became a ghost?" Jennifer asked as she pressed closer to me. "I'm not surprised he killed her, the big jerk. Her boyfriend probably helped the punk bury her. He should have punched the warlock in the nose."

Chrissie laughed. "Yes. And she is a ghost to this day. She wanders the bad man's house where she talks to his guests when he has company. But the guests don't know she is dead. They think she is a real person on account of she looks and acts alive. Sometimes the boys fall in love with her because she is so pretty, but then she has to kill them and hide them away where no one will find them because they remind her of her stupid boyfriend who was afraid to punch out the warlock's lanterns."

"Ex-boyfriend," Jennifer said.

"How did she find out where the secret hiding place was located?" Laura asked.

"She found out when the bad man warlock person killed her and buried her there. Now she knows where it is because

188

she lives there, except she's not alive. She's dead. That's how come she is a ghost."

Laura asked, "Did the police arrest the bad man?"

"Not yet, Mommy. She still haunts his house and talks to his guests. She doesn't talk to all of them. Just the ones who can see her and hear her speak."

I thought about Brigitte, which embarrassed me because Jennifer sat next to me and was still ticked off at me despite having my arm around her shoulder while she leaned in close against me even though she no longer faced the back seat.

"What was her name?" I turned to face Chrissie and brushed my lips against Jennifer's ear as I did so.

"It's time to talk about something else," said Jennifer. "No sense scaring the little girl with ghost stories. And it is late. I'm sure Laura would prefer she fell asleep now." Jennifer straightened up and removed my arm from around her shoulder.

"It's okay, Jennifer. Let her finish the story." Laura patted Chrissie on the head.

"I'm not sure of her name," said Chrissie. "Bridgette or Barbara or something like that."

I held my breath when Chrissie said "Bridgette." It sounded too much like "Brigitte."

"Where is she now?" Gilbert asked.

"In heaven except when she haunts the bad man's house. She's still there to this day. The end." Chrissie nodded her approval of her story.

I planned to have a long talk with Brigitte the next time I spoke with her.

CHAPTER 22

TURPELATOR OR JENNIFER?

"Quit your job with Turpelator." Young Jennifer's right hand flew up to within a micro inch of scraping boogers from my nose. We stood on the front porch of Hawkins House. She slapped her hands on her hips and leaned way forward of straight up and down.

This girl was pissed although I thought the little arm on the shoulder thing on the ride to Wheaton had restored our relationship or at least had pointed the journey in that direction. "And if you don't, I will break up with you, Bryan Ganarski."

Talk about how to make me the happiest twenty-first century teenager in nineteen twenty three. "Wow, that's great news, Jennifer. Thanks."

"What? You want to break up?"

"Of course not. I'm glad you didn't break up with me. That's the great, wonderful news. I thought you never wanted to see me again after James got fresh with you while I stood there like an idiot."

"I can forgive you for that, Bryan. It came as a shock to you, and you don't respond rapidly to danger. Instead, you stare with your mouth open or wait for the bullet to bounce off your hard head. I can live with that, if you mature the problem out of your system as we get older. At first I did dump you. I just didn't tell you."

"It was obvious to everybody, Jennifer."

190

Jennifer sat down on the glider. "I should have said something to you like 'you're dumped' or whatever. So I'm gutless, too. If you want to be gutless together, it's okay with me. But you can't work for that jerk ever again. You have to quit. No notice. No sweating your paycheck. It's him or me, Bryan."

I sat beside her. "It's you. It's always been you." I may be a gutless teenager, but I hugged my Jennifer without a second thought.

Lilly Blackstone approached on the street. "Isn't that a sweet picture?"

"Oh, hi," Jennifer said.

Lilly leaned on two canes and she wore a bandage on her right hand. "Is your big sister home, dear?"

"What happened to you?" I asked.

"Lost another of my nine lives, Bryan. Not to worry. My back's not broken but it sure is sore. The doctor wants me to remain in bed for eight weeks, but I need a bed buddy for a date of that duration. Let me know if your Jennifer dumps you. I could use younger meat."

Jennifer stood with hands on hip. "Hey, we just got back together. Leave him alone if you know what's good for you."

"Don't get your claws out, honey. I was just teasing."

***

Once I told Ernie I quit working for him and James Turpelator, I was ready to head for our home time. I wasn't sure bootleggers were allowed to quit without a funeral, and I didn't want to stick around long enough find out.

Frank, Tony, Daniel and Gilbert joined the two Jennifers and me in Great Grandma Hawkins' living room. Ernie was out on a bootleg assignment at the time. Gilbert declared he wanted to go home before I could speak.

"I second Gilbert's motion. It's time we went home," I said.

Tony insisted we stay for the holidays including the big Christmas party at James Turpelator's mini-mansion.

"Why?" Gilbert asked. "We have to find Maria and head home. We already missed a lot of school."

"I'm homesick, too," young Jennifer said. "We need to get back to our parents. We must be on every plastic milk jug and junk mail circular in the country by now."

"Children, children, you still don't understand the magic of time travel," said Tony. "You haven't missed a single second of your lives back home. All we have to do is arrive back when we started."

"You're kidding, right?" I asked. "Time has moved forward for us since our arrival in nineteen twenty-three. Doesn't it make sense our home time moved on without us? Search parties have looked for us for months and given up by now. We're dead to our families. Our photos appear on cereal boxes and junk mail."

"We will not allow that history to be created," Tony said.

"We won't?" asked CJ.

"By returning on the same day we left, no one will realize we were gone.

"But we'll be older," said CJ. "Look at me. Plus there are two of me. How do I... or we... explain to Mom and Dad?"

"Dibs on my room," young Jennifer said.

"No problem, little sister. I'm old enough to live on my own. I won't move back home, but still, I haven't seen Mom and Dad in a very long time. I prefer to not freak them out too much. You talk to them first and I'll hang out somewhere else until they're ready to meet me."

Tony rubbed his chin. "College girl, let's not worry about you for the moment. We'll get you back where you belong. As for everyone else, when you show up a year older but on the same day you left, your parents won't notice the physical changes, and they'll appreciate your new maturity."

"But will my mom believe what happened to us?" Gilbert asked.

"Of course not," said Tony. "That's why you won't tell them. Instead, you'll smile and thank them for noticing how much you have grown up."

James Turpelator continued to host his weekend parties. He had a houseful of guests for the holidays, but young Jennifer and I avoided him and his parties. The others went because, as Tony said, "He apologized. As Christians, we have to forgive him."

Jennifer wasn't ready to dole out forgiveness and I supported her decision. The man hurt her and was no longer trustworthy, not that we trusted him before. He was a bootlegger after all and a Turpelator.

Gilbert kept an eye out for Brigitte but he never saw the curly-haired blonde. With school in session, we assumed she was in Switzerland or wherever she went to high school.

***

The black panther attacked the house the Friday after Thanksgiving. We know that day as Black Friday in the twenty-first century but in nineteen twenty-three it was Friday or "left-over turkey" day. Why the pesky panther broke through the back door is more than I can figure. The door was unlocked and half open because the kitchen was so hot from Great Grandma cooking turkey soup and baking some kind of turkey cheese casserole.

The cat knocked me to the floor on its way to rip my Jennifer to shreds. My dear friend Snpgrdxz came to our rescue by transforming his arm into a large hammer and smacking the big cat across the kitchen. The cat landed on its feet the way cats almost always do. It crouched for the attack. Snpgrdxz by this time had transformed into a black panther. The two panthers met in midair and wrestled across the linoleum.

Snpgrdxz worked the panther towards the backdoor despite the panther's attempts to break free. With so much scratching and clawing, I became concerned about Snpgrdxz becoming too scratched up and maybe bleeding alien blood all over the place.

While watching the cat fight, I missed what the ladies were up to until my Jennifer and Great Grandma Hawkins came into the kitchen with shotguns. Gilbert came in behind them with his Glock.

Tony arrived back from a shopping excursion to ask, "What's going on."

"Cat fight," Great Grandma Hawkins said.

Snpgrdxz succeeded in backing the predator out the door and into the backyard. Once the attacking panther was in the yard, Snpgrdxz tore off around the house. The panther hesitated long enough for Gilbert, Great Grandma and my Jennifer to open fire. The panther escaped over the back fence, but trailed blood behind.

***

Ernie and I shared a beer in his backyard the week before Christmas when he blurted, "Jennifer hates my guts."

"She loves me." I stirred a pile of leaves with my rake. We should have burned them a month or two earlier, but with so much activity, like the gunshot wound to my head, this was the first chance any of us had to rake and burn. The ground froze which made the raking difficult, but the snow hadn't fallen yet.

"Not your Jennifer, my Jennifer." Ernie sipped his bottle of Troll beer.

"If she was your Jennifer, she wouldn't hate you. CJ doesn't hate you. She likes Frank and Chauncey. She wants to marry Chauncey." I stepped back from the heat and smoke. "Young Jennifer and I double-dated with them."

Ernie waved his beer bottle around the air. "She hates me and I don't know why."

"Okay, let's say she hates you. What possible reason could she have?" I asked.

"I don't know. I'm a likable enough guy, a combat veteran war hero and a fine writer, if I say so myself."

"What have you written?"

Ernie rubbed his chin as his face reddened. "Nothing yet, but when I move to Paris next year I'll write about my adventures in the Great War. I'll combine the horrors of the trenches with a love story where I, I mean my main character, is wounded and falls in love with a nurse. She dies of course. Great love stories end in a death. I'm basing it on you and young Jennifer. I think I mentioned it to you guys once."

"Wait. You mean you're that Ernie? I had to read your book last year in high school."

Ernie scrunched up his cheeks and closed one eye. "Last year? Are you nuts? I didn't start to write it yet. Then I have to find a publisher although I hope to make contacts in Paris. You never know who you'll meet when you reach out to other artists and writers."

"So you love our CJ, huh?"

Ernie spun around. "Yes, I'd like to marry her but don't tell her I said so."

"I don't think she loves you, dude." I poked at the fire again to stir up the flames.

"Dude?"

"Man." I raked the leaves into a more concise pile.

"Man?"

"Ernie."

"She loves me. I can feel it, but something holds her back. She must have a secret she hasn't told me." Ernie pounded his fist.

"Yeah, like she loves Frank and loves Chauncey, and oh by the way, Turpelator is hot to get into her panties. And did I mention she's leaving town. She is one busy lady."

"She is?" Ernie's face fizzled.

"We all are, dude. Man. Ernie. Whatever."

"Where to?"
"Home."

***

Christmas at Hawkins House included a huge evergreen in the living room that blocked half the doorway into the entrance hall. When you came through the front door, you ran into the tree branches sticking out of the living room. It had an odd set of old lights and colored glass ball decorations and smelled of fresh pine forest throughout the house.

A train set ran around the tree with tiny paper and cardboard houses to make a village. Smoke with a nasty metallic oil smell poured out of engine's tiny smokestack.

On Christmas Eve, Tony read the ancient story from the Book of Luke after dinner. Tony translated the King James into his left over slang from the sixties and eighties where he deemed appropriate like when the shepherd said, "Dudes, like we should truck into town and check this gig the angels sang about." Don't ask me what happened to the seventies slang. I asked Tony once, and he replied, "Dude, the seventies were the sixties." Go figure.

After the reading, we sang carols around the fireplace. This led to a series of Christmas songs that weren't written yet like *Chestnuts Roasting by an Open Fire* and *Rudolph the Red Nosed Reindeer*. The nineteen twenty-three people commented with, "Gee, I don't know that one" or "Did Paul Whiteman's Orchestra play that one?"

Everyone, including little Chrissie, shared a glass of eggnog spiked with rum contributed by Ernie.

Laura sent Chrissie to bed at nine so she would be asleep when Santa visited. Except for the period decorations and the goof-ups on the song selections, we could have been celebrating Christmas in the twenty-first century. As I thought of home, I realized terms such as "twenty-first century" sounded like expressions from a science fiction novel. I was about to mention this to young Jennifer when she burst into tears.

"What's wrong?" I pulled her into a hug. The gang gathered around us.

"I want my mommy." Jennifer had been so good the months we stayed in nineteen twenty-three. With her incredible courage, she shot those two mobsters and saved me from the panther that stalked us.

She nursed me back to health after I cracked my head open with someone else's bullet, so her tears came as a surprise to me. But as I watched her chest heave and her nose run and the unstoppable tears flow, I realized this young lady was only fifteen or sixteen depending on how you counted, and she hadn't seen her mom or dad in a long time when you added the six months in this time plus our travel time among the trolls. And I realized we were a semester or more behind in school. But then I remembered what Tony had said about arriving back home at the same time we left. To our friends and family, we were never gone. But we would remember.

Tony wanted us to stay longer for the educational experience and the maturity we would return with, but one peek at my little Jennifer told me we had to go home now.

I hugged Jennifer and whispered, "Let's take a walk."

Jennifer nodded and I grabbed our coats. The temperature was in the mid-twenties as we stepped into the darkness of Wheaton. Snow had not yet fallen this year, and we could see stars above the downtown Wheaton Christmas lights. Crisp, clean air chilled our faces.

"I'm sorry, Jennifer. We should have gone home a long time ago. We would have if I hadn't been shot." We turned on Jefferson and headed toward Main Street.

"I know we'll arrive home the same time we left, but I can't help missing Mom and fuddy-duddy Daddy. I'm sorry I'm such a baby." Jennifer took my arm.

"You're not a baby. You're lonesome for your family. I miss my family, too. I miss Katie, which I never thought would happen."

"We don't have to go home yet, Bryan. I just need to grow up a bit."

"May I tell you something, Jennifer?"

"What?"

"I wanted to wait until we opened presents in the morning, but it's better here in our own hometown even if this is our town long before our time." I shrugged and shivered in the cold. I had to tell her now. I had made the commitment, but no one told me it took guts. "Aren't the windows beautiful with the candles?"

"You brought me out into the cold to talk about candles?"

I grimaced. I bent over to pick up a rock but changed my mind when I considered that knocking out a neighbor's window was not a good idea. "No, Jennifer, what I wanted to say was... oh, why can't I just say it?"

"Because you're a wimpy afraid to commit boy?"

"Anyway, I love you."

Jennifer gazed into my eyes and breathed on my chin. Her smile revealed her wonderful white teeth.

How come no one had noticed how great our teeth gleamed? Chrissie's mom Laura was in her thirties, but she soaked her teeth in a jar every night. Tony looked forty and had perfect teeth. Nobody else we met in this time that old had any teeth left. Back in the summer, no one noticed we didn't have huge round scars on our upper arms from the small pox vaccine. You could place a quarter over their vaccination scars and still have a corona wrapped around it.

"You love me even though I'm a big crybaby?" Jennifer laid a quick peck on my lips.

I wiped a tear from her cheek. "Especially because you miss your family. It proves you love them, and I want my girl to love and honor her family like Mr. Corbin says in youth group."

"I kind of like you, too, Bryan Ganarski."

"Like but not love?"

"You make me smile when I'm sad. And you are my one great joy in this world. Well, meeting myself makes me happy, too, but it's confusing when I try to figure out how she is me if I'm me and how come my other self is so much older than me? I mean how does that happen? And will I become like her or will I do dissimilar things and become a different me?"

"The old change-the-subject dodge, eh?"

Jennifer stretched up and kissed me on the lips with one of those mouth open zingers I didn't realize she knew how to do. A long time later, I led my girl back to her house although we arrived a couple of generations before she called it home.

"Hey, I still live in my own bedroom, the one I grew up in. It's pretty cool to live in your own house a gazillion years before you were born. Gives you a better perspective on where you live. And you get great decorating ideas, especially if you like antiques." She ran up on the porch.

Before she busted through the front door, my Jennifer Hawkins spun around to face me with the biggest shit eater I ever saw. "I love you Bryan Ganarski, forever and ever."

CHAPTER 23

THE CHRISTMAS PRESENT

Christmas morning we opened presents before breakfast as Chrissie would have it no other way. CJ came over to Ernie's house to round up "my boys" as she liked to call us. "Ernie, you can come, too. Santa left your present under our tree for some strange reason."

"Probably because we didn't put up a tree," Ernie said.

Without an advance discussion, we decided on a camping theme for presents. I bought my Jennifer a flannel shirt and a pair of blue jeans.

"You bought me man pants?" Jennifer asked.

"Yeah, in case you need an extra pair. I couldn't find girl pants. I guessed at your size, but I'm close, right? Your blouse is the right size because I cheated and peeked."

"You peeked down my blouse?" Jennifer's cheeks turned the prettiest shade of pink.

"Yeah. You weren't wearing them at the time."

"Next time check with me in them, okay?"

"Yes, dear."

Jennifer smacked me hard on the lap.

After we exchanged presents, Tony said, "I have one more present for our little troop of adventurers."

Everyone perked up in anticipation of one last present from under the tree, except the bottom of the tree was as naked as can be.

"My present to you is the gift of a journey home, gang."

***

Chauncey visited after lunch. We gathered in the living room for conversation. It's something you do if you are someplace where television hasn't been invented yet. Radio wasn't even around yet, except for a few people experimenting with crystal sets on the airwaves.

Jennifer and I shared a chesterfield with Chauncey and CJ, which made for a crowd.

"We need more room." Chauncey stood up.

CJ tapped him on the arm. "That's not necessary. I can sit on your lap."

Chauncey knelt down.

"Oh shit. Is he going to do what I think he's going to do?" asked my Jennifer.

CJ turned beet red. "No, Chauncey."

Chauncey gazed into CJ's eyes. "No? I haven't asked you anything yet."

"I mean we need a private moment if you're planning to ask me what I think you're going to ask."

Laura said, "He already began, CJ. Let him finish. We don't mind watching."

"Yeah, I want to see you kiss," said Chrissie.

"We need a little privacy here," said CJ.

Chauncey took CJ's hands into his own. "Jennifer Hawkins, will you honor me by becoming my bride?" Chauncey dug a fist into his suit jacket pocket and yanked out the biggest diamond rock I had ever seen.

CJ cried.

Chauncey stood and lifted CJ off the chesterfield. "Please, darling. Be mine."

CJ smiled through a face full of tears. "Okay."

Snpgrdxz and Gilbert whooped.

***

Brigitte whispered in my ear from behind. "Come to the basement. I'll meet you." The time was one in the morning at James Turpelator's Christmas party.

The evening began as his parties always did for our gang with a chow-down session for the guys in the dining room while the ladies wandered the halls and byways in search of adventure. Jennifer asked me to attend despite her disdain for James Turpelator because it would be our final fling in nineteen twenty-three, except for the wedding of course. And my Jennifer didn't want to stay home worrying about her parents.

Before I could head to the basement in search of Brigitte, Gilbert punched me harder than usual on the shoulder. "Daniel turned into a girl again. Check her out."

By the time I turned around, Brigitte was nowhere to be seen. Instead, my eyes beheld an attractive young lady who appeared to be Daniel Brickmaster's twin sister. She had his face, eyes, hair color, but bobbed in the twenties fashion. She wore a dress I'm sure was purloined from an upstairs closet or a local bordello. With her was Lilly Blackstone.

"Danielle," Gilbert called.

"Isn't she beautiful?" Lilly was covered in deep scratches. She hunched over a cane. She no longer wrapped her right hand in a bandage, but she displayed a fresh scar the size of a kitchen knife on the back of her hand.

Danielle Brickmaster placed an arm around both of us for a group hug. She gave me a quick peck on the cheek which I tried to duck. Gilbert received a healthy lip lock that lasted from the time my Jennifer entered the dining room until she snagged carrots and celery from a tray along with onion dip and made her way to us.

"What's with Gilbert and Snpgrdxz?" Jennifer asked.

"Something new," I said. "I have to meet someone in the basement, and I'd like you guys to come with me."

"Basement?" Gilbert asked.

"Yes, Brigitte wants to meet with me," I said.

Jennifer poked me on the shoulder. "Are you cheating on me, Bryan?"

"No. She wants to tell me her big secret or show me where Turpelator buried his treasure. I don't pretend to understand. She confuses me."

"I'll pass," said Lilly. "I'm not getting along with basement stairs at the moment." Lilly limped off with her cane.

The four of us wandered through the crowded kitchen to the basement door. On the way, we ran into CJ and Chauncey making out by the kitchen sink.

"Watch out, you guys. No make out sessions in public," my Jennifer said.

The lovebirds ignored us. They disregarded Turpelator who sat at the kitchen table drinking beer. When we entered the kitchen, Turpelator sighed, grimaced and headed for other places in the house.

"Get a room," I whispered in Chauncey's ear.

"Great idea," Chauncey said.

"What is?" asked CJ.

"A room," said Chauncey.

"Here?" CJ asked.

"Turpelator has a house full of bedrooms," Chauncey said.

"Cool," said CJ.

"I'm hot," said Chauncey.

I shook my head and guided my Jennifer to the cellar door. "It's locked."

Danielle Brickmaster reshaped her finger into an old-fashioned skeleton key and slid it into the keyhole. He wiggled his finger around a bit to get the lock mechanism right. The lock clicked, and Danielle opened the door. She indicated I should go first, so I led the group into the basement.

"Brigitte?" I called.

"Over here." Her voice led me through the maze of beer cases to the same spot we stood the last time I was with her in the basement. "Dig here," she said.

I didn't see Brigitte.

"Where is she?" Jennifer asked.

"I don't know. I heard her, but I didn't see her." I peered around a stack of boxes like an idiot playing hide and seek.

"She's not here, is she?" Gilbert asked. "We didn't hear anyone but you."

"She must be nearby. She told me to dig here."

"Why should you dig up James's basement?" Danielle asked.

Gilbert did his best ghost voice, "It's where the bodies are buried, my dear."

We searched around for a shovel. Gilbert found one in a corner. "Bryan, you're the one who wants to dig." He tossed me the shovel.

"Here?" I dug the shovel into the dirt floor.

"Yes," said Brigitte.

"The others can't hear you," I said.

"I know. I don't know why. Only certain people are sensitive enough to know me."

I dug a grave size trench about six feet long and two feet wide. I dug it out to a depth of about one foot when Robin the hobgoblin approached out of the darkness of the basement beer maze. "Why are you people in the cellar?"

"We want to find our friend," Danielle said.

"She ain't here," Robin snarled. I noticed a revolver in his hand. "Fill it back in."

Based on the logic of a pistol, I shoveled dirt back into the hole. When I finished, I patted the dirt down to minimize the hump. "How's that?"

Three quick shots rang out.

Robin said, "What was that?"

I breathed hard. The shots confused me. A gun went off, but no fire flared out of Robin's weapon and no holes appeared in my body.

Danielle must have noticed my confusion and the others appeared muddled. She said, "The shots came from upstairs."

Robin stormed out of the basement with the rest of us not able to keep up a hobgoblin pace.

At the top of the stairs, Jennifer tugged my arm. "How did Robin know your friend was female? We never mentioned it."

***

James Turpelator lay face up on the dining room floor with three bullet holes in his chest. His mouth dripped blood like an overflowing vessel. His body was swollen and beet red.

Police sirens grew louder. A short man with graying blond hair was restrained by three men I recognized as drivers in James's bootleg organization. One of the three dangled a pistol in his hand as three police officers rushed into the room. "What happened?" the sergeant asked.

"This man shot Mr. Turpelator," said one of the drivers.

.We learned the shooter was Jens Wurzburger, father of a long missing teenage girl named Brigitte. The DuPage County State's Attorney later charged him with murder.

CJ plodded into the room with tears streaming down her face. Her chest heaved. "He's dead."

Frank received CJ into his arms. "We know, darling. Some German guy shot him."

"Not Turpelator, Chauncey." CJ fainted.

Frank lifted her into his arms "Officers, there's been another killing."

The sergeant asked, "Where?"

My Jennifer patted CJ's cheek. The universe did not collapse, but CJ opened her eyes. She pointed to the stairs.

"Which room?" the sergeant asked.

"Third floor, middle room," CJ said.

The sergeant ordered one of the officers to remain with Turpelator's body. He and the other officer took off upstairs. Frank stayed with CJ as Tony, Danielle Snpgrdxz, Gilbert, Jennifer and I followed.

We ran into Lilly Blackstone limping down the hall on the second floor. "What's going on?"

"Someone shot James Turpelator," I said.

"Breaks my heart."

"I thought you and he were buds," Gilbert said.

"Buds?" asked Lilly.

"Friends, buddies," Tony said.

Lilly said, "Oh, why didn't you say so. Let me tell you a few things about your Mr. Turpelator – "

"No time now," Gilbert said.

We tore off for the third floor leaving Lilly behind."

"We can discuss him later." Lilly limped down the stairway.

On the third floor, we made our way to the middle bedroom. The two police officers checked Chauncey. His body was white as alabaster, except for two streaks of blood on his throat. His dead eyes glared at the ceiling.

"We'll have to interview everyone," Officer Darnell said.

"Turpelator did this," said Tony. "Examine his bloody mouth for extra-long vampire incisors."

The officer prodded Chauncey's mouth.

"Not him. Check Turpelator downstairs. Have your coroner look for it," said Tony.

***

We postponed our departure long enough to attend the funeral for James Turpelator. We had mixed emotions about him. He was a powerful bootlegger, a friend of the scar faced man. James ran liquor operations in the towns west of

Chicago beyond what were considered the suburbs in nineteen twenty-three. These were farm towns for the most part including Wheaton, Naperville, Warrenville and other small nearby communities.

The funeral director's people loaded James's casket into a horse-drawn black wagon and covered it with flowers. There was no church service so we marched in procession from the funeral home to the Wheaton town cemetery on the south side. At the cemetery gates, we were asked to line up along the dirt road that wound through the cemetery to the gravesite.

James Turpelator was a prominent local gangster and drew a large crowd to line the roadway.

Despite his many associates and bootlegger friends, James had no family and no one closer than our little group. Tony, Snpgrdxz, Ernie, Gilbert and Fireman Frank served as pallbearers along with Scarface. I declined the opportunity in deference to my Jennifer.

The pallbearers lifted the flower draped casket from the wagon at the cemetery gate. The casket was constructed of solid oak boards. Gilbert told me later it had weighed a ton. I couldn't help but notice the pallbearers grunt as they lifted it to their shoulders.

The Wheaton History Museum had a collection of old newspaper photographs that showed the funeral of James Turpelator. You can find them mounted behind glass in wooden frames in the men's room on the second floor above the urinals, a place my Jennifer would find suitable. A man can do his business and contemplate the folly of his kind in a single rest stop. The photos also appeared in one of those public television shows about the roaring twenties.

The caption doesn't identify the pallbearers shown in the photographs, but you can see Tony, Scarface and Frank on one side of the casket. Tony carried the front corner. Scarface trudged in the center position, barely touching the casket. The backend was on Frank's shoulders. The casket leaned down on Frank like a car with a flat tire. On the other side, you can see the top of the heads of the other pallbearers.

As the casket passed between the rows of people lined along the road into the cemetery, they dropped into place behind it for the solemn procession to the gravesite.

The pallbearers set the casket down over the open hole and backed away. Scarface made his way to the head of the grave.

"Such that we should remember our friend James, let us bow our heads in silence," said Scarface. After a few seconds, he said, "James was a man of the people who enjoyed his work. You cannot ask for more out of life. Let him rest in peace."

The funeral director and his crew lowered the casket into the hole with ropes. They passed a shovel to Scarface who chucked in the first dirt. He passed the shovel to me to toss my soil onto the casket. I passed the shovel on. Once the grave was full we left.

Unlike modern funerals, the Scarface mob didn't offer luncheon afterwards. Ernie invited our little group to his house for sandwiches, but the rest of the funeral attenders dispersed. I imagine they each formed their own little groups at local restaurants or headed to someone's house.

Ernie asked Scarface to join us, but he declined. "Such that the mayor should honor our loyal support of his candidates, I must decline yous invite and visit wid hizzoner."

Gilbert grabbed our attention after lunch as we munched apple pie and drank hot cider. "Major problem for you, Jennifer."

Young Jennifer replied, "What?"

"Chauncey's body has gone missing," said Tony.

"Someone stole his body?" CJ asked.

"More likely he's turned nosferatu." Tony pulled a Glock out of his belt and laid it on the table.

"He'll be around to suck our blood, won't he?" Gilbert asked.

"No need to look for him. He'll find us." Tony pulled a crucifix from his suit coat pocket and placed it on the table.

"What about Turpelator? Won't he return to suck our blood?" my Jennifer asked.

"Jens Wurzeburger had the good sense to use lignum vitae bullets. I found out when my friend, Doctor McCully performed the autopsy. He cut Turpelator's heart out. Separating the heart from the body is one way to kill a vampire. A wood stake to the heart also works. In this case, the wooden bullet suffices as long as it lodges in the heart."

"Doctor McCully is the coroner?" I asked. "You mean the guy who poked and prodded my brain is the same guy who chops up dead people?"

"Yep," said Daniel Snpgrdxz.

"We have to do something," CJ said.

"He'll come for you first, my dear," said Tony.

CHAPTER 24

NEW VAMPIRES, OLD JOURNEYS

New vampires aren't always the brightest of creatures. We're talking about a monster working with a dead brain and someone else's blood. The noise in the Hawkins House attic put me in mind of a ghost moving with too many things bumping in the night.

"What's he doing up there?" Gilbert asked.

"Tearing up the attic junk in search of CJ," Daniel Brickmaster, aka, Snpgrdxz said.

"It's one in the morning," said my Jennifer. "We didn't bring you boys over here from Ernie's to talk about Chauncey. I say we go up there and stake the sucker."

"Hey, that's my fiancé we're talking about," said CJ.

Frank joined us with a step ladder at the top of the third floor stairs. The entrance to the attic was in the hallway ceiling above our heads.

As Frank set up the ladder, Tony said, "How do we know Chauncey isn't up there right now looking for the exit so he can climb down here and blood suck us all?"

"We don't," said my Jennifer. "But we do know how to stop a vampire. I'm sorry, big sister, but we have to stake him. He's a demon-possessed monster masquerading in Chauncey's body. That monster is not your dead boyfriend."

Frank held a stake and hammer.

Tony passed around the M16s and lignum vitae clips. "Everyone ready?"

"Who's going up first?" Frank asked.

"You're holding the stake and hammer," said CJ.

A loud thump shook the attic entrance.

"He's right there, right now," whispered Gilbert.

My Jennifer shook her head. She grabbed the stake and hammer from Frank. "I'll go."

"No," I said in a loud whisper, which if you think about it, is a dumb way to communicate. Loud is loud.

My Jennifer climbed the ladder. She turned around to glare at each of us. She looked me in the eye last with a look of love so deep I almost fell to my knees. She smiled. I smiled back. Jennifer pushed the attic door up into the attic.

A very naked Lilly Blackstone dropped out of the attic. Did I tell you before how beautiful Lilly Blackstone was? I mention this purely from an aesthetic viewpoint mind you. From the floor, she said, "Oh! How did I get here?"

I don't think Lilly noticed how nude she was because she made no attempt to cover up. CJ ran into a bedroom while the rest of us gawked.

My Jennifer poked her head into the attic. "Flashlight."

Tony passed her a flashlight.

CJ returned with a blanket she draped over Lilly.

"Thanks," said Lilly. "I think I broke my ankle."

"Clear," my Jennifer called down from the attic. She dropped the door back into position and climbed down the ladder. "What were you doing in our attic?"

Lilly wiped dust from her scratched up forehead with her scarred right hand. "My sore back is killing me so I'm going to lay here for a while if you guys don't mind."

Great Grandma Hawkins stumbled out of the master bedroom. "What's going on here?"

"Lilly fell out of our attic," said CJ.

"What was she doing in our attic?" asked Great Grandma Hawkins.

We all glared at Lilly.

"I don't know. I was home asleep in my bed, quite alone mind you, when I woke up in somebody's attic. I had no idea it was yours, and I have no idea how I got there. I thought it was a dream. Maybe it was a dream in which I sleep-walked my way into your attic. Then somehow it all became real. Or perhaps I'm dreaming still."

"That doesn't explain how you came to be up there. You need a ladder to reach the attic," said Frank.

"I think I jumped," said Lilly.

"In your condition?" my Jennifer asked.

"Yeah, I am kind of a mess, aren't I? In my dream, I must have jumped. How I ended up there I have no idea."

I don't know where the thought came from, but it spun in my bullet-cracked, insane brain so I said, "Maybe that black jungle cat that roams around here could have made the jump and pushed its way into the attic through that door."

***

Chauncey didn't strike until the next night.

After the previous evening which ended with Frank driving Lilly to the hospital to have her fractured ankle placed in a cast, we set up a watch system. The ladies slept in their bedrooms as usual while the guys took turns posted at the top of the stairs below the attic. When we weren't on surveillance, we camped out in the living room.

Ernie joined us for the guard duty because he was afraid to sleep alone in his house. Everyone except Chrissie slept with a stake, crucifix or gun loaded with wooden bullets.

I awoke around two in the morning to the sound of a bat flapping around. One of the problems with old Victorians is you are liable to find an actual bat or two in the house on occasion. I mean real bats, not vampires. In this case, I managed to capture the beast in a kitchen towel and flip him loose in the backyard. The tiny flying mouse lifted to the skies until I spotted that large bat flapping around the roof line. I went back in and woke the guys. "He's here."

Chauncey rang the doorbell a few minutes after I had alerted our gang. Tony answered the door while wearing a foot-long crucifix draped around his neck and carrying a pint bottle of holy water in his hand.

"May I come in and visit CJ?" Chauncey pushed on his upper teeth like he was adjusting a set of false teeth. His fangs must have dropped down while thinking about his CJ. He held his left forearm up to cover his eyes.

"No, you are not welcome in this house," said Tony.

"Tony, you know me. Let me come in."

"No. You are forbidden entry to this house now and forever."

"Don't you think you should ask CJ?"

CJ made the mistake of coming downstairs to see who was at the door. "Oh, Chauncey. I'm so glad to see you. Come on in."

Chauncey glared at Tony who stood his ground with the crucifix and holy water.

"You take one step forward and I'll cover you in holy water," said Tony.

"But you heard CJ. I'm invited."

Tony pushed the crucifix against Chauncey's chest. Chauncey backed away while smoke and the smell of burning, rotting flesh filled the night. Chauncey's voice deepened the way monster voices do in the movies, "I'll be back."

"Wasn't he supposed to use a German accent?" Snpgrdxz asked.

***

We maintained a standoff with Chauncey throughout the next week. He attempted to enter Hawkins House while we frightened him off with holy water, crucifixes, wood stakes and wooden bullets. After a few nights, CJ worked up the gumption to revoke her invitation to enter. This was a difficult decision for her because she was deep in mourning for the real Chauncey and had to learn to deal with the idea that a vampire is nothing more than a demon in possession of a dead person's body.

The last night we saw Chauncey, he announced that he was leaving Wheaton to return to college. We tried to warn college officials and even contacted his fraternity brothers but to no avail. They all laughed off the suggestion that vampires were real. That's why that famous fraternity is still filled with vampires to this day at the U of I and helps explain the success of the university's basketball program.

***

"You're stuck in a time loop, Jennifer Hawkins," said Gilbert.

We gathered in the Hawkins House living room at the end of the night's vampire watch. The sun shone above the eastern horizon so we relaxed. Great Grandma Hawkins brewed coffee in the kitchen.

Gilbert said, "The other Turpelator, our teacher back at Lincoln High, remember him? Our Mr. Turpelator's Rule Two of Time Travel has kicked in in your case. You'll live from nineteen eighteen to nineteen twenty-three and back again to nineteen eighteen forever. Good news is you'll never die. Bad news is you will become awfully bored. The other good news is you'll stay young forever."

I wanted to scream so I did. "What are you talking about? Jennifer will return to the tunnels with us."

Gilbert shook his head a few times. "And she'll end up back in nineteen eighteen by herself again."

"What do you mean again?" asked Fireman Frank.

Tony's expression turned from dazed to the Buddha. "Like, dude, you reached me big time. How often has CJ gone through this experience already? Once? A million times? She ain't saying because she doesn't want to confuse us. Wild Thing, life for you is wilder than we thought."

"I don't get it." And I didn't. "What do you people mean? What time loop?"

"What is a time loop?" young Jennifer asked.

Gilbert stood up. "Mr. Turpelator explained it in our physics class."

"I'm not in your physics class, remember?" young Jennifer asked.

"I know," Gilbert said. "You're a sophomore. The way Mr. Turpelator explained it to us juniors was a time loop is when you cycle through time over and over again. In this case, you are looping, or about to loop, through the same experience many times over."

"Why me," Jennifer asked.

CJ jumped in. "If the young version of Jennifer, the one we know and Bryan loves, comes with us back through the tunnels, she will be with us when the zombies attack. She'll jump through the Wheaton When Portal to get away because she will be first in line to jump with Bryan holding her hand. But the zombies will jump Bryan, and Jennifer will pass through the time portal by herself. She'll land in nineteen eighteen and pee her pants because she'll be so scared. She will meet Chauncey and stay here until nineteen twenty-three when we show up. Then we'll do this dance all over, taking her down to the tunnels, letting go of her hand and sending her to nineteen eighteen by herself. Jennifer has nowhere else to go and no way out of the loop. She's stuck forever. And I'm the proof after twenty-seven times around that stupid loop."

"Chauncey's dead," Frank said.

"Not in nineteen eighteen," said CJ.

"But I thought we landed in a different when every time we crossed the Wheaton When Portal." I sounded confused because I was.

"Too true," Tony said. He slipped deeper into sixties clichés the more crazy our situation became.

"Not true in this case," said Gilbert.

"Gilbert's right," said Snpgrdxz. "When Jennifer goes through the Wheaton When Portal, she'll repeat the same action as before at the same moment in time. The portal is always aligned to the same time because it is the same time. It's a time loop. For us, it'll be a normal passage of time and we'll keep on through time as always. For our young version of Jennifer, here, she's about to loop into nineteen eighteen again and wait for us to show up in nineteen twenty-three and then it's time to do it again. She'll bounce back to nineteen eighteen over and over again forever. Sorry, Jennifer."

Young Jennifer's hands flew to her hips, which being so skinny, she almost missed. "This will not happen to me. First off, it will be different because we'll have two Jennifers with us, and we'll both make sure numbnuts, I mean Bryan, doesn't let go of my hand. Second, I know what's about to happen. I obviously didn't know the first time through. Now, I do, so I won't let this happen."

Snpgrdxz took Jennifer's hand. He slid a little hand action across her hips which ticked me off until I remembered he's an alien and might not have all of our touch-no touch rules down after only about seventy years on our planet. "Jennifer, we don't know how many times you've cycled through this loop already, CJ says it has been twenty-seven by her count, but it could be more. She just happens to be the Jennifer we ran into in this loop. In any case, this isn't the first time for you because old Jennifer went through it before you. This of course is absurd because you are she."

"So we can take precautions to make sure this doesn't happen again. We can go through at a different time then when old Jennifer went through last time." Jennifer pounded a fist into her hand.

"Or you can remain here and not come with us," Snpgrdxz said.

"No way will I stay in nineteen twenty-three." Young Jennifer did another fist pound.

"You can go through the Wheaton When Portal anytime you want, except when the rest of us go through." Gilbert said.

Tony jumped in. "Of course. Wild Thing, you wait here for a while, a few days or a few hours. Long enough to pass through the Wheaton When Portal at a different time than the rest of us. Then you pass back into our world, and you break the loop. You'll arrive at a different when in the same old Wheaton."

"That's it, isn't it? What do I do by myself in a different time? I could come out anytime. How do I get back to my regular time in the twenty-first century?"

Tony rubbed his stubbly chin. "Jump back and forth through the Wheaton When Portal, Wild Thing, until you arrive back home. You may never arrive at the exact time you left, but if you return home within a decade or so of when we left, you'll have the opportunity to re-connect with your family and with numbnutz."

"How many times will I have to jump back and forth?" young Jennifer asked.

"As many as it takes," said Snpgrdxz. "It could happen on the first try or take a few dozen, but the odds are you will end up close to our original time period."

"What odds?" young Jennifer asked.

Snpgrdxz rubbed his Daniel Brickmaster chin. "Who knows, but it appears we don't stray too far in time when we go back and forth, do we Tony?"

"I wouldn't worry much about straying too far from your present."

"You all better go," CJ said.

"What about Chauncey and that pesky black panther?" I asked.

Laura said, "They are problems in this time. They are not your problems or your time. It's best to leave now or you may end up here forever while you chase other people's problems. We shouldn't have out-of-time weapons and people here. Sooner or later the authorities will find out and investigate you."

"You do not want the feds investigating you," said Snpgrdxz. "They'll kill you so they can investigate your innards. Laura is right. We have to return to our own time and deal with our own issues then."

Young Jennifer asked, "What about CJ?"

"I could go with you, if you like. It won't make any difference to me since I'll end up on another round of the time loop anyway."

"What do you mean?" Gilbert asked.

"If I go or stay, it ends up the same way. Young Jennifer lands in nineteen eighteen. Like I said, twenty-seven times. If I go, I'll be embarking on try twenty-eight."

"It's hard to believe that you've been around the time loop twenty-seven times," Snpgrdxz's jaw dropped.

"That's five years of life in the loop. And twenty-seven cases of Spanish flu, darlings." CJ sat on my lap, put her arms around my shoulders and kissed me. "I have missed you, Bryan. Sorry to say but I also have been angry with you for five years times twenty-seven."

"That's a long time," said Gilbert.

"One hundred thirty-five years," said CJ.

Snpgrdxz reached down and picked his jaw up from the floor. He reattached it to his face. "Have you thought about killing yourself?"

"I died a few times, but I always wake up in the tunnel outside the Wheaton When Portal in nineteen eighteen." College age Jennifer raised her eyes to the ceiling and back to Snpgrdxz.

"We died?" asked my Jennifer.

"You can't always get past the trolls. They're pesky critters and so are the zombies. I don't want to talk about vampires, werewolves and the other monsters that inhabit the troll world," CJ said. "And the other monsters are the scary ones."

Young Jennifer folded her arms across her chest with a defiant glare. "I will remain here. If I don't go through the tunnels, I can't go back to nineteen eighteen. And I'll skip the monsters, thank you. And I'll live longer."

"You'll go," said CJ. "You'll miss Bryan and try to catch up with him. The best I've lasted so far is three weeks."

"But if I wait three weeks, I'll come out some when else," said young Jennifer.

CJ said, "Nope. You're stuck in a time loop. You'll always come back to nineteen eighteen."

"I will stay with my Jennifer," I said.

"That's new." CJ kissed me on the lips and sauntered away.

"What if young Jennifer crossed a different when portal?" Frank asked.

"What other when portal?" Snpgrdxz asked.

Tony scratched his chin. "Other portals exist, but locating them is dangerous. You have to cross deep into troll territory. No telling if we'd make it."

CJ kissed Tony. "I'll do it! And my twin little sister will come with me. The worst that can happen is the trolls or spiders will eat us. The best is we'll come out in some other when and some other place. We have to try, little sis."

"Spiders?" asked Snpgrdxz. He transformed into a troll. In his best gruff voice he said, "Let's go. I love an adventure and it's not like I'll ever return home. Jennifers, I know how you both feel except for the twenty-seven cases of Spanish Flu deal. That's one I'd as soon skip."

"Adventure calls. I'm in," Frank said.

The others nodded and stood up like it was time to go, and Frank headed for the front door.

My Jennifer remained in her seat on the sofa or chesterfield or whatever the thing was called in January nineteen twenty-four. Tears flowed down her cheeks. "I can't go with you."

"Why ever not, little sister?" CJ asked.

"If I go, I'll become stuck in the time loop with you. If I stay, I'll move forward in time from here. I'll live in the wrong time but at least I'll move in the right direction."

Great Grandma arrived like the cavalry in a silent movie except in color and not as grainy. She pulled young Jennifer up off the couch and into her arms. "You can go with them, darling."

"I can, Great Grandma?" Jennifer wiped a tear.

Great Grandma patted young Jennifer's cheek. "Yes, dear. No worries as your generation says. You have a choice. Either way works because it's not the time you live in, it's how you spend the time you live."

"How can you know for sure, Great Grandma?" Gilbert asked.

"Trust me. Great, great, great whatever I am to young Jennifer here Grandma is hip to the score."

My Jennifer snuffled. "Okay, Great Grandma, I'll go."

Great Grandma grabbed CJ. "You can't leave without a hug, my dear. I've loved you since the moment you arrived here back in nineteen eighteen. I nursed you through the big flu epidemic, remember?"

CJ chuckled. "And then I nursed you through it. And we both came out okay."

Great Grandma wiped a tear from her own cheek. She removed a small watch she wore pinned like a broach to her dress. "Take this watch, my dear, to remind you of the wonderful times you and I have had together and to remind you there is no time like the present no matter which present you find yourself in."

"Thank you, Great Grandma." CJ pinned the watch on. "I'll cherish it always and never let it out of my sight." CJ hugged Great Grandma Hawkins.

Great Grandma pulled back from the hug. "I have to tell you something important, Jennifer, darling. When you go into the land of the trolls, you will face one of those life and death decisions. Make the right one this time."

"This time?" Snpgrdxz cried.

Great Grandma sighed. "Yes, this time. The last time you did this, you made the wrong decision. And whatever you do, don't let anyone steal your watch."

CJ stared at Great Grandma with wide eyes and open mouth.

Young Jennifer put a hand to her mouth and pulled it away. "Great Grandma, are you trying to tell us you're another Jennifer, another me?"

Great Grandma laughed. "What a wild imagination you have, child."

***

"Convert your money into simple gold rings," Tony instructed. We stopped at a jewelry store in downtown Wheaton on our way back to Lincoln High and the Wheaton When Portal. "Save a few ten-dollar gold coins because you'll need at least one."

"What for?" I asked.

"You'll know when the time comes," said Tony.

After a stop that made a jewelry store owner happy to unload a bunch of cheap wedding rings, we headed into the tunnels beneath Lincoln High School.

"How come we haven't run into ghosts, goblins or trolls this time around?" my Jennifer asked.

"We're not at the portal yet," said Tony. "Sometimes they're simply not around. Other times they hide in the shadows where they can pop out at the first sign of weakness. My guess is the word got around about us from our last time through. Do you think the creatures of darkness want to mess with us after the last time they tried to attack?"

Tony made sense except that was the moment ten vampires dropped from the ceiling in front of us. Young Jennifer flashed her crucifix while the rest of us fired lignum vitae bullets and oak-shafted arrows. The vampires vanished in a cloud of smoke. I spun around expecting them to attack us from the rear, but they didn't. Tony was right. The bad undead knew us and now they would leave us alone.

As we made our way to the Wheaton When Portal, I thought about those crazy days back in our home time when Jennifer Hawkins assassinated my crucifix and Snpgrdxz bayoneted her. I realized the visitations of those days were manifestations of my time traveling friends, but the love of my life had no reason to shoot me now. Gilbert and Snpgrdxz had no reason to kill Jennifer.

Was I as insane at this moment as I was back then? Or did we somehow change the past so those manifestations of Jennifer and my friends were no longer valid? Would we return home to discover their visits never happened? Or did more insanity await us in an as yet unexplored future?

As we joined hands in a circle to pray at the Wheaton When Portal, I was sure of one thing and it wasn't my sanity. No matter what happens, you have to trust your own mind's sense of reality, and you have to trust your friends. We broke the prayer circle, and with our hands joined together, entered the Wheaton When Portal not knowing when we would end up.

THE END

Thanks for choosing the Snpgrdxz series.

Purchase more of my books, including **Snpgrdxz and the Time Warriors**: Book 2 of the Snpgrdxz Series by searching Snpgrdxz on www.amazon.com.

Or keep reading the Snpgrdxz series now…

SNPGRDXZ AND THE TIME WARRIORS

BOOK 2 OF THE SNPGRDXZ SERIES

BY PAUL R. LLOYD

CHAPTER 1

CURIOUSER AND CURIOUSER

In the speediest move I ever saw her make, sixteen-year-old Jennifer Hawkins opened fire with her M16 and charged down the long, grassy slope. I never loved Jennifer more than at this moment as she protected me against a horde of three-foot tall troll-zombies.

Jennifer sported long, straight brunette hair tied in a ponytail that bounced as she ran. Her fair complexion reddened the harder she raced. Fat ruby lips and high, sweaty cheekbones complemented her beauty. She was a bit on the skinny side but tall. Like me, she wore twenty-first century blue jeans and a t-shirt. Our brown leather boots were sourced from a shopping spree in nineteen twenty-three so they were brand new. I turned my attention back to the troll-zombies before I accidentally pointed my rifle at the back of the beauty I admired.

The troll-zombie horde split to go around our rifle fire. Yes, by this time I had worked up the gumption to support

Jennifer with my M16 without shooting her in the back. The malodorous critters were not as attractive as the zombies we had seen in the movies, and I doubted they would do well on the SATs. But they knew the nearest path to brains wasn't through a hail of gunfire.

At the bottom of the hill, Jennifer smiled but punched me hard on the right shoulder. "Bryan Ganarski, you almost got us killed."

"I'm sorry, but the sight of those creatures made my head hurt." I had my skull fractured by a glancing bullet wound about six months earlier. Stress brought on headaches, and our time travels kept us under constant strain.

"No excuses. We have to catch up." Jennifer shouldered her rifle and headed across the field towards the woods.

"How will we find the others?" I hurried to match Jennifer's pace.

"Follow these footprints." Jennifer pointed to the grass.

I didn't see anything at first, but eventually noticed slight disturbances and color differences in the grass about the size of a boot. I lost the trail in the woods. "Now what?"

"This way. They moved in a straight line." Jennifer continued in the lead as we headed deeper into the trees to catch up with our friends.

Like our world, the land of the trolls had its share of mosquitoes, flies, spiders and other tiny creatures that lusted for our blood. "Hold up," I said.

"Bryan, we can't stop."

"Mosquito repellent won't take long." I rifled through my backpack but found none.

"Don't be a teenage wuss." Jennifer messed around in her backpack. "Here, hold these." Out popped her hair dryer, clips of silver bullets, makeup kit, clips of lignum vitae bullets, personal lady supplies, case of diet coke which I dropped, two hand grenades and mosquito repellant.

While she repacked, I sprayed the goop on my clothes and exposed skin. I lacked the muscle to qualify for high school athletics despite my six-foot frame. Instead, I hung out with Gilbert in the pursuit of academic excellence and girls. I found the young lady of my dreams in Jennifer Hawkins while Gilbert prowled in vain. Although if we ever find the long missing Maria Gonzalez, Gilbert's luck could change. Or not. It was hard to tell with Maria and her imitation Goth ways.

Jennifer placed one arm around my neck, swiped her mosquito stuff back and kissed me square on the lips. She backed away, sprayed and returned the repellent to her backpack. She passed a bottle of ibuprofen to me along with a canteen of water. "This is for bravery in action. Keep up your courage and we'll be fine. And remember, you did not see that box of personal items."

I was about to thank her when we heard Frank say, "Sound advice."

Frank Bronson meandered in our direction from twenty feet away where he must have been hidden in a stand of buckthorn. He possessed the broad shoulders of a football player but on a small college team due to his five-foot-ten-inch frame. In his mid-twenties, his athletic career had ended in favor of firefighting in our hometown of Wheaton, Illinois. Like us, he carried an M16 rifle and a backpack stuffed with ammo, grenades, rations, clothes and first aid gear.

"Where is everyone?" Jennifer shouldered her repacked backpack.

"Tony led the team along a trail up ahead. I volunteered to stay behind in case you guys survived the troll-zombie horde."

"We did, no thanks to Bryan," said Jennifer.

"Cut your boyfriend a break, Jennifer. He's walking wounded."

Jennifer placed her right arm around my shoulders and kissed me on the cheek. "I did. And Bryan, you were wonderful charging down that steep incline with me. I didn't know you had the guts. Too bad you tripped earlier at the top of the hill when the others took off."

"Who knew a root stuck out of the ground? There wasn't even a tree nearby, but you were awesome staying back with me. You saved my life." I awarded Jennifer with a kiss.

"Let's catch up with the gang," Frank said.

Jennifer and I followed Frank through the woods until we reached the trail five minutes later.

"This way." Frank pointed out the uphill path to the left of us.

"Downhill is the other way," I said.

"Zombie-troll village is downhill. Our friends trudged uphill."

About fifteen minutes later, we began to smell rotten eggs mixed with baby excrement. We heard the troll-zombies stagger out of the woods onto the trail.

"Run," Frank yelled.

We clambered up a rise in the path. At the top, we followed a right turn. The troll-zombies moved slowly but they were the most persistent of creatures.

Jennifer hollered, "Halt."

I stopped while she and Frank bent over to catch their breaths. I scanned the trail behind us with my rifle locked and loaded.

"We better take off," Frank said once his breathing returned to normal.

I opened fire on a group of troll-zombies that came into view at the curve behind us.

"Hurry," Jennifer yelled.

We sprinted another fifty yards where CJ jumped out of the bushes. "You guys okay?"

When traveling in time, you risk the unlikely possibility of bumping into another version of yourself, and Jennifer had. Now we journeyed with two Jennifers, including my girlfriend, the original or "young Jennifer." The guys sometimes called her "that Ganarski girl" as if we were hitched, which we are not. We're still teenagers after all. Tony, our art teacher and basketball time keeper from back at Lincoln High, was the only one who got away with calling her "Wild Thing."

We named the second version of Jennifer "College Jennifer" or "CJ" because she was college age, five years older than my Jennifer girlfriend. The age difference had to do with CJ ending up in nineteen eighteen and having to wait five years for the rest of us, including herself (don't ask) in nineteen twenty-three.

What would we do if a third Jennifer Hawkins showed up? How many ways can you refer to the different versions of a girl named Jennifer? And don't even think about how College Jennifer was no longer my girlfriend while her high school same-self sister was. CJ matched my Jennifer in every way except for a few extra pounds and her age. Like *Alice in Wonderland*, time travel became curiouser and curiouser.

"We're fine, but we won't be for long." I opened fire with my M16. The others fired on the troll-zombie horde bearing down on us with no signs of stopping or reversing course.

***

Unlike human zombies, troll-zombies retain enough intelligence to know it doesn't make sense to attack rifle fire with your teeth and outstretched arms. After dropping ten of the troll-zombies with head shots, the remaining monstrosities reversed course and disappeared into the woods down the hill from us.

"Let's catch up with the others," said Frank.

"They aren't too far in front of us," said CJ.

We met up with Gilbert, Tony and Snpgrdxz twenty minutes down the road. They had discovered a large rock outcropping by the side of the trail and used it as a bench to take a break.

"You guys thirsty?" Gilbert held out a canteen. Gilbert Armstrong was my best friend from Lincoln High. He stood half a head taller than me with the broad shoulders and barrel chest of a football linebacker. However, he tackled math, not athletics.

"Bryan has a headache," Jennifer said.

"So what else is new?" asked Tony Romano, our leader who was responsible for us becoming lost in time. He sported the shoulder-length salt and pepper hair older guys grow into. On the skinny side, Tony usually needed a shave.

"I don't think we should remain here long," said Snpgrdxz. As you may have guessed, Snpgrdxz was not your usual teenager. Instead, he was our shape-shifting, space alien comrade. He had survived a flying saucer crash back in our world decades before we met him. Despite his years on earth, he still considered himself a teenager.

Most of the time, Snpgrdxz appeared as Daniel Brickmaster, making him both the easiest and hardest friend to describe. The easiest because he appeared as a nondescript teenage boy with brown hair and eyes. Everything about Daniel smacked of average such as his height, weight, clothing choices, lip thickness, nose size, and teeth color. The difficulty of describing him stemmed from his averageness, but he believed "average" was the secret to keeping below the radar of the men in black.

His alien culture did not use vowels which made his name a nuisance to pronounce. The easy way was to insert the letter "I" everyplace you thought a vowel belonged. So it was pronounced "Snip-grid-ix." We went back and forth calling him "Daniel" or "Snpgrdxz."

Frank passed a bottle of ibuprofen to me. "You guys realize we have an army of undead sleepwalkers between us and the only way out of the troll world."

CJ handed the canteen to me and paced with her arms flying above her head. "If you guys would take a moment to reflect on our conversation way back in nineteen twenty-three, which was back this morning, we agreed to cross the troll world in search of another exit."

"CJ is right. We move out in this direction." Tony headed down the trail away from the Wheaton When Portal, the place of our crossing into this strange but beautiful underworld.

"Wait, the horde turned around," my Jennifer said.

"Run," Tony shouted.

Troll-zombies moved at the speed of overgrown snails, but running rarely succeeded in losing them. Persistence and general stupidity kept them on your trail. Sooner or later, you tired and they didn't. Think ugly used car sales people here. We scurried, but we were tired.

To fight off the pesky brutes, Snpgrdxz transformed into a giant troll-zombie master who commanded them to go away. Snpgrdxz spoke in his own version of the troll language. When that didn't work, he switched to zombie speak, a set of meaningful groans, moans and undead body noises. When he mixed the undead noises with basic troll, the troll-zombies paid attention. To make sure the troll-zombies understood, Snpgrdxz transformed into an even bigger zombie.

The transformation process scared the bejeebers out of the meandering automatons. They took off leaving their giant master behind and the forest trail to us. Snpgrdxz returned to his Daniel Brickmaster form and put his clothes back on.

"We have to save Maria Gonzalez," Frank said.

Maria Gonzalez instigated our time journey through no fault of her own when a troll kidnapped her out of Lincoln High. Our group would head home immediately and abandon the search for Maria to the professionals if we could. But once we crossed the Wheaton When Portal the first time, we learned we knew no way to control it. Returning to our home time involved as much guesswork as a multiple choice test in Miss Throngbottom's English class.

"I'll go." Snpgrdxz mutated into a giant troll-zombie again as he lumbered off in the direction of the troll village. The last time we travelled this way, the territory was in the possession of small three-foot tall forest trolls commonly known as *Huldrefolk*. The trolls must have been involved in a zombie apocalypse since our last visit and now we faced all the joy of dealing with trolls combined with zombies.

The rest of us hunkered down to wait while Snpgrdxz learned if we timed our entry into the troll world perfectly to meet up with the captured Maria Gonzalez. If so, we could rescue her before the trolls boiled her. This made no sense since one of the trolls kidnapped Maria before the zombies invaded. If you think about time travel, it will make you crazy so instead we prepared ourselves for anything without regard to proper time placement.

Our journey began about a year ago when Tony swore we would find the missing Maria Gonzalez alive and return home in time for dinner. So far, we had discovered Maria's boiled and chewed bones in a troll encampment, and our moms must have stopped holding meals for us months ago.

While Frank Bronson and CJ Hawkins intertwined fingers, Gilbert parked against an oak tree.

My high school sweetheart, Jennifer Hawkins, stood over me. "Bryan Ganarski, why aren't you securing our perimeter?"

"I'm busy with more important things." I stretched my lanky body along the ground, yawned and stood up.

"Like what?" Tony asked.

"Making out with my girlfriend." I kissed Jennifer.

"I like your ideas." Jennifer snuggled close.

"We better stay locked and loaded," Gilbert rubbed his Black, bald head before he assumed a defensive position by the oak tree, rifle at the ready.

"Retreat," Snpgrdxz shouted from fifty feet down the trail.

"This way." Tony took off away from the troll-zombies.

"Don't we have to stay and fight?" CJ asked.

"It's safer to escape along this troll path to where it meets the werewolf trail. We'll sneak past the vampire cave and the werewolf village undetected." Tony hollered over his shoulder. We followed.

Snpgrdxz yelled, "Lock and load. Here they come." He snagged his clothes and backpack as he passed by us.

Tony stopped us. "I guess CJ was right. It's too late to run. Take up positions behind these trees and wait for my signal to open fire."

We didn't have much of a time lag before Snpgrdxz dressed again and the troll-zombies struck. For some reason, they didn't send their army after us the way they had the first time we arrived in their territory.

A hunting party of twelve troll-zombies meandered down the path toward our position. Tony waited longer than I would have before he shot the first troll-zombie in line.

The rest of the troll-zombies dragged their buddy with them as they beat a hasty retreat. Troll-zombies aren't used to modern firearms so you could startle them with a little instant death.

"Remind me to never walk point," said Gilbert.

"This way." Tony headed in the direction of the vampire cave. This may start to sound like a dumb horror story to you, but the last time we found ourselves in the troll world, we ran into vampires and werewolves. To cross the troll world, we had to pass by their hangouts.

"How will we sneak past the vampires?" Frank asked.

Tony scratched his head. "The nosferatu will be asleep and the werewolves will be regular people. They'll think we're werewolves from another village."

"Let's not forget about the troll-zombies," my Jennifer said.

"You're right, Wild Thing. We could run into another of their hunting parties, or these guys might become brave again, but at least we're away from their village now. I suspect they'll spend the remainder of the day in search of easier pickings." Tony pointed in the direction of the troll-zombie community in the valley below.

The two suns in the western sky shouted mid-afternoon so we needed to make time passing the twin monster lairs. The shadows stretched a long way by the time we reached the cave of the vampires.

We would have passed by safely if it weren't for the trap we fell into. The vampires had dug a hole in the ground and covered it over with sticks hidden under a layer of dirt. The trap held our weight until our entire group traipsed on it. A cracking sound provided the first hint of trouble. We dropped through sticks and bellowed the universal oomph as we hit bottom.

***

My head hurt and my knee ached. Gilbert grasped his Black, bald-shaved cranium where our heads had collided.

"Everyone okay?" Tony asked.

"No, Bryan bashed my head in," said Gilbert.

"He bashed my head, too," said my Jennifer.

"He bashed both your heads?" Daniel Snpgrdxz Brickmaster asked.

"My head hit Gilbert and my knee must have hit Jennifer. Are you okay, honey?"

"Yes, dear. Just be more careful next time," my Jennifer said.

"Anyone else injured besides Gilbert and the old married couple?" Tony asked.

"Somebody scraped my shin with their boot," said Frank. "I think it was CJ."

"Hey, you know we aren't married yet," said my Jennifer.

"Yep, it was me. I just can't get close enough to you." CJ clutched Frank's arm to pull herself up.

"I'm okay and so is Daniel. Everyone else suffered minor injuries. Does that about cover it?" Tony asked.

"What about Bryan's bullet-shattered cranium?" my Jennifer asked. Tears streamed down her cheeks so I figured she was remembering the months I spent in nineteen twenty-three recovering from a bullet that grazed my head during an attack by a bootlegger gang. The bullet caused a fractured skull but it didn't penetrate to the brain.

"My head hurts but not so bad that I have to worry about a fracture," I said. "Besides, I clunked the other side of my skull." I didn't have the courage to ask Jennifer why she said "yet" in the same sentence as "marriage."

Tony messed around in his backpack to yank out a rope with one of those hook devices you see in the movies when somebody needs to scale a high wall. "Stand back as far as you can."

We smushed together into a corner, but the hole was tiny so there wasn't much room. I felt my Jennifer's body heat against me so I hugged her from behind. She pushed against me more so I kissed her on the neck.

Tony threw the rope.

"I got it," a voice said from above. "You fell into Glimtuckmucker's troll trap. And there's not much time before Glimtuckmucker and his band of hearty nosferatu wake up so you better scramble up here."

"I'll go first to see if this guy is safe." Tony pulled a pistol out of his backpack. "Silver bullets." He shouldered his backpack and an M16. "Lignum vitae bullets." Tony climbed the rope and disappeared over the top.

Tony reappeared with another person peeking over the edge. "Guys next so we can pull the ladies up," Tony said.

Gilbert climbed the rope followed by Frank.

Snpgrdxz said, "Plastic Man can go last."

My Jennifer and CJ clambered out of the hole next. Neither of them needed any help. Daniel stretched his arms up to the top of the hole and pulled himself out of the trap.

We recognized Growlpucket from our last visit to the werewolf village.

"You better leave us alone or we'll shoot you full of silver," said Tony.

"Do you think you'll have time to shoot all of us?" Growlpucket clapped his hands once and a crowd of people scampered out of the trees and bushes. Our only escape was the vampire cave so our choices included having our blood sucked or serving as werewolf meat.

To continue reading **Snpgrdxz and the Time Warriors,** please search Snpgrdxz on www.amazon.com.

ABOUT THE AUTHOR

Paul R. Lloyd writes fiction that explores the monsters and strangers among us. His offbeat characters reveal the horror and humor of the human condition. He investigates themes such as cowardice in the three-book Snpgrdxz series, forgiveness in Amazon top seller HAGS, redemption in Amazon top seller FULFILLMENT, and the nature of love (and hate) in STEEL PENNIES. Paul teaches workshops and speaks on how to reach the next skill level as a writer. He heads the Write Time Writers Group and serves as a member of the DuPage Writer's Group, the Chicago Writers Association and Lively Arts, a group of Christian artists and writers. Paul recently completed a 30-year career as head of a marketing communications firm.

Visit him online at: http://paulrlloyd.blogspot.com

To read more paperback books or ebooks by Paul R. Lloyd, including the next book in this series, please search Snpgrdxz on www.amazon.com.

FICTION BY PAUL R. LLOYD

NOVELS

Fulfillment

Hags

Steel Pennies

Snpgrdxz and the Time Monsters
Book 1 of the Snpgrdxz Series

Snpgrdxz and the Time Warriors
Book 2 of the Snpgrdxz Series

Snpgrdxz and the Time Hunters
Book 3 of the Snpgrdxz Series

SHORT STORIES

Angel Thorns

Little Miss Forgotten

Egbert

To Dwell Among Us
Prequel to Fulfillment

Paperback and E-Book versions available on
www.amazon.com.